The Birds, the Bees, and You and Me

Swoon READS

Swoon Reads
New York

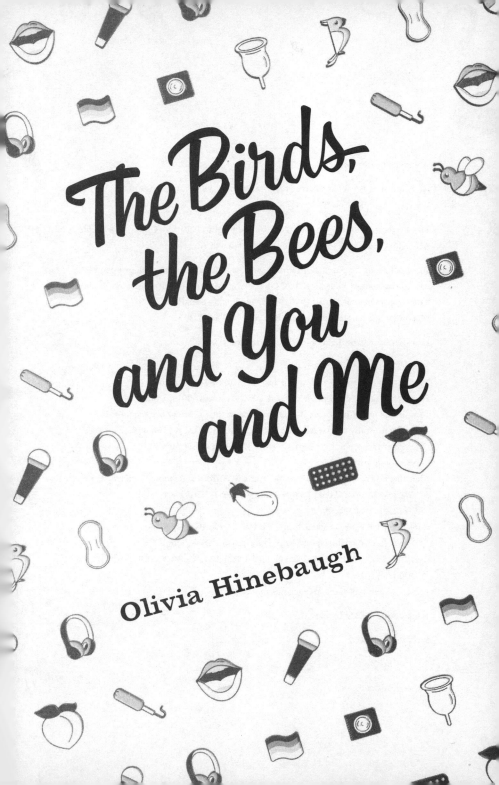

The Birds, the Bees, and You and Me

Olivia Hinebaugh

A Swoon Reads Book

An Imprint of Feiwel and Friends and Macmillan Publishing Group LLC
175 Fifth Avenue, New York, NY 10010

Our books may be purchased in bulk for promotional, educational, or business
use. Please contact your local bookseller or the Macmillan Corporate and Premium
Sales Department at (800) 221-7945 ext. 5442 or by e-mail at
MacmillanSpecialMarkets@macmillan.com.

Library of Congress Cataloging-in-Publication Data

Names: Hinebaugh, Olivia, author.
Title: The birds, the bees, and you and me / Olivia Hinebaugh.
Description: First edition. | New York : Swoon Reads, 2019. | Summary:
    Seventeen-year-old Lacey Burke responds to the failure of her school's
    abstinence-only sexual education curriculum by handing out advice
    and contraceptives in the girls' bathroom, even as her own life
    gets complicated.
Identifiers: LCCN 2018020069 (print) | LCCN 2018030166 (ebook) | ISBN
    9781250192660 (E-book) | ISBN 9781250192653 (hardcover) | ISBN
    9781250192660 (ebook)
Subjects: | CYAC: Sex instruction—Fiction. | Friendship—Fiction. |
    Dating (Social customs)—Fiction. | Bands (Music)—Fiction.
Classification: LCC PZ7.1.H5685 (ebook) | LCC PZ7.1.H5685 Bi 2019 (print) |
    DDC [Fic]—dc23
LC record available at https://lccn.loc.gov/2018020069

Book design by Liz Dresner

First Edition, 2019

10 9 8 7 6 5 4 3 2 1

swoonreads.com

For Jason, the best partner and
co-parent I could ask for.

One

One

"I think I finally have my audition piece," I say to my best friend Evita. I plop into the chair next to her and start unpacking my lunch.

"Huh?" she asks, pulling out ear buds that I hadn't noticed under her mane of curls.

"You're not supposed to listen to anything too loudly," I remind her. It's a rule she came up with anyway. She needs to preserve her perfect hearing for when she's a famous record producer/singer/DJ. "But if you are going to listen to something . . ." I hold up my phone.

"What's that?" Theo asks, sitting opposite us.

"Possibly my audition piece," I tell him.

Evita sits up a little straighter and puts her game face on. "Hand it over."

"Why does she get to hear it first?" Theo asks.

"Get over here," Evita tells him, holding out one of her ear buds.

"It's obviously just a MIDI file, but, you know, I could do it on viola. With maybe piano, but it's kind of . . ." I gnaw on the side of my thumb.

Theo shoves between us, balancing precariously across our two chairs. I hand Evita the phone. She hits play. The piece is two and a half minutes.

A long two and a half minutes.

Beyond an occasional bob of her head, Evita makes no show of emotion. Theo, thankfully, is much less opaque. First, he raises his eyebrows at me. Then he mouths "Wow!" He's probably at that set of arpeggios from the viola that melt under those big chords.

"What are you listening to?" Theo's girlfriend, Lily Ann, asks as she sits down with her lunch tray.

Theo puts a finger up, telling her to wait.

When it's over, Evita finally smiles. "Yes, Lacey. Absolutely. We should record it ASAP."

"It's great," Theo says, throwing an arm around me and giving me a squeeze.

I can't keep the smile from my face. "Awesome."

"You nailed it," Theo says as he stands and joins Lily Ann on the other side of the table.

"Can I listen?" Lily Ann asks.

"Of course," I say with a forced smile.

"So, if we can record this today after school, we can send it in by Wednesday. Or even tomorrow. You know I don't mind pulling an all-nighter," Evita says.

"That's not necessary," I tell her. "Let's just do it Saturday. We were going to rehearse other stuff this afternoon anyway, right?"

"Okay. It can wait until the weekend. But you have to slate the entire weekend for this endeavor and band practice."

"The whole weekend?" I ask. "I have that other project, though . . ." Evita knows I'm working on a piece for Theo's birthday next week.

"Pretty sure that's almost finished," Evita says.

"What is?" Theo asks.

"Nothing!" Evita and I say in unison, grinning conspiratorially.

"Weirdos," Theo says.

"We have absolutely nothing going on other than rehearsals and audition recordings. The sooner we send them in, the sooner we get accepted and the sooner we look for an apartment," Evita says.

The three of us are applying to Berklee College of Music in Boston. It's been the plan since before we even got to high school. Play music. Listen to music. Study music. Leave our small town in North Carolina for college in Boston. Play even more music. Conquer the world.

It's only October, so we don't need to rush. And Berklee has rolling admissions, so it doesn't really matter when we submit, but Evita wants us to send them at the exact same time, so we hear back at the same time. She wouldn't cop to feeling nervous that one of us won't get in, but none of us has a backup plan. It's Boston or bust. It's funny we're so set on Boston, especially since none of us has even been there.

Theo is listening again, sharing the headphones with Lily Ann this time.

Seeing them all cozy together always bothers Evita.

"Your face is going to get stuck like that," I whisper to her.

Her somewhat bushy eyebrows are scrunched together, and her upper lip is sneering.

"Not true. This is just my resting bitch face."

"It's a face that only appears at lunch, oddly enough," I say.

Theo kicks me under the lunch table. "Secrets don't make friends, girls."

"No secrets here," Evita says cheerfully.

"It's good!" Lily Ann says too loudly. She's either totally oblivious that Evita shoots daggers at her any chance she gets, or she really doesn't care.

"Thanks," I say.

"You guys heard Theo's audition piece?" Lily Ann asks once she's done listening.

"Evita mixed it," Theo says through a mouthful of sandwich. He also definitely played it for us during quartet rehearsals. Lily Ann and Theo and I, along with this other guy Scott, have a string quartet that meets last period every day for an independent study credit. Apparently, Lily Ann doesn't recall that. Or maybe she just likes to keep the conversation spinning around Theo.

"Oh yeah. It's just super good, right?" Lily Ann asks. She turns to Theo and puts a hand on his arm. "You should seriously send it to some of the conservatories I'm applying to."

"I'm not a conservatory kind of guy," Theo says, kissing her on the forehead.

"You're just such a brilliant cellist," Lily Ann says with a pout.

Evita crosses her arms. "Just because someone *can* play classical music doesn't mean that's all they should do."

4

"I know he's more than just a good cello player," Lily Ann says defensively.

"Right. He's also hot," Evita says. "And an epically good kisser."

"Evita," Theo groans.

This is Evita's MO: say something to make Lily Ann uncomfortable by bringing up her own history with Theo, even though, historically, it's not something she talks about all that often. No one mentions the brief period when Evita and Theo were together, or the even more painful period after they broke up, unless it's to rub Lily Ann's nose in it. The subtext is always: "It's not as if it's a feat to get Theo to sleep with you." Lily Ann seems infuriatingly immune to these comments, but Theo always caves in on himself when it comes up.

"I have to pee," I say, grabbing Evita's arm and pulling her with me. "We'll be back." The hallway is mostly empty since it's still the middle of lunch. "Do you really need to do that?"

"I honestly can't help myself. The two of them make me want to vomit."

"You didn't always hate Lily Ann," I point out.

Evita's the one who adopted Lily Ann at the start of the year when she moved to town. Evita picked her out of the crowd the first day in August as a "lonely new kid." It's the exact same way she saved me when I was the new kid on the first day of sixth grade.

As soon as she found out that Lily Ann played violin, Evita asked her to sit with us at lunch, since Theo and I also play in the school orchestra and were already hoping to find another violinist for our quartet. Lily Ann didn't know the history with Theo and Evita. She didn't know that Theo was sort of spoken for. Before we knew it, Lily Ann and Theo were a thing, and our "perfect senior year was ruined," as Evita likes to say.

"I just wish he'd date someone deserving of him," Evita says, pushing the bathroom door open.

There's a girl at the mirror adding mascara to already-mascaraed eyelashes. She glances over at us. This school is small, and everyone is always up in everyone else's business. One of the things I love about Evita is that she does not care who knows her business. But I prefer to be invisible.

"You don't think anyone would be good enough for him," I say quietly.

"Well. Right."

"Okay, but, he's with Lily Ann now, and what do you think is going to happen if she decides she doesn't want to put up with your scowling and under-the-breath comments?"

"She'll break up with him?" Evita says hopefully, but she obviously doesn't believe this. She sighs. "Okay. You're right. I will attempt niceness."

"Honestly, nice would be amazing, but we could all probably settle for civil," I tell her. "You do not want him to have to choose between Lily Ann and us. Somehow we haven't lost him yet." I can't imagine facing high school without Evita and Theo.

"I'll make an effort," Evita mumbles.

"Hey, Jess?" a voice from a stall asks the girl with the mascara.

Jess peels herself away from listening intently to our conversation. "Yeah?"

"Do you have a tampon?"

"No, sorry," Jess says.

I reach into my bag without a second thought and pass a tampon under the door. My mom always tells me to carry more feminine protection than I need. Part of her "sisterhood" philosophy.

"Thanks!" the girl says.

"So . . . ," Evita says, "do you actually have to pee?"

"No."

"Okay. Meeting adjourned. I will be nice." Evita throws the door open.

Back at our lunch table, Evita makes a barely audible apology and we all move on. Theo catches my eye and mouths "Thank you." I shrug.

The bell rings, dismissing us from lunch. Theo, Evita, and I go one way to our senior seminar class, while Lily Ann goes to a different class. She has complained about this fact every day for the last two months.

"I don't know why I didn't sign up for that class," Lily Ann moans.

"Because it's boring and you don't like taking easy classes with no homework?" Evita offers unhelpfully.

"It really is boring," Theo agrees. So far, it's mostly been about college or trade schools or community college or job applications. "It's fine, babe, I'll see you in independent study."

At the word *babe,* Evita turns to me. I shake my head before she can pantomime vomiting. But, let's get real, when people call each other *babe* it's sickening.

"Okay," Lily Ann says. She pouts and Theo puts his arms

around her waist and whispers something in her ear that makes her grin.

"Ugh. Come on," Evita says, linking arms with me.

~

Evita and I drop our lunch stuff in Theo's locker because it's the closest to the senior seminar classroom. We're the first to arrive, so we claim our usual table in the back. Theo slips in right before the bell, sitting a row in front of us.

There's this nervous-looking guy sitting behind the teacher's desk. Our teacher, Mrs. Einhorn, introduces him as the guest speaker.

"We're starting a new unit on healthy life choices. Mr. Robbins is here to kick this unit off. He has a lot of wisdom to share, so I hope you give him your attention."

Evita and I exchange a look. We're generally on the same wavelength. Without saying anything, I know she's as skeptical as I am that our backward school will ever teach us anything useful in a health unit. Evita and I have more than just music in common. We were both raised by single mothers. Single, liberal, feminist mothers. My mom was a teenager when she had me, and she has spent my entire life talking to me about "healthy life choices." Things like safe sex and consent and women's health.

Mom and I still laugh about how my sophomore health class was a lot like the one in *Mean Girls*, where the gym teacher is so uncomfortable discussing sex that he basically tells them just "don't do it," then hands out condoms. Our class was a lot like that . . . minus the condom part. When I told her about that class, my mom threatened to take the issue of abstinence-only sex education to the school board. But at the end of sophomore year, she found out she was pregnant with my little brother, Dylan, and a few things fell by the wayside. We still smash the patriarchy in smaller, subtler ways.

"To get us thinking about the impact our choices have on our lives, Mr. Robbins is going to be talking about the choices he has made. Some were healthy, and some were not. I'm hopeful you'll learn a lot from his experiences," Mrs. Einhorn says.

Mr. Robbins stands up awkwardly and grips index cards that he starts to read from. At first he's mostly talking about alcohol. His story is familiar. Half the kids here could probably relate to it. First, he was just drinking at parties, then whenever he was with friends, then all the time, even when he was alone. Theo, Evita, and I are generally too busy with music to go to parties in the mountains or at the nearby college campus. But we still hear all about them. From everyone.

Half the class is doodling or fiddling with jewelry or chewing on pencils, even when Mr. Robbins talks about dabbling in other drugs. But then Mr. Robbins starts talking about sex. Everyone sits a little taller.

But instead of going into anything useful about sexual health, he just lists it as a regret. Being drunk and high all the time caused him to do the unforgivable: he had life-ruining sex! The kind where you get a girl pregnant.

Mrs. Einhorn starts chiming in with how sex is not something you can take back. She and Mr. Robbins are demonizing sex at every turn and my hands flex and un-flex. I bite my lip to keep from blurting something out. They are completely skipping an important issue. If you're going to talk about drugs and sex, then you should be talking about consent and how tricky the issue is when you are drinking. Or about—I don't know—contraception!

But *of course* they don't talk about contraception. Because if you get pregnant, then it's obviously your fault for making bad choices. Shame on you!

This whole talk reeks of stigma. And if my mom has taught me anything, it's that demonizing and stigmatizing sex prevents everyone from getting information on *safer* sex. That stigma hits girls extra hard. And my mom knows about that, because she was once a pregnant teenager. Instead of getting support from her family and friends, she got a lot of judgment. If I could travel back in time and punch my mom's unsupportive friends in the face, I would. And I'm not generally a violent person.

I keep fighting the urge to raise my hand and give them a piece of my mind, but I always chicken out. Just when I don't think I can keep these thoughts to myself any longer, the bell finally rings. I get out of there as fast as I can. My face is burning, because this whole class feels like an attack on everything I've been taught and believe in.

Theo and Evita catch up to me and Theo hands me a tally sheet. If they can tell I'm upset by the class, they choose not to address that.

"What's this?"

"Eye rolls, Burke. Yours."

"You sit in front of me," I point out.

"Yes, but you make this sound when you roll your eyes," Theo says.

"I do not!"

"Yeah, you do, like this little *pfffff* through your front teeth."

I roll my eyes and, yeah, that sound is automatic. "Shit!" We stop by Theo's locker, drop our binders in there, and grab our government stuff. "You do realize," I say, "that that lecture was basically fearmongering. I did not sign up for that."

"It's an easy A. What more could you want?" Evita asks.

"I just . . ." I get this annoying prickle between my shoulder blades. Under all my feminist rage, my insecurities are simmering. Namely: Do I even know what I'm talking about? Aside from listening to my mother all my life, do I know anything? I have never even been kissed. No one has ever wanted to kiss me. So what do I actually know about sex?

"What?" Theo asks. I swear no thought I have gets past him.

"It's like, I've had a few drinks before—"

"We were there," Evita interrupts.

I sigh. This whole topic is embarrassing, even if, intellectually, I know it shouldn't be. It's that damn stigma. "Well, even when I was buzzed or whatever, it isn't like I suddenly lost control and jumped anybody. They make it seem like if you have a drink or kiss someone you'll just . . . I dunno . . . lose control and the next thing you know you've contracted an STI and gotten knocked up. But, for real, is that it? Are we all just ticking time bombs, waiting to lose control?"

"It's not like that," Evita says. She knows I worry about this. My mom is the smartest person I know. But she had me at sixteen. There are probably half a dozen pregnant girls in our school at any given time. What other explanation would there be for so many people making so many mistakes?

"Not for you," Theo says. Evita seems to brush the comment

aside, but we both know that he's still hurt by the fact that his and Evita's sexual experimentation ended when Evita concluded that sex wasn't for her. She just didn't want much past kissing and cuddling. And even though she has been totally clear that it wasn't Theo's fault, and that she isn't sexually attracted to anyone, it still seems to make Theo insecure.

"My asexuality aside," Evita says to me, "you don't lose control. And *you* are the least out-of-control person I know. And you know more about sex than any other virgin I've ever met."

"Vita, you know that virginity is such a patriarchal construct," Theo deadpans.

"My mother would be so proud of you," I say, a smile finally creeping back onto my face. "I just wish I had some experience to speak of. I wish someone *wanted* me." The minute I say that, I'm mortified.

"Seriously, Lacey, I'm sure people want you. We'll just get you that first kiss. And you'll see, it's not like this slippery slope," Evita says.

"Wait . . . ," Theo starts. Then he shakes his head, his cheeks suddenly blooming with color, as he closes his locker.

"What?" I ask him. I've recovered from being mortified, and now I'm just annoyed that he'd have the gall to be embarrassed by this conversation. After all I've heard about him sleeping with Evita and even tidbits about Lily Ann.

"You haven't kissed *anyone*?" he asks.

"For real, Theo? Where have you been?" Evita asks him.

"I dunno. Like, never at camp? Or, like, on the bus as a dare? Or at a middle school boy-girl party?" Theo asks.

"You *knew* me in middle school," I point out. Being the new kid at that age was awful. I was awkward, and I didn't know anyone. Theo and Evita saved me from certain hell. They cared way more about the fact that I was into music than the fact that I wore childish clothes or that I was shy or a dorkily overeager student. They saw me through two sullen years of complaining about my mother getting married and how my life was over. They even boycotted a middle school party because the girl throwing it didn't want to invite me.

"Yeah. But you're not Lacey Burke, prepubescent dork, anymore," Evita points out.

"Thanks," I grumble.

"No. You know what I mean. Now it's cool to be smart. Or cool*er*. And, like . . ." Evita opens and closes her mouth, as if she can't think of anything else nice to say about me. Super helpful for how insecure I feel at this moment.

"Stop. You really don't have to try to make me feel better about this. Let's just drop it."

"You're a catch," Evita says firmly. "I'm sorry I brought it up. I'd be happy to make out with you if it would make you feel better. You know I've always wanted to kiss more girls. Softer lips." Before Evita came out to us as asexual, she came out as bi. Previously bisexual, currently biromantic. She tells us her identity is a never-ending work in progress. And, yes, she has often bemoaned the fact that there aren't more gay or bi girls at our tiny school, even in the Genders and Sexualities Alliance, which she's the president of. Her backpack is practically a shrine to all things pride, the black, gray, white, and purple asexual flag pin being her most beloved pin.

In this moment, I wish I could have things half as figured out as Evita does. Or be even a quarter as comfortable talking about sex and attraction. "Can we just change the subject? I'm getting twitchy."

"Good twitchy or bad twitchy?" Evita winks.

"Stop! Bad twitchy! Definitely bad twitchy." I shoo her away.

"Hey, Lacey, you're fine," Theo says. He affectionately tugs one of the short pieces of my grown-out bangs that always fall into my face.

I bat him away. "I'm a delicate flower." I don't want them to see just how embarrassed I am to have asked about this. But it's obvious, so Theo throws his arm around my shoulders. Evita shimmies her way under his other arm, and we walk toward government.

"My delicate flower and my prickly porcupine," Theo says.

Two

Sometime in the last month, the three of us went from best friends jamming on our instruments to an actual band. Theo plays the last of the melody on his cello, I lay down a huge chord on my keyboard, and Evita fades it all out from her console. I'm grinning. I can't help it. We sound *good*.

"The extra keyboard is magical," Evita says.

"Yeah, but I need major practice," I say. I'm not a pianist; I've just taught myself what I can. The viola is still my instrument of choice.

"Let's do that one again, then," Evita suggests. She ties her long mop of hair into a high bun and pulls one leg of her sweatpants up past her knee. "I think we should record a demo of this one to try to get gigs. What do you think, Lacey?"

"It's very us," I say. Our music falls somewhere between epic film score, trippy electronic music, and pop. Dramatic and catchy.

"Sounds amazing. But twenty minutes 'til you have to shut it down," Evita's mom, Janice, says as she picks her way through cables and clutter on her way to the kitchen.

"Let's start at the top, then. Time to run through it five more times," Evita says. Without even a moment to catch our breath, Evita spins the beat up. I pick up my viola and look at Theo on his cello. We lock eyes, I take a deep breath in through my nose, and we start in unison.

~

With all the equipment shut off, the three of us pile onto Evita's deep couch. This is our routine. We play until it gets late, then we watch TV or do homework until we all crash in Evita's room. My mom and stepdad don't mind that I spend most of my nights here. And Theo's parents don't seem to care. He says it's a benefit of being the youngest of four kids.

I pull out my biology textbook to try to get some reading done, when Evita jumps up.

"I almost forgot!" she says. "I think I have a name for our band!"

"Do tell," Theo says. We have been drawing blanks for weeks on this. Every name we suggest either seems too fluffy or like we're trying too hard.

She holds up both of her hands in a gesture like *wait for it!* "The Sparrows," she finally says.

Theo and I look at each other, our grins mirroring each other's perfectly. "Yes!" I say. "I love it. It fits."

"But where did the name come from?" Theo asks. "Aside from you being a tiny little bird of a person?"

16

"The inspiration is not important. It works, right?" Evita says. Her eyes are huge and she's nodding enthusiastically.

"I'm just glad it's not Evita and the Something-or-Others," I say.

"Well. Right. So, the name comes from an Eva Peron quote . . . so it is tangentially related to my name," Evita says.

"Ha. Knew it," Theo says, laughing.

"Whatever. It's good, right?"

"It's good," I say. "Now you can put a label on the demo we record."

"Oh my god, yes! I need to sketch a logo!" Evita scampers into her bedroom to grab a notebook and then doodles little birds while I read.

Theo's phone rings, and he goes into Evita's room to answer it. Evita looks at me with her eyebrows raised.

"That just kills my good mood," Evita says, climbing up onto the couch next to me and covering us both with a blanket.

"Don't let it," I tell her. "He's allowed to talk to Lily Ann on the phone."

"I know. I can't help it," she says, resting her head on my shoulder. "I guess I'm a little jealous," she whispers.

"I understand," I say. I really do understand. It was hard for me when Evita and Theo were together. It was stressful when they broke up. And it's hard now, knowing that Theo always has this other person on his mind when Evita and I are used to being the only ones.

"I wonder if I shouldn't have ended things with him," Evita whispers.

I snap my head toward her. She's never seemed anything less than certain that splitting up was best for both of them.

"But I thought you didn't want to be with him like that."

She bites her lip, like she isn't sure if she should say anything more. "Okay, so that's the thing. I couldn't stand it when he would look at me that way."

"What way?"

"You know, that sort of searing stare where the person wants to take your clothes off and is feeling all sexy?"

"I don't know that look," I say grumpily.

"Okay, well, that look made me anxious. It made me like him less. Like having sex was kind of fine. Like it could feel good sometimes. But I hated him wanting me. I hated knowing he was feeling things I wasn't. I felt like I was pretending to be into it. Pretending is *so* not my strong suit. I wanted to slow things down, not speed them up. Like if we could just kiss and cuddle forever, I'd be happier. We were totally not on the same page. I like him so much better when he doesn't want me like that."

"That makes sense," I say.

"But that's the thing," she says, playing with a loose thread on the blanket and scooting closer to me. "I'm asexual. Not aromantic. Because that's a totally different thing."

She's talked about these parts of her identity before. Theo and I both joined the GSA when she did, and there's a lot of discussion of identities there. I know that even though she's asexual, she's alloromantic, meaning she experiences romantic attraction. And sometimes she specifies biromantic, because she has romantic feelings for guys and girls.

I know that she still wants to date. She wants to fall in romantic love. But she's never said any of this in relation to *Theo.*

"So . . . like . . . maybe you *love* him?" I ask her. The words feel so heavy.

She nods, tight lipped. I want to talk more about it with her. She spends so much time being bright and bubbly and untouchable. But the moment is over, because Theo comes back in and plops down on my other side.

"Let's see the sketches," he says, reaching for Evita's notebook.

All I can do is give Evita's arm a little squeeze under the blanket and then marvel over her sketches with Theo. When Theo has his face in the notebook, Evita glances at me. She shakes her head ever so slightly. She doesn't want me to ever tell Theo any of what she's just told me. I nod. We're on the same page, like always.

Three

After school on Tuesday, I drive to the hospital to meet my mom. She's a labor and delivery nurse. I could meet her at home, but whenever I meet her at the hospital, she gets this goofy grin that I just can't pass up. My earliest memories are of her working toward this career, and I love seeing her so happy.

I park in the hospital garage and take the elevator to the fourth floor. When I get off the elevator, I see a bunch of familiar faces at reception and down the hall at the nurses' station. I volunteered here over the summer. Mostly I restocked postpartum kits for the new moms and made coffee runs to the cafeteria, but since school started, I only come by when Taco Tuesdays coincide with Mom's shifts.

I say hi to some of the nurses I know. I don't see Mom, so she must be busy with a patient. I head to the large waiting area. It's brightly lit and pleasant. There's an older couple sitting across from the seat I choose. They're holding a bunch of balloons and looking both tense and excited. Probably waiting for the arrival of a grandchild. I smile at them and they smile back.

Glancing around, I realize with a shock that I recognize someone here. Sitting off in a corner is my friend Alice. Our eyes meet, and my first instinct is to pretend I haven't seen her. Because she might be here as a patient. She's almost definitely pregnant, judging by her belly and the way she rests a hand there. A few doctors and midwives see prenatal patients at the hospital, and she's sitting in the corner of the waiting room near the offices. The way she's sitting, with her shoulders shifted away from the room and her back curled, I don't think she wants to be noticed.

I'm not sure what would be kinder, pretending I don't see her or walking over and saying hello. I glance back over. She's studying her shoes, which is not exactly an invitation. But this is Alice. Soprano Alice. GSA Alice—at least until her mom made her quit. She's a junior. Last year Evita declared that she wanted to be her mentor because "The girl has got some serious pipes," and "In a sea of non-queer people, it's nice to have a bi friend," and "She's like a taller mini-me." I haven't seen her all school year. And her large belly possibly explains why.

Before this awkwardness can go on, I grab my bag and walk across the waiting room toward her.

"Hey, Alice," I say, taking a seat near her.

"Lacey! Hi!" She looks relieved I came over. "How are you? How's Evita?"

"We're good. Doing a lot of music stuff. How are you?"

She looks down at her belly and smiles. "You know. Good. Kind of huge. But good. Everything's good. Are you . . . ?" She nods at my belly.

"Oh. No." It comes out defensive. Which makes me sound judgmental. And I want to say something to make Alice more comfortable. "My mom's a nurse here."

"Cool. Obviously, I'm here as a patient," she says with a shrug.

"We miss you at school," I say. "You should get in touch with Evita. She'd want to know how you are."

"I know I should. But I'm sort of embarrassed. My mom thought it would be easier for me if I just homeschooled this year and got off Facebook and stuff."

"Gotcha," I say. But this is exactly the stigma that makes me angry. Why should she hide? I search for something else to say. Anything that isn't the rant I have building in my head. "Do you like homeschooling?"

"It's kind of all right, actually. I'm trying to fit junior and senior year into just this year. So that'll be good. I just do my schoolwork online and watch a lot of TV. Occasionally come to appointments and stuff."

I nod. I'm already being super awkward, especially since I'm trying not to look at her with pity. But her life now sounds so isolating. It's not like she'd be the only pregnant girl in school, either. I guess sometimes the teen moms drop out, but most of the time they keep going to class right up until they deliver.

It sucks that someone's own parent would encourage them to drop out of school. My mom would never. But then, she continued going to school before and after she had me, even when it was difficult. Even when it took her twice as long to graduate and get through college.

"It's really fine," she says, even though in this situation, I feel like *I* should be putting *her* at ease.

"Is anyone here with you?" I ask, looking around.

"Nah. My mom says that if I'm old enough to get myself into this situation, I can handle it all by myself."

"Sorry, but that's bullshit," I blurt out before I give it a second thought. I clap my hand over my mouth. "Oh my god. Sorry. It's just . . ." There's no end to that sentence. Or rather, there are a thousand ends. She deserves better. She should have more support now, not less. She shouldn't be punished for this.

But Alice smiles. "It is, isn't it?" She sighs. "It's really awesome running into you."

"Are you still singing?" I ask her.

"To myself. To him." She pats her belly.

"It's a boy?"

She grins. "Yeah. Eli James."

"That's an awesome name. I have a baby brother. He's so sweet." *What stupid things to say*, I think. Maybe I should just be polite and wish her well and go find my mom. Or else I'll probably keep saying stupid, unhelpful things. But maybe if I were in Alice's shoes, I would be tired of people being afraid to say the wrong thing. I think maybe what she needs right now is a friend.

"I volunteered here over the summer," I say. "And I came with my mom for all of her appointments when she was pregnant with my brother. You know, if you ever want company for appointments or anything . . ."

"I've been coming to them by myself and it's mostly okay," she says. "And now I have to come every two weeks. So this place is like my home away from home."

"Okay. But if you do want someone. I mean . . . I'm here. And

I happen to like doing the baby thing. Hearing the heartbeat." My palms are legit sweating. It all feels like a bad pickup line.

"That would actually be really great," she says, smiling. "Even Eric doesn't want to come. He's the dad. Do you remember Eric?"

I nod. Eric was her boyfriend last year. I didn't know him that well. I'm grappling for things to make this conversation less awkward than it already is. "I'm really not trying to pry. Is he still . . . ?" *Oh my god. That is totally prying.*

"Oh. I don't know. He's going to be around for the birth and wants to be a dad and stuff, but, honestly, the whole thing is kind of a lot for him. It's a lot for me, too, not that anyone ever asks." She pauses. "So . . . actually, you could come with me, if you want. Or . . . if you don't mind. And I'd love to see Evita and hear about choir and GSA. I just feel so weird that I didn't tell anyone about the baby and then to be so huge and, like, spring it on everyone? That would be so awkward."

"She would love to see you. You should come jam with us sometime. Evita isn't totally satisfied with my backup vocals. Not that she'd come out and say that to me. But I bet she'd love to have another singer to record stuff."

"You guys are recording stuff?" she asks.

"Well, not like an album or anything. Audition pieces for Berklee. Other than that, just some tracks and samples for the stuff we want to perform live."

I start telling her about the band name and the instruments we play and how we've been collaborating when we write stuff. Once we start talking about music, the awkwardness just falls away.

My mom walks over in her Pepto Bismol–pink scrubs that all the labor and delivery nurses wear. "Lacey, the other nurses said you were here," my mom says. She's so energetic, you'd never guess she's coming off a ten-hour shift.

"Mom. This is Alice," I say. "She's a singer," I add, instead of saying "She's pregnant." My mom has this rule about never commenting on another woman's pregnancy. It's up to the mom to tell you she's pregnant. And, unless you see a baby emerging, you don't assume.

My mom holds out her hand. "Nice to meet you, Alice."

"Nice to meet you, too. I'm here for an appointment with Kelly," Alice says.

"Kelly is the best," my mom says. "She delivered Lacey's little brother and oversaw Lacey's volunteering hours this summer."

"Really?" Alice asks.

"Yeah," I tell Alice. "You are absolutely in great hands." Then I tell my mom, "I'm actually gonna hang with Alice for her appointment if you just want to meet at home."

My mom gives me a decidedly uncool grin. I kind of wish she could let her feelings fly under the radar just a little bit. "Sure. I'll save you a taco."

"Have I ever eaten just one taco?" I ask her.

"I will save you twice as many tacos as I think you could possibly eat," my mom says with a laugh. "See you at home. Have a good appointment, Alice."

"You really don't have to wait if you've got plans," Alice says once my mom is gone.

"My plans involve eating tacos, and as you heard, my mom will save me some."

"That's really nice."

I think maybe Alice's eyes are watering. I keep talking music in case she wouldn't want me to notice her tears. "Actually, we're probably going to record my audition piece this weekend."

"A viola piece?" she asks.

"Yeah. I wrote it for viola, but we might add in some other stuff. I don't know, I want the admissions people to see my composing just as much as my playing."

Kelly pokes her head into the waiting room and calls Alice back. She gives us both a smile. "Nice to see you again, Lacey."

"You, too," I say.

"Is it okay if she stays for my appointment?" Alice asks.

"Totally, if you want," Kelly says as she holds the door to her office open for us. "I wondered if you guys knew each other."

They go on with their appointment, and I just feel glad to be included. Alice is thirty-two weeks along, so she's nearing full term. They discuss birth plans and preparations and a lot about easing her discomfort. Then comes the magical moment when Kelly uses the Doppler to hear the baby's heartbeat. It's like a small microphone that glides over the belly and amplifies the little *whoosh, whoosh* of the heart.

"I don't think there's anything better than that sound," Alice says, grinning.

"There really isn't," I agree.

"Everything looks good with little Eli," Kelly announces. "And, Lacey, I'm glad you're here, because I wanted to talk to you about the possibility of an internship. I talked to a radiologist last week, and he is sponsoring one of your classmates doing an independent study. I know the year has already started, but when I heard there were kids from the high school doing internships here, I thought of you. I'd love to sponsor you. I know you completed doula training over the summer."

"Lacey, you'd be awesome," Alice says eagerly.

I'm stunned. Volunteering here over the summer was great. I loved seeing the new babies and the happy new families. But that was the summer. I had plenty of time outside my weekly shift to play music.

"I have an independent study already," I say.

"Oh. That's too bad. I was just thinking that if you were interested in working something out so you could try attending births as a doula, going through the school is a great way to go, liability-wise."

"I did think the training was really interesting," I say. Doulas provide support to women during birth and beyond. It isn't a medical job. It's more about supporting them emotionally and physically, trying to ensure they have all the help they could want. Mom and I took the training together over the summer. I observed childbirth classes, learned all about labor and birth and what kind of help women need. "I'll think about it and let you know."

Kelly looks so hopeful. I want to say yes just because saying yes is always easier for me than no. But I just don't see how it would work.

"Of course. But if you want to try it out, you could just drop in on Sunday for a shift. We can totally run it past the hospital as you shadowing me, to consider an independent study or something," Kelly says.

"I'll let you know," I repeat.

"Awesome. Alice, I'll see you in two weeks," Kelly says. She gives us both hugs.

Back in the waiting room, Alice turns to me. "Thank you so much for hanging out."

"Are you kidding? This was fun. And exciting," I say.

"It's really cool that you know about this stuff. If I had known that you were into this, I might have told you about Eli sooner."

"Well, I'm glad I know now. And I could come to other appointments if you want. Just let me know when they are, and I'll make it work," I say.

"I would love that," Alice says. "Thank you." She lets out a big exhale and then smiles. She already seems so much more at ease than she did when I first spotted her. "You should go get those tacos. And tell Evita I said hi."

"I will. She'll be glad to hear you haven't moved away or something."

"Could you maybe just let me tell her about the pregnancy and stuff?" Alice asks.

"Oh. Absolutely. I wouldn't mention anything."

Alice looks relieved. "I just feel like such a moron. You know? Like, obviously, I knew this was a possibility, but somehow I just didn't think I would get pregnant, and now I know just how stupid that was. You must think it's dumb."

"No way. My mom had me when she was our age, and she's the smartest person I know. But just because you're smart doesn't mean you make all the right choices. Not that . . . you chose this . . . You know what I mean," I say.

She laughs bitterly. "Yeah. I do. I would not have chosen this. But, well, I guess it's happening." She shrugs. "And I love Eli already. That's not it . . ."

"You'll be great," I tell her.

We exchange phone numbers, and I put her next appointment in my phone. I give her one last hug. I am hungry for tacos and tired from a long day, but I'm also energized. I really like Alice, and I'm honestly honored that she let me into her appointment and in on her secret. I probably won't do the doula thing—not yet anyway—but I can do this. I can support Alice in whatever ways she needs.

Four

Mom wraps me in a hug the moment I walk through the door. "I'm so proud of you! Supporting your friend at her appointment."

"Yes, Mom, I know. You made that obvious," I tease.

"We haven't eaten yet! Come grab a taco," my stepdad, Charlie, calls from the kitchen. "Big day. Dylan is going to try his first solid food!"

Dylan squeals at me from his high chair. He's been sitting at the table with us for about a month, eyeing our food, but he has yet to actually try any. I take the seat next to him and kiss his chubby cheeks.

"Food at last!" I say to him in the singsong voice that doesn't seem to belong to me but comes out whenever I'm around my baby brother.

I help Charlie get all the taco fixings on the table while my mom carefully mashes an avocado.

"I can't believe my baby is about to eat solid food," my mom says sadly.

"And your other baby is almost eighteen. Time flies," Charlie says.

I wait until we are all sitting and digging in to tell my mom that Alice asked me to come with her to her next appointment.

"What did you say?"

"That I'd love to. Kelly even asked if I wanted to try volunteering as a doula, like work it out as another independent study credit. She said I could try it out this Sunday."

"Oh, Lacey, you have to," she says, clapping her hands together. "You know you'll be amazing at it!"

"No. I know it could be cool, but weekends are kind of full as it is."

"But birth is so special, Lacey. I have this feeling that if you tried it, you'd love it. In the moment of birth, it's like nothing else exists. I mean, it's impossible to think of anything other than the fact that you're about to meet a human for the first time and bear witness to a woman's strength." My mom thinks for a second. "Or I should say, a birthing person's strength. I suppose not everyone who gives birth identifies as a woman." She shakes her head. "Regardless of a birthing person's gender, it is the most magical thing on the entire planet. Calling it beautiful doesn't even scratch the surface."

Charlie and I exchange a look.

"You are way overselling it, darlin'," Charlie says. "And I'm not sure it's helping your case."

"I get it, Mom, I really do. I just have to think about it," I say.

The way she's grinning at me, I want to give it a try. At least on Sunday. Her enthusiasm is always infectious. And how can I argue that birth is special? I was there when Dylan was born. But that was different. He's my baby brother.

"I'll probably go this Sunday," I say. "But I'm not sure I'll even like it. I'll feel like I'm intruding. It's kind of nerve-racking."

"You just gotta make that leap. Jump in and help. You'll be wonderful." My mom grins. "I am *so* proud of you. You've always been a helper. You're a people person. You know what people need and you help them get it. This is a natural fit for you, Lacey. You'll see."

I put up my hand to stop her. "All right. Stop trying to talk me into it or I'll change my mind."

I can tell my mom is fighting the urge to leave me with just one more piece of wisdom, but she changes the subject and asks me if anything fun is happening in school.

"Oh yeah, I almost forgot," I say, remembering that before seeing Alice, I was excited to tell her all about our guest speaker. "We had an awesome abstinence-only lecture. It was infuriating."

"You're joking! What was it this time?" She's just as outraged as I thought she'd be when I tell her what happened.

"Because only drug users have sex," she says, shaking her head. "Can you imagine sitting there as a sexually active teenager and feeling that guilt laid on you?"

"I'd imagine it was awkward for them. Not that I totally relate," I say, with an eye roll. I have the only parent on the planet who would probably be totally fine having a sexually active high schooler, and instead she's got me.

"So is there going to be a whole unit of this? Or was it just the guest lecture?" Charlie asks.

"I think this might be just the first of many. Apparently, we're discussing 'healthy life choices,'" I say with air quotes.

"You have to keep me posted on what y'all talk about," Mom says. "I want all the details."

"I'll take notes."

"Oh, would you?" Mom asks.

"I'll probably get teased mercilessly, but I will." I get up to clear my plate. "I've gotta work on this project for a bit, but don't put Dylan to bed before I can give him a kiss."

"You got it," Charlie says.

Down in my room, I put on my headphones, sit at my old desktop computer, and open my music composition software. I've been working on Theo's birthday present for over a month. It's this sort of Celtic-sounding piece I'm composing for our quartet. Theo and I always complain about the Haydn and Mozart we play. The cello and viola parts are boring, so I set out to write a quartet that would give both of us some of the best melodic lines and epic supporting harmonies. I'm giving the violins a lot of syncopation. It's sort of an in-joke. On viola I always play these lines that are syncopated, falling after the beat. And Theo and I tease our violinists who can't play off the beat, because they've never had to learn.

I started working on this just to try to trip up our violinists while showboating Theo's cello skills, but once I got started on it, I got really into it. I decided to add other movements and variations. I can't wait to give it to him, because I can already imagine how much he'll like it.

Now with my headphones on, even with the lackluster MIDI synth this computer has, I get sort of lost in it.

~

"Lacey!" Charlie calls down to me. "You've got a guest!"

I know it's either Theo or Evita, so I quickly save and quit the program and go upstairs. Theo's standing in our foyer with his cello and two coffees.

"Thought you might want to jam. Or you could work on your Berklee audition piece?" he asks.

"Definitely." It isn't totally like him to show up here unannounced. Evita's apartment is the usual hangout place. It's kind of an awesome surprise, and I smile at him and jog up the stairs to take one of the coffees.

"You guys can play until eight, and then it's Dylan's bedtime," Charlie says.

"I know the drill," Theo says, smiling. He lifts his cello case and raises his eyebrows at me eagerly. He's always dorkily excited to practice. He follows me down the stairs, and I can tell even from the way his feet fall on the steps that he's happy about something.

He starts unpacking his cello. I'm sitting on my desk chair. I bite my lip. I sort of want to show him the quartet, but his birthday isn't until next week.

He notices me watching him. "Hey," he says as he rosins his bow.

"Hey," I say. I'll show him soon. I cross my room and start unpacking my viola.

"So. Why did you want to come here to practice?" I ask. "We only have about twenty minutes until Dylan's bedtime." I wish

I weren't curious about why he's here, but he was hanging out with Lily Ann this afternoon. And Lily Ann is, objectively, a better player than me. She's been first chair violinist since she moved here. She's one of those kids who's been playing forever, starting with the Suzuki Method when she was four or five.

"Oh. I'm not allowed to stay at Lily Ann's house after dinner," Theo tells me. "Her folks think it's inappropriate to hang out after dark. Even though, like, we are all just sitting around the dining room table together."

And it must be obvious that this pings for me: that Lily Ann's strict parents are the only reason he's here.

"No. No, no, no, no. I'd be here anyway. I can't betray our anti-violin ways! Plus, you'll give it to me straight. Lily Ann gets sort of swoony when I play."

"Dude. Everyone swoons when you play."

His ears turn red. "You know what I mean."

"Yes. I will tell you when you make a mistake."

"Exactly!" Theo holds the neck of his cello in one arm and swings the other arm around me and pulls me in, kissing the top of my head. "Let's tune up."

We start on this boring étude that our orchestra teacher gave us to practice. Then Theo decides we should play it at the same time, but he transposes it up a tritone so it's really dissonant when we play together. It messes both of us up, and we are laughing so hard, he's snorting. Before long, my mom comes down and knocks on the door and we put our instruments away.

We join Charlie in the family room, where he's watching sitcoms. Theo plops onto the loveseat and I sit next to him. My mom comes down looking exhausted, staring at the video baby monitor. She snuggles into Charlie and kisses him. I roll my eyes at Theo. They're as bad with PDA as some of the kids at school. But Theo just puts his arm around me and pulls me into him. Theo doesn't like to be outsnuggled by anyone. It's a point of pride. Evita and I always list his snuggling as one of his best qualities. Evita likes to mention this in front of Lily Ann especially.

"Where's Evita?" I ask him, realizing she hasn't texted me all evening.

"Oh." He clears his throat and whispers in my ear, "She's 'spending the night with me.' But actually, she's at a club listening to this big DJ spin."

"She's such a wild child," I whisper back conspiratorially.

"Oh, of all the—" Mom points to the TV. "This is bullshit! Sexist! That woman is being sexually harassed and they're mining it for comedy. You might as well tell young girls to use their cleavage to get a job."

"Mom. It's a joke. It's a joke the character is clearly in on," I say.

"What's wrong with using what you've got?" Charlie asks.

My mom gasps. Charlie's joking, knowing just how to push her buttons. He laughs as he dodges a swat.

"I solemnly swear to wear turtlenecks to job interviews," I tell her.

"And auditions," she says.

"I will wear a nun habit," I joke.

"At the same time, Lacey, I want you to take charge of your sexuality. It's yours and yours alone." My mom is suddenly serious. And I want to die—she can say whatever she wants in front of Charlie, but Theo is different. This conversation can go a couple of ways. If she brings up the fact that she bought me a vibrator, because I should "know how I work," I will never be able to look at Theo again.

"Mom. Please." I look at Theo, communicating how mortifying this is.

But he's laughing.

"You are a whole person. You don't need to hide any aspect of yourself. And you don't need to give any part of yourself away if you don't want to. You know that, right?" she asks, shutting off the TV. Charlie starts to complain, but she shushes him.

"Yes, Mom."

"You, too, Theo. Pressure on men can be just as damaging. Don't be afraid to embrace your own femininity."

"Oh. God." I groan, because I feel a lecture coming on. And Theo is the last person who needs this particular lecture. He isn't averse to showing his emotions, and he'll wear "girls' clothes" if he likes the way they look. *Affectionate* and *sensitive* are probably the first two adjectives I'd use to describe him.

"No, Lacey, your mom is right," Theo says. "But, Ms. Burke, you don't need to worry about that. I was raised by a pack of females. My cycle even syncs up with theirs," he jokes. But I groan again, because he has no idea what he just stepped into.

"Oh, Theo. No. No, no. We don't call women 'females.' And we *definitely* don't joke about the menstrual cycle. Men have used that for centuries to discredit women and their emotions."

"Oh, I really was joking—"

"I know. But that's just as bad. Other men aren't as evolved as you are."

"Can we please just turn the TV back on?" I beg.

"I better shove off anyway, Lace," Theo says.

"Oh, honey, I didn't mean to embarrass you," my mom apologizes. She jumps up when Theo stands.

"What part of bringing up the menstrual cycle isn't embarrassing?" I ask her.

"Lacey!" she says, shocked. "You can't be embarrassed by your beautiful body! Have I taught you nothing?"

"You know, she might just be objecting to you saying all this in front of company," Charlie says gently.

"I'm gonna walk Theo out," I say. "I promise I love my body and all of its life-giving functionality." I grab Theo's hand and pull him up the stairs to the foyer before my mom can say something else.

Outside it's surprisingly warm for the end of October. "I can practically feel my cello going out of tune," Theo says as he puts it in his trunk.

"Where are you headed?" I ask him. Since the youngest of his three older sisters went away to college, Theo avoids being home as much as possible. He doesn't really talk about it, but Evita and I know.

"I guess I'll try to catch up with Evita."

"You want company?" I ask him.

"Nah. Don't you want to see how the sexist TV show pans out?"

I really don't want him to leave. "You should stay. We can just hang out in my room. I have something . . ." But I shake my head. I should wait until it's totally finished.

"I gotta catch Evita at some point anyway. Unless you'll miss me too much," he says. He's joking. I think. But something in the way he says it makes me think he's fishing for something, wondering if I miss him when he's not here.

"Nah. Have fun. I'm tired." *And I want to work on your quartet.*

He nods. "All right. Good night, Lacey." He hugs me. "Please don't wear turtlenecks for auditions. I don't want to be embarrassed to be seen with you," he deadpans.

"Sexist pig," I joke.

"Is it sexist to tell you that you smell good?"

I laugh at this. He's always asking Evita and me about what shampoo we use, because he wishes his hair smelled good. "No. But it's weird."

"Okay. See you later." He folds himself into the driver's seat of his dad's old muscle car. I watch him drive off, kind of wishing he would stay.

Five

Wednesday, I'm heading into senior seminar ready to note every ridiculous detail of whatever lesson Mrs. Einhorn has planned. It's more than just wanting to report back to my mom, though. I get a little thrill at being outraged. I've prepared for this class like I'm going into battle, armed only with common sense, statistics, and memorized lectures from my mom. I'm just hoping to prove someone wrong. But, then again, maybe it's ridiculous that I'm going into this class feeling like I know anything at all about sex.

Theo holds up a sheet of paper. "I'm going to tally again."

"And I am going to try very hard to roll my eyes silently," I say.

When the bell rings, without saying a word, Mrs. Einhorn carefully places two clear plastic cups on her desk. In the first one, she pours an inch of water from a pitcher. "This is you. Your body is healthy and pure."

I draw in an audibly loud breath. Screw being silent. I might be healthy, but I'm not *pure*, and that whole idea is bullshit. I know exactly where this is headed.

Then she fills the second cup, only this time she adds a dozen drops of blue food coloring. "Can anyone guess what this is?"

Evita raises her hand. "From what I understand from television, that's menstrual blood." She's completely deadpan. Everybody giggles.

"Evita. You can see me after class," Mrs. Einhorn scolds. "This is another person. And they have been exposed to a sexually transmitted infection."

I could scream. Or, at the very least, I feel a big eye roll coming. Theo turns around and raises his eyebrows at me even though I'm pretty sure it was a silent eye roll.

"And if the two of you engage in sexual activity . . ." Mrs. Einhorn takes the two cups and pours the water back and forth between the two of them a few times. "Now look at your body."

"Hey! But my sexual partner's STI has cleared up a little!" Evita calls out. There are more snickers, but Mrs. Einhorn ignores it.

"This is an apt illustration, don't you think? It perfectly shows the exchange of bodily fluids." This comment elicits a slew of groans.

She pulls out half a dozen more cups and fills them all with water. She begins to mix the cups, pouring them back and forth, demonstrating sex in the stupidest way possible. I can feel my palms clenching and sweating, I'm so personally offended.

I think of what Alice would feel if she were here. She said she was embarrassed to have gotten pregnant. And that's without any-one telling her she isn't pure or that the sex she had with her boy-friend was nothing but a gross exchange of bodily fluids. Alice deserves better. We all do. Because what if some of these kids in this class believe what Mrs. Einhorn is saying? Even just a little bit.

My mind is racing with problems with this demonstration. It's completely ignoring sex that isn't heterosexual intercourse. It's presenting virginity as a state of purity, when it is just *some-one who hasn't had sex yet*. And what about victims of sexual abuse? What would they say about this "purity"?

I am so tired of hearing this same shit over and over and not having it help anyone.

And something just clicks into place for me. A crucial piece of information is missing from this equation.

I tap Theo, and even though I don't want to know the answer, I ask him, "Do you have a condom on you?"

"Uh . . . seriously?"

"Yes!" I whisper. "If you do, hand it over."

He digs through his backpack and produces one.

"Gross, dude. Were you gonna do it at school?" Evita whis-pers to him.

I snatch it and march to the front of the class. "Mrs. Einhorn," I say, my voice sounding more confident than I feel. "It's a pretty good demonstration, but perhaps we could provide a few more variables."

She's shocked that I would interrupt a lesson, so she's speech-less as I unwrap the condom and stretch the opening over the top of one of the cups of now-light-blue liquid. I turn the cup upside down over a "pure" cup.

"And, look, we have prevented the transmission of the STI," I say. The class applauds.

Mrs. Einhorn shushes the class and turns to me. "You can see me after class as well. Return to your seat."

I sit back down. Theo turns around and whispers, "I hope that's the last time you walk around without being prepared. You never know when—"

"Theo! You may see me after class also," Mrs. Einhorn calls. She turns back to the class, trying to get their attention back on the inane cups of blue liquid. "Perhaps the transmission of disease can be somewhat lessened."

"Eighty percent reduction in incidence of HIV," I call, armed with that particular statistic from one of the brochures my mom has given me.

She ignores me. "But what of the emotional consequences?" She tries desperately to regain the class's attention, but it's too late; everyone is whispering and giggling. I even get a couple smiles and nods of approval. "You may use the rest of the class to do homework and to ponder the demonstration."

Evita reaches her hand under the table for a low five. "You are such a badass."

After class, Evita, Theo, and I stay in our seats. We're gonna be late for government, because Mrs. Einhorn makes us wait before she says anything.

"I have been teaching at this school for almost twenty years," she says. "I have never, in all those years, been so disappointed in my students as I was today."

My heart speeds up. I have never been in trouble at school. I still remember when a teacher had to raise her voice at me for giggling with Evita during a lesson. My cheeks burned with shame for almost an hour. The pounding of my heart isn't actually unpleasant this time, because her lesson was bullshit, and I'm righteously furious.

"I expect you all to listen to the knowledge I'm imparting. You need to trust that I am trying to teach you. That I care about you."

"We don't doubt that," Theo says. He glances at me, and I think maybe he's trying to draw the heat off me, since, obviously, I was the most disruptive. "But if we have opinions or questions or other thoughts, shouldn't we express them? Start a discussion that benefits all of us?"

"Not how you did it," Mrs. Einhorn says, looking right at me.

"Are you saying that condoms don't lower the transmission of sexually transmitted infections?" Evita asks.

"I'm saying that interrupting and derailing my demonstration was rude, disrespectful, and inappropriate. I'm not going to be taking official disciplinary action, but as this class's grading mainly focuses on class participation, you all have some work to do to bring your grades up. You will each hand in five pages on healthy life choices on Monday if you want to improve your grade. And any further inappropriate outbursts will not be tolerated." Mrs. Einhorn, who's normally a mild-mannered teacher, practically glares at me when she says it.

The bell that indicates our tardiness to our next class rings. Evita squeezes my hand under the table. She knows I hate being late.

"Gladly. Thanks for the chance to make it up," she says. "Can we go?"

Mrs. Einhorn nods. I grab my backpack, eager to leave as soon as possible. Theo puts his arm around me as soon as we're in the hall.

"Don't let the man get you down," he says.

"No way," Evita says reassuringly. "You were and are amazing."

"Guys. I am surprisingly unruffled. I kind of feel awesome." I just did that. *Me.* Straight-A Lacey who hates to make waves. But today felt right.

"I would write a million papers to see you rip open a condom like that again."

I just blink at Theo.

"Oh god. I just heard myself say that out loud and I'm mortified. No. Not like that," Theo laughs.

"Suuuuuuuuuuure," Evita teases him.

"You guys are nuts," I tell them, but I'm laughing along with them.

Six

Even with Theo and Evita giving me puppy-dog looks and begging me to hang out at Evita's, I get in my car after school to drive home.

"I gotta check in with my mom!" I tell them. "I'll catch up with you guys soon. I promise."

"I will buy you a coffee!" Evita says from Theo's car, which is parked next to mine.

"But no one will appreciate the condom demonstration like Ms. Burke. She's gotta go tell her," Theo says to Evita. "Although you will be missed." He smiles at me, then asks Evita, "Do I get a free coffee? I supplied the condom."

"Actually, I don't have my wallet. So the coffee has to be on you," Evita says with a toothy grin.

Theo rolls his eyes playfully and shuts his door. He waves after he starts his car. Evita sticks her tongue out at me as they back out of their spot, but then blows me a kiss. I follow them out of the parking lot, and drive home.

My mom is folding laundry when I walk in the door. She puts a finger up, letting me know that Dylan is napping. She points to the bouncy seat where he sleeps. I nod and sit on the living room floor next to her, helping her fold.

"How was your day?" she asks me.

"It was . . . interesting," I whisper. "I actually couldn't wait to tell you all about the sex-ed drama."

"Oooooh. Tell me."

I start recounting the blue water demonstration. My mom is appropriately outraged.

"So, I borrowed a condom from Theo, marched up to the front of the class, and put it over the opening of a cup."

"Genius!" my mom whisper-yells. Dylan stirs.

"Yeah. Well. The teacher wasn't too happy about it."

"I guess she probably wasn't. But that's okay."

"I have to write a five-page paper as punishment."

"About what?"

"Healthy life choices."

"Such as . . ."

"Well," I say, folding together a pair of tiny socks, "I'm not sure it'll help my grade, but I thought I could write it about condoms."

"Yes. Absolutely. In fact, I bet if you were armed with statistics about how freaking stupid abstinence-only education is, you might even convince her."

"That's a little more optimistic than I am feeling. But I just don't feel like I should totally cave."

"You know if you get in any kind of trouble about it, I've got your back, right?" my mom says.

"I'm sort of counting on that," I tell her.

47

"I can find some scholarly articles for you, too. About abstinence-only education, or maybe some big public health studies about condom use and efficacy. You can't argue with facts," she offers. "I love a good medical study."

"I know you do." I laugh. When she was studying for her nursing degree, she used to share studies that fascinated her. She loves public health stats. Proof that her job makes a difference in the big picture.

"You know . . . Speaking of this paper, and medical studies, and volunteering at the hospital . . ." Mom is going for a segue, and it's not very subtle.

"Were we talking about volunteering?" I ask.

"I still think you might want to submit an application for a nursing program or two. There are so many great in-state schools." She gets up from where she's sitting. "Hang on a sec."

She walks to the kitchen and I hear her rustling through the junk drawer where we keep chargers and pens and notepads and other sundries. She comes back with a manila envelope. She shakes the contents out on the carpet next to us. They're college brochures.

"Mom. Seriously. How long have you been squirreling these away?" I ask her.

She shrugs guiltily. There's a reason she hasn't shown me these before, and I'm guessing it's that she knows these go against all my plans.

"I've just been setting them aside. There are some really great schools in state, you know," she says.

"Yeah. I know. Boston has sort of been the plan, though," I tell her.

"There are some for Boston schools, too!" She shuffles through the pile and points to some in Boston and the surrounding area. She has obviously researched this. "I just want you to leave your options open. I think about how into nursing and pregnancy and stuff you were as a kid, and I just don't want you to discount that. You could really make a difference. Look through them. Pick one or two. It'll take you an hour—just submit an application. What would it hurt?"

I look at her hopeful face. She does have a point. There was a time when I dreamed of nursing. But I don't think it's any different from the armies of kids who want to be astronauts or vets or artists. I wanted to be a nurse because I was surrounded with anatomy textbooks and because my mom has always been my hero.

"Yeah. Why not?" I say. "And I think I'll volunteer this weekend."

My mom claps her hands together, excited, but it makes Dylan stir. She leans over the basket of laundry to give me a giant hug.

"I'm gonna get started on the paper and stuff," I tell her.

"I'm proud of you," she whispers.

Once I'm in my room downstairs, I spend an hour researching condoms. It actually all feels so unnecessary. Like, who doesn't know that condoms protect against STIs and pregnancy? Nonetheless, I find a couple abstracts of scholarly articles that I wonder if my mom can access. And, mostly so I can tell her I gave it a shot, I look up the websites for some of the schools in Massachusetts.

I start by mapping how close they all are to Berklee, but then I'm totally won over by UMass Amherst's website. The problem is, when I map it . . . It's not that close to Boston. Of all the schools I'm looking at, though, it fits my interests the best. They highlight this nurse who worked for Planned Parenthood, even when the people around her told her that was morally questionable. Her story is kind of awesome. And if the school wants to highlight her story, then maybe they would like to hear about my condom demonstration. Or about this paper I'm about to write.

Before I second-guess the decision, I apply. It's quick and painless. Even if I'm not going to end up there, I know it will make my mom really happy that I've entertained the idea, even just for this afternoon. When I ask to borrow her credit card for the application fee, I'm pretty sure I see a couple of proud tears.

"This does not mean I'm going there," I say. "It's a whole hour and a half away from Boston, I might add."

"What's an hour and a half from your friends?" she asks. "You'll be—what—twelve hours away from me."

"It would make it pretty hard to all share an apartment."

"I guess. I'm still really glad you're applying," she says, pressing her lips together, likely trying to fight the grin that she wants to give me. She hands me her card. But then she giggles joyfully.

"Real subtle," I say to her.

With the application sent in, I put on my headphones and work on the quartet for Theo. Lily Ann wants to pick new music in independent study tomorrow, so it's the perfect time to give it to him.

I fiddle with dynamics and other markings and nuances. I listen to it one more time through the software, making sure there isn't anything else I would change. I'm prouder of this piece than anything else I've done, including what I just wrote for my audition. I print a score, and then copies of each of the individual parts. And I just flip through the pages.

I've only been composing for a couple years. And I'm mostly self-taught. I've had private viola lessons with students at the nearby college on and off since middle school. But when Mom and Charlie got married, we got Charlie's family's old piano, and suddenly I got my hands on whatever I could to learn more. I watched YouTube tutorials on how to play. I downloaded free software to try composing. I did an online course in music theory. I started paying attention to how the parts of a quartet fit together. I studied the scores for the pieces we played in orchestra instead of just worrying about the viola part.

This past summer with Theo and Evita, the composing finally started to make sense. It's amazing to have two people on the same wavelength as me. We collaborate seamlessly. Evita can take whatever I write and make it way more interesting and complex and catchy. She can write lyrics, which is something I don't do. And Theo can play anything. He's got this killer combination of a musical ear and crazy-good rhythm and the kind of coordination that makes picking up new instruments and percussion parts super easy for him.

I suddenly wish Evita and Theo were here. It's going to be hard to even wait to show Theo until tomorrow afternoon.

I text Evita.

Project quartet is complete!

Yes!!!!!!! I want to hear it!

I email the MIDI file and text her to check her inbox.

> This is like epic fantasy movie
> shit. Like a theme for a gladiator
> and his elven princess girlfriend

I love that she clearly dropped everything to hop on her laptop and listen.

> You're not waiting a whole week
> to give this to him, are you?

> **No way. Tomorrow during**
> **quartet. Also, Mom is fully on**
> **board with the condom**
> **demonstration.**

> Of course she is! Because you
> have never been more of a
> badass : . . except maybe that
> time you wrote some epic film
> score for your best friend's
> birthday.

I grin. Tomorrow cannot get here fast enough.

> Honestly, I might see if I can't
> bring my own independent
> study from the library to the
> orchestra room

She also has an independent study last period, but hers is dedicated to running the Gender and Sexuality Alliance. She's done a lot as the GSA's president. She's organized field trips to pride events. She's booked speakers for our monthly meetings and she's contacted presidents of high school GSAs all over the country. Nothing would ever overtake music as Evita's greatest passion, but she pours a lot of love into the GSA as well.

That might tip him off

Fine. Somehow you have to take
a picture of his face, though.

I run my fingers over the black notes on the crisp white pages and wonder if I should wrap the music and make him open it. But something about that seems silly and frivolous in a way that Theo would surely appreciate, but that Lily Ann would not. If I want our quartet to actually work on this, I have to introduce it more like a project for all of us and less like an inside joke with Theo. Still, I doodle birthday balloons on the printout of the cello part. The balloons look embarrassingly spermlike. Maybe that's the condom research getting to me.

Seven

The next day, I'm walking to lunch with Evita when this girl Victoria stops me in the hall. I've had a few classes with Victoria, including senior seminar. She's standing in the hall with her friend Hailey. The way she sort of jumps toward me from where she was leaning on her locker makes me feel like they were just standing there waiting for me. Both of them hang with the popular crowd. I wish I weren't like this, but that fact makes me nervous to be around them and I fight the urge to smooth my hair, which is always futile.

"Lacey, we were wondering if we could talk," Victoria says.

Hailey nods. "Maybe in the bathroom?"

"Oh." I'm taken aback. "Sure."

In the bathroom, Victoria looks under the stall doors to make sure no one is listening. It feels very cloak-and-dagger.

Evita asks them, "You're not about to give my girl a

beatdown or something, are you? Cuz you will definitely have to go through me."

Victoria waves her off and looks at me. "Okay, so you know all about this stuff, right? Like condoms and sex and stuff?" she asks.

"Well . . . ," I say.

"She does. Yes. Give yourself some credit!" Evita says to me.

"But your demonstration in class. I was wondering if . . . okay . . ." Victoria turns red.

"You need to know how to use a condom?" I ask her.

"Well, the guy always takes care of it, for, like, sex and stuff, but for other things . . ." Victoria looks like she wants to shrink away to nothingness.

Hailey chimes in, "What about oral sex?"

Oh. "What *about* oral sex?" I ask.

"Like. I don't know. Condoms are just for sex-sex, right?" Victoria asks.

I take a deep breath. Some of this is stuff I've read up on, but a lot of it is stuff I just seem to know, like I absorbed it by osmosis by living with my mom.

"So, first off, I would consider oral sex, sex. And I'm assuming that 'sex-sex' is heterosexual vaginal intercourse," I say.

They nod.

"Obviously, with intercourse, there is the possibility of pregnancy, so we normally think of condoms for preventing pregnancy," I say. "But condoms can be used to prevent STIs during any sex act. Counting oral."

"I told you," Hailey mumbles.

"Second of all," I say. "It's awesome that your partner or

partners are using condoms, but you can't just dismiss it as 'something the guy takes care of,' you know?"

"Well . . . it's his . . . penis . . ." Victoria sort of nervously giggles.

"Yeah, but you need to be in charge of your health. So, it's best if you know how to use them properly. You might have to show a guy one day. Or maybe someone might use one incorrectly and you'd only know that if you know how to use one. And it doesn't hurt to keep some on you. You know, prevent the 'Oops, I don't have a condom, but who cares if it's just this once' kind of thing."

"Yeah. But, like, I'm not going to go *buy* condoms," Victoria says, horrified.

"Why not?" Evita asks, more harshly than I would.

"It's mortifying."

"It's a rite of passage," Evita says. "Right, Lacey?"

"I think you might feel more empowered if you take charge of it," I answer.

"Everyone knows this trick," Evita offers. "Fill a basket with some shampoo, some chocolate, and a magazine. Then add the condoms to the basket. Try to time it so that you get an old lady to ring you up. Then talk about her hair or *whatever*, just nervously chatter while she rings you up."

"And she won't notice the condoms?" Victoria asks skeptically.

"Oh, she'll notice, but she'll know you're nervous, so she'll try real hard not to look judgmental about it," Evita says.

"Or you can go to the clinic. You know the one across the street from the college campus? They just have a bowl of them right there," Hailey says.

"For real?" Victoria asks.

"Where do you think I get mine? They even have flavored ones. Which—oh my god—makes total sense with oral," Hailey says. "Anyway. Thanks, Lacey."

"Yeah, thanks, Lacey. You're the best," Victoria says.

"Everything said in the office is confidential, so don't worry about that," Evita assures them.

Victoria and Hailey thank me and then leave.

"Dude. You know your shit," Evita says to me.

"Evita. Come on. You knew all that stuff."

"But there's no way I would have had that conversation with them without scaring them off."

"That's probably true. Did you really do that trick at the drugstore?"

"Oh. Totally. Theo's a total wuss about buying condoms. He thinks everyone is trying to picture him naked when he buys them."

"He does not," I say, shocked. No friend of mine should be a wuss about buying condoms.

Evita shrugs. "The point is: you know your shit." We walk out of the bathroom and head to the cafeteria.

"I'm writing my paper for Mrs. Einhorn on condoms, by the way."

"Rebel!"

"And now I'm thinking I should make people read it before I turn it in. There's more to know than you would think. Stuff like types of lube you can use, or concerns with breakage and slippage."

It's loud when we get to the cafeteria, so I worry less about people hearing me, but then Evita squeals.

"Slippage and breakage? Are those official terms?"

"Actually, yeah," I tell her.

"But seriously, why not show everyone your paper?" Evita asks. "We could, like, distribute pamphlets. That'd show them!"

"Pamphlets on what?" Theo asks.

"Slippage. Breakage. That sort of thing," Evita says with a wry smile.

"That's not a bad idea," I tell her. I'm glad Victoria and Hailey sought me out, but how many of my classmates are too nervous to talk about this stuff? Especially when it's been made clear to us that these are questions we should feel ashamed to have. Like, which is better for keeping us healthy: shame or information? It seems like a no-brainer.

Eight

Our quartet meets in the orchestra room last period. The orchestra teacher flits in and out of the room. She's overseeing our quartet, but she also wants us to handle things like repertoire and gigs and running our own rehearsals, just like professional chamber music groups. Our second violinist, Scott, is the first one there, so we all tune off him.

"New music?" Theo asks when we're all settled.

"Please," Lily Ann says. "Any suggestions?" She looks to Theo as if Scott and I don't even exist. Though Scott's never shown an opinion about what we play. It's just as well. The three of us have enough opinions as it is. Lily Ann wants to make sure we have all the basic repertoire down, so we can get more wedding gigs. Theo wants to go more modern. I just like pretty and emotional things.

"Schubert?" I offer.

"Anything but Haydn," Theo says. "Schubert could be good."

"Not all Haydn is boring," Lily Ann says. "But I like Schubert."

"Actually . . . ," I start. But, no, maybe we should start with Schubert, and I should offer my piece at the end of the period, so if no one else is thrilled by it, I don't have to know. "Ideas for Schubert or should we just play through some?" I hop up to the shelf of music and grab a folio of Schubert. The card stock of the covers is so worn it feels more like felt than paper. Worn sheet music is one of my favorite things, but I keep thinking of the crisp white sheets I brought with me. Lily Ann and Scott reach for their parts, but when I try to hand Theo his, he just raises an eyebrow at me. I don't know how he does this, but he always knows when something is on my mind.

"Did you have another suggestion? Care to share with the class?"

"No. Well. I don't know if anyone but you will like it," I tell him. God. I wish I didn't sound so freaking bashful and uncool in this moment.

"Even better. Pass out whatever it is you have in your bag that you keep looking at." Theo is smirking.

"Yeah. Okay. But be kind. It's sort of a birthday present. And . . . I haven't really tried to write a quartet before."

"You *wrote* one?" Lily Ann asks excitedly. "That's awesome!"

The folder is out of the bag and in my hand before I can change my mind. "Happy birthday, Theo."

Theo looks at his part and my cheeks burn. They're all looking their parts over, and part of me feels so naked. I'm not sure how I'll feel when we're actually playing it.

"We should play it," Lily Ann says.

"Sure," I say, tightening and then loosening my bow. It's my nervous habit. I'm never sure I've gotten quite the right tension.

"How fast is it supposed to be?" Lily Ann asks.

I pat my knee in beats of two and make a little tick with my tongue in sets of three eighth notes, counting out the six/eight time. Lily Ann nods and puts her violin up. I glance at Theo before we start, and he gives me this goofy look with wide eyes and high eyebrows and my nerves disappear. Lily Ann cues us, and we jump in.

It's rough since we're sight-reading. The syncopation messes Lily Ann up like I thought it would. And Scott shakes his head when his endless eighth notes don't let up. But Theo sounds great. By the end we're all grinning, because it was so fun, but I'm sure my smile is the biggest.

"Lacey!" Theo says. "This is by far the coolest present I have ever gotten! When did you even manage to write it?"

"It's really good," Lily Ann says. "And totally film-soundtrack-worthy."

"Yeah?" I ask. "Should we actually . . . work on it? I mean, if you guys have suggestions for things to change . . . I'm totally up for notes."

"Well . . . ," Lily Ann says, "I think we should play classic stuff, too." She always says this. But for some reason it's coming off as extra condescending today. "But . . . sure. Theo sounded amazing," she says with a predictable swoony sigh.

"Thanks. No one has ever *written* something just for *me* before," he says, looking at me with this sort of puzzled look that is impossible to read.

After a few more run-throughs, we pick a nice Schubert piece to practice, too.

"You guys want to go for coffee or something?" I ask when we're packing up. I hold up my phone. "Apparently, Evita cut out of class early and has been there for twenty minutes and can't believe we didn't also cut out early and teleport there."

"She is something else," Lily Ann says. The way she says it is critical, and I wait for Theo to jump to his best friend's defense.

"I have youth group," Lily Ann continues when Theo doesn't respond. "I wish I didn't."

"God won't mind if you skip," Theo says, buckling his case shut.

"My mom will, though. She's sort of a tyrant about this stuff," Lily Ann explains to me. And I pretend like this is news, as if Theo hasn't been complaining about Lily Ann's mom since they started dating.

"We will just have to hang out *after* youth group," Theo says, kissing her nose.

I walk a little behind them through the music wing and out to the parking lot. I text Evita to tell her we're on our way.

I put my viola and my backpack in the trunk and lean against my car waiting for Theo. Theo is bent in half to kiss Lily Ann through her open window.

I text Evita again:

> I take it back. We aren't on our
> way because one of us is
> making out.

> Well, obviously it's not you.

I'm about to be kind of offended at the suggestion that kissing is out of the realm of possibility for me ever, but then she adds:

> . . . because I doubt you'd send
> me a text to update me if that
> were the case.

62

I send her five eye-rolling emoji, because they're still kissing. I slide into my car and turn on some music until finally Theo hops in the passenger seat with the exuberance of a puppy.

"Lacey Burke!" he exclaims. "You sly creature!"

The muscles in my stomach I didn't realize I was clenching relax. "Happy early birthday."

I put the car in reverse, and Theo puts a hand over mine and guides it back to park. All at once, I notice an unwelcome flock butterflies in my stomach.

"What?" I ask.

He shakes his head. "Just. Thank you. I had no idea. And . . . you just *get* me."

"Did you notice the complete lack of unison when you and I played?" I ask him.

"Except for the awesome, epic double-stop chords! And that theme is killer, Burke. Like. I had no idea. You are a musical genius."

"Shut up."

"Lacey. No. Thank you." His gaze is intense. Then he breaks into a grin. "Got it? I loved it. And you're super talented."

"Yeah, okay."

"No. You're amazing," he says. "You have to believe me or I won't let you go anywhere."

"I'm amazing," I say with a laugh, and he puts the car back in reverse.

He moves his hand, although I immediately wish it were back over mine.

"Could you hurry up? I want to treat you to coffee," Theo says.

Nine

Evita sits with this older, intentionally scruffy-looking guy and waves us over excitedly. I give Theo my order and join her. She forgets to introduce me to the guy she's with, but it doesn't matter; Evita makes friends with everyone. They're talking about some show they went to last week.

"He's a grade-A musician," Evita tells me.

I look at him and smile politely. He's at least college-aged. Half the people in this town are college students. I have this uncomfortable feeling Evita is trying to set me up or something. I don't even know his name.

"Bruno plays bass," Evita says.

I look at Bruno. "Like bass guitar?"

"Double bass. Jazz mostly," he says.

I nod appreciatively.

"We're trying to figure out how we can combine our talents," Evita says. "Just brainstorming here, but some bass might round out our sound a bit, or something. I mean, he could play with the Sparrows, or even just record a few riffs. Something."

The poor guy looks at Evita like she's the coolest person ever, like he's drinking in every word she's saying. And it's funny to me that despite her wacky clothes (sweatpants tucked into tube socks and this drapey poncho thing that looks like it swallowed her whole) and her complete lack of flirtation or interest, she's still attractive to him. I mean, she's gorgeous. Despite all the effort she is putting in trying to get me to talk to these guys, I don't compete.

I'm not great at flirting, I'll admit. But maybe that's because I'm always next to Evita. Even when she totally shuts people down (like "I'm not giving you my number" or "I don't date people I don't know"), they still look enamored. And yet, here I always am. I probably *would* give half those guys my number. I totally would go on a date with someone I didn't know that well. But it doesn't matter, because no one asks me.

"Yeah. You guys might be good, but Lacey here writes intricate and nuanced and emotional string quartets," Theo says, handing me a coffee drink that's as much cream and caramel as coffee.

"Oh. That's awesome," Bruno says. "I'm into a more relaxed, improvisational vibe than that, probably. But I think we could do wicked stuff with some of your mixing." And his attention's squarely on Evita again.

"Let's do that soon," she says enthusiastically. "But you should let me get to my family dinner. Cool running into you."

Bruno gets the hint and saunters off after making sure he has Evita's number—which she actually gives him.

"You just gave him your number," I say when he's out of earshot.

"A professional thing. He knows that," Evita says.

"I'm not totally sure he does," I tell her.

"No, he does. I already told him he's not my type. Like, ick, facial hair?" Evita scrunches up her nose. "Lumberjack dudes are more your thing than mine."

"Who says I have a lumberjack thing?" I ask defensively.

"Um. Hello. You lust after the dude from the Civil Wars. And you have a poster of Ray LaMontagne."

"I took that down," I mumble.

"But you didn't throw it away, did you?" Evita teases.

"Can we please talk about something more important? Something amazing, in fact?" Theo asks with a grin.

"So, your birthday came early, did it?" Evita asks Theo.

"You knew about the quartet?" Theo asks. "And you somehow kept it from me? Color me impressed."

"I am a tomb," Evita says mysteriously. "Where's *my* drink, Theo?"

"You don't look like you need any more."

"Not the point."

"I got Lacey's because she wrote me an entire quartet," Theo argues.

"Yes, but that was a birthday present. And one that was free, I might add."

I roll my eyes at Evita. But Theo gets up to order something for her.

"Evita, were you . . . Was that . . . that guy . . ." I fumble with the words.

66

"Is there a question in there?" Evita asks, enjoying my discomfort.

"I get the feeling you're trying to set me up," I say.

"I mean, yes, but no. Not really. I mean, *why* would I do that to myself? We've already lost Theo to the dark side. What would I do if you had a guy? I'd be no one's number one on speed dial," Evita pouts. "Actually, what are you doing tonight?"

"Umm. Doing homework at your house? Or mine. Why?"

"Cuz Bruno's throwing a party. There is a good chance it'll be, like, dismally small and totally lame and a bunch of guys smoking up and spouting pseudo-intellectual-whatever, but it could still be fun."

"That really doesn't sound like my scene," I say, sipping my drink. "I have a paper on condoms to write. And possibly a pamphlet, too."

"You should totally distribute a pamphlet," Evita says. "But, then, shouldn't you practice what you preach? This party could be an excellent time to . . . explore your options."

"Evita."

"What?"

"Are you trying to get me laid?"

"I mean. Not actively . . . ," Evita says. "You just seemed so worried about that stuff the other day."

"What stuff?" I ask her.

"The sex stuff, Lace. I mean, you even say virginity shouldn't be that big of a deal, but it seems like it is for you."

"What's a big deal?" Theo hands Evita a coffee. "That's decaf."

"Jerk," Evita grumbles. "And we were discussing Lacey's deflowering."

"See!" I say, my cheeks growing hotter by the second. *"Deflowering!* What an awful, awful way to put it. But, regardless, for me it's more about . . . you know . . . only doing what I'm comfortable with."

"Which is what, exactly?"

"Evita, lay off. She doesn't want to talk about it," Theo says.

I hate that he feels like he needs to come to my aid. "Theo. It's fine." I take a sip of my drink and then sigh. "It's not like I'm averse to the whole kissing thing, you know. And I'm not a prude, in theory. It's just a lack of . . . opportunity."

"Which is why we should go to this party," Evita counters.

"What party?" Theo asks.

Evita ignores him. "Blow off your homework. Your grades are great. Come to the party. Get a little drunk. Kiss someone. I mean, round second base if you want. But I think it'll help you not be so uncomfortable when it comes up, you know?"

"How old is he?" I ask.

"I don't know. Twenty?"

"The whole idea of going to a party to get my first kiss out of the way is mortifying," I tell her.

"I'm pretty sure that's why people go to parties," Theo says.

"True!" Evita says.

"Still. No," I tell them.

"Whatever. Okay. The real reason for this coffee date: I have news!" Evita squeals.

Theo looks at me. "And she's going to make us beg her to tell us."

Evita ignores him. "Drumroll, please."

68

Neither of us provides her a drumroll, but she forges ahead. "We have a gig!"

"Are we really ready for that?" I ask her.

"Duh. Yes. It's at that college bar The Map. It's an all-ages night next Wednesday. Bruno says they've just started doing live music and open-mic nights and stuff. It won't be too much pressure. Apparently, their setup is pretty nice."

"That's awesome!" Theo says.

"Yeah. I mean. We can prepare at least a short set," I say. Theo and Evita's excitement is contagious. "So I do have a little news of my own. I'm thinking of volunteering at the hospital."

"When?" Evita asks. Her smile drops.

"I don't know yet. I could still just do Sundays. Kelly said I could be a doula. Like, actually be involved in the births. So, I don't know if I'd be on call or do shifts or what. But it doesn't mean I don't want to be totally there with the Sparrows," I add when I see her scrunch up her face. "I'm going to try it out this Sunday and then figure it out from there."

"That sounds good," Theo says unconvincingly.

"Like, how long on Sunday?" Evita asks. "We need all the rehearsal time we can get. Is this gonna be your new thing? First condom demonstrations to prevent pregnancy, but when that doesn't work you're gonna deliver the babies?" Still scrunched.

"I hadn't tied it all together like that, but, no. It's not my thing. It's *a* thing. Maybe. I'm good at it." I'm holding my ground. Evita probably hopes that if she raises issues with this, I'll just decide not to do it. "How often do you really find something you enjoy and are good at?" I ask her and Theo.

"Not often. So far that's only ever been music," Theo says.

"I still love music," I say. "And. Full disclosure . . . My mom asked me to maybe apply to nursing school. So I sent an application to UMass Amherst."

Both Evita and Theo suck in a gasp.

"Just applying. Not going there. I'm just keeping options open. It doesn't change the whole 'Boston or bust' thing. I'm not breaking up the band." I look back and forth between their dismayed faces. "I have to know exactly how I feel about doing the doula thing and the nursing thing. I mean, it's likely it just won't be for me, right? So, I'll know for sure. But it was important to my mom. And . . . I don't know," I ramble.

"If you think you might want to do that, then you should try it out," Theo says. "I mean the volunteering. I don't think you should try going to a different college . . . but . . . yeah, maybe it'll help you figure stuff out?" He shrugs and looks at Evita.

Evita's face is still scrunched, but she must see my conviction. "Yeah. You do you. I mean, right? It could be cool. Babies. And stuff. You like that stuff."

"Evita. It's okay. You don't have to get it," I say.

"Okay." She's quiet for a second. Then she laughs. "You should see your face."

"What?" I ask.

"You look nervous. I'm not *that* scary, am I?"

"Yeah. Sometimes you really are."

"Okay, but, I support *you*. I just like to know what's going on. Talk to me about stuff, you know?" Evita says. "We're a team."

"We're a team," Theo repeats.

"That's incredibly sappy." I smile.

"I do want you to be happy. Both of you. I just also want the

Sparrows to be our thing. I guess it doesn't have to be our only thing. Right? So, yeah, volunteer, and just get your butt over to my house as soon as you're done."

"Sounds good," I tell her.

"Theo," Evita snaps.

Theo is suddenly engrossed in his phone and typing something quickly.

"Sorry. Lily Ann is hoping to hang out after youth group," Theo says, his head still buried in his phone.

Evita and I roll our eyes at each other. And sure enough, a *pfffff* escapes my lips.

"I heard that," Theo says, not looking up. "Is it cool if she hangs out with us later? Her mom extended curfew for an hour tonight."

"Veto," Evita says.

"Do you really need to be like that?" Theo asks.

"Sorry. That was mean. I don't want to hurt your feelings. But I also don't need to hang out with someone I don't like. And I *do not like her.*"

Theo sighs and shoves away from the table. "Her church is only half a mile from here."

"It's getting cold out," Evita says. Theo pauses, and I'm sure she's about to give him reasons not to leave. "But you can have my mittens." She hands him these hideous orange jack-o'-lantern mittens, which he accepts.

"Yeah. Bye, Lacey. Thanks a million for the best birthday present in the entire world." He gives me a half smile. "Evita, try to be cool?"

She shrugs. The way she does it is so cold, Theo just sort of crumbles. His face falls, and he seems to shrink a few inches. "Bye," he mumbles, and walks out of the café.

"Evita. Seriously? Wasn't that a little harsh?" I ask, draining my coffee. "We've talked about this. Hang on." I get up and follow Theo out the door before I can fully formulate what I even want to say to him. I just hate seeing him defeated like that. "Theo!" I call.

He turns around and gives me this grin like he hadn't just been bummed out a second ago.

"Lacey, where the hell is your jacket?" he asks when he sees me holding my bare arms.

"I just wanted to say how glad I am that you like the quartet." Which is a pretty stupid reason to chase after him. "And, like, don't let Evita being grouchy ruin a good day."

"She did not ruin it. I just really wish she could get on board with Lily Ann."

"I know."

"You guys should maybe actually go to that guy's party," he says.

"Stop! I do not need you trying to hook me up, too."

He looks surprised for a second. "No. I wasn't. I just meant that you and Evita should do something fun so, you know, you guys don't miss me too much," he says. "That sounds super conceited. I just mean that . . . I don't want you guys talking trash when I hang out with Lily Ann."

"I swear."

He reaches over with those ugly mittens and rubs my cold arms. "I'm gonna go get Lily Ann. Today was fucking awesome. Thanks so much for the song." He smiles. "Again. A million times."

Back in the coffee shop, Evita is chatting with a barista. She cannot go even a few minutes without human companionship. But as soon as she spots me, she blows off the barista and sits back down. "Now that Theo's gone, I can finally ask you: What on earth should I get him for his birthday?"

"You haven't gotten him something yet? His birthday is on Tuesday."

"I could buy him something from the grocery store. Jelly beans or Hot Wheels or something. What else is still open?"

"You should just officially give him that Bjork shirt he loves so much."

"Oh my god. Yes. Perfect." She leans back in her chair.

"Do you maybe think the Sparrows could use another singer?" I ask her, remembering Alice. I am way too aware of the fact that I shouldn't bring her up right after talking about volunteering or birth.

"It depends on the singer."

"Remember Alice?"

"Alice? Evans?" Evita asks. "I haven't seen her all year. She must have moved or something."

"Yeah. No. She hasn't moved. I ran into her the other day," I say.

"Where has she been? I miss her!" Evita says.

"Oh. She's . . . homeschooling, I guess."

"Homeschooling? Is it . . . like . . . a religious thing?" she asks like it's a dirty word. We are in the minority at this school for not being active in any youth group. We're not even the kind of people who go to church on Christmas, let alone every Sunday.

"I don't think so. But she's still around. Kind of lonely, I think," I say.

"What? Seriously? Did you get her number? Alice would be *perfect*! Not to diss your vocals or anything."

"It's fine. Here." I pass my phone to her. She puts the number in her phone.

"She'll be perfect. But, oh my god, adding another singer would be a lot of work. But, like, she'd be really good. Okay. I'm excited. I'm gonna call her right now."

"You really don't need more caffeine." I laugh.

"We. Have. A. Gig. I'm freaking excited," she says, putting the phone to her ear. "Alice! It's Evita. Where have you *been*? I miss you! So you have to come sing with us."

Evita keeps filling Alice in on the details. She's so excited and happy, I can't help but smile. This is everything we've been wanting.

Ten

Maybe Evita was joking when she suggested I make a pamphlet, but I am totally into the idea. Evita decided to go to Bruno's party, so I'm at home with my mom. She's predictably thrilled with the pamphlet idea.

She gives me her laptop so I can work on it while we watch *Mean Girls*. Charlie has Dylan at swim lessons at the rec center, so it's just me and her, just like the old days. *Mean Girls* is the perfect movie, because we essentially talk right through it and pause our discussion for the best lines.

"So, like, instructions for when and how to use condoms," I say.

"You need an illustration for that. They are on all the inserts when you buy them," Mom says. "And maybe add where to get them for free. Like the clinic. Or the college health center. Honestly, they should have them at your school. But I guess hell will freeze over before that happens."

"Probably."

We pause the discussion for one of our favorite scenes. My mom says the "cool mom" lines along with the TV.

"And stats about how much it protects you from STIs. You could even add an illustration with the cups," she suggests.

"You really are the cool mom," I say, putting the laptop aside. "I'm gonna get us sodas."

I pause the movie and head upstairs when I hear a knock at the door. I answer it and my heart gives a thud. For the second time in two weeks, Theo is here. Without Evita. "Hey."

"Hey." He grins at me. "Just wanted to come hang out with my favorite composer."

"Beethoven has been dead awhile," I joke.

Once he's inside, he leans over the banister to wave to my mom. "Hi, Ms. Burke."

"Come on down, Theo," she calls up to him.

"You want a soda?" I ask him.

"I got it." He gives my arm a little squeeze before he helps himself from the fridge.

We get settled back in to watch the movie. My mom's on one arm of the sectional and Theo and I are on the other. It's cold down here, so I reach for a throw blanket and without missing a beat, Theo arranges it over both of us and puts his arm around me. I tell him about the pamphlet, and if it embarrasses him to be talking condoms with my mom, he doesn't let on.

After the movie we go to hang out in my room. "Oh, you want to see this piece I was writing with a bunch of timpani and, like, bodhrans and taiko drums and stuff? I totally think that with Evita's drum sounds it could be a cool beat." I start to boot up my ancient computer, and I'm acutely aware that Theo is suddenly sort of tense.

"Sounds cool." He says it like it's anything *but* cool.

There's this awkwardness with us sitting here. And I hate it. Especially because I don't know where it came from. Things are easy with us. They always are. But Theo looks tense.

It's weirdly formal, but Theo reaches out and grabs my hand. He pulls me to stand from my desk and leads me to sit on the edge of my bed. Our fingers intertwine, and he leans back and looks at me.

"Okay. So. I feel so shitty about this . . . ," Theo says, and my heart starts galloping. "Lily Ann doesn't think we should play the quartet you wrote."

I pull my hand away in surprise. "What? She said she liked it."

And just like that, I've lost his eye contact and he stares instead at his now empty hand. "She thinks it's weird that you wrote it for me."

"Weird?" My gut drops.

"Like. Inappropriate?" he says.

My mouth goes dry. I don't know if I should defend why it's perfectly appropriate, or rage against Lily Ann's stupidity like Evita would. Why can't we have this talk with Evita here? "I thought she wanted to play it."

"No. She did. But the more she thought about it, she said it seemed a bit like . . . a grand romantic gesture." He's so crestfallen, I almost don't want to be angry at him, but I suddenly am.

"So what did you say? Because that's ridiculous. I mean, you wrote me a song for my birthday two years ago. I don't think you were trying to woo me."

"Right. I guess . . . this maybe feels different."

"Oh." I scoot as far away from him as I can. "So, you think . . ."

"No. I don't. But she's not comfortable with it. And I think we need to respect that, you know?"

"No. I mean. God!" I jump up from the bed. "I'll tell her it's not a romantic gesture. We always make music stuff for each other. Did you tell her that? Does she get total veto power? I mean, there are four of us. I've had to play through stuff I didn't like."

"I don't think she gets veto power for the quartet necessarily. But she sort of does with me." He finally looks at me.

"That's bullshit," I say, trying not to let my voice get too loud. I pull my knees up to my chest and start fiddling with the edge of one of my sleeves.

"I know it is. But I get what she's saying. Not that . . ." Theo stands up. "Fuck. This is the worst."

"I just don't get it," I say. "You should have stood up for me." Because that's what best friends do.

"Look. She's a little threatened by you."

"By *me*? Seriously? Because I have all this boy-charming power?" I scoff.

"Lacey, you don't ever give yourself enough credit."

"Oh good. Yes. Tell me you're not gonna play the thing I spent hours of my life on, but go ahead and make it okay by telling me how wonderful I am. Then I'll totally forgive everything."

"That's not why . . ."

I give him a second. Maybe it's because part of me is dying to hear just how desirable I might be, or maybe it's because I don't actually want to pick a fight with him. Except I do.

"You are so full of shit, Theo. And this is mortifying. Like I'd be so underhanded. Or pathetic. That I'm sitting over here pining over you. And why are you even here? You didn't have anything better to do than crash a movie night with my mom? You were just biding your time before you insulted me and my intentions and my present. So. Right. Now I don't want to play the quartet, either. Good. Only now I don't know what to say to Lily Ann tomorrow. Like, do I apologize for overstepping? Or is that like admitting some undying love I have for you?" I squeeze my eyes shut tight, because those words just feel wrong to say. "Or I guess I should pretend not to know about the talk you two had about me, because I bet she wouldn't be too thrilled with you hanging out with me alone, would she?"

"Well . . . she was gonna come up with another reason not to work on your piece. Because she thinks she lined up a wedding gig for a month from now. So we should probably work on other stuff anyway." He picks at a loose thread on my comforter. He won't even look at me.

I growl in frustration. "Why did you bother to tell me the real reason? You could have spared me. Like, why are you here?"

"I don't know. Because I was upset." He's dejected.

"Well, good. Now I am, too!"

We stare at each other, in a standoff.

"I'll just go," Theo says.

"Okay."

"I am sorry." He looks at me again, waiting for me to accept his apology. But I don't. I'm angry and defensive, and I want him to leave. Now. He must get that because he stands and slumps out the door.

Once he's gone, I realize that I'm shaking. My heart is pounding against my ribs, because it's possible that Lily Ann was a little bit right. I mean, of course I love Theo. I've always loved him. But there's the way I feel elated when he drops by, and how I always wish he were sitting closer to me. Or the thrill I get when he does little things like grab my hand or tug on my hair. I really do have romantic feelings for Theo.

I rub my eyes, as if I could just erase these feelings or somehow go back to ignoring them. That realization makes me feel sick. Partially because of Lily Ann. But more because we have this perfect friendship.

Suddenly I feel like I swallowed a rock, because I think of Evita. She just told me she still loves him. He's probably the last person on the planet I should develop feelings for. At least for Evita's sake.

Eleven

O rchestra is our first class in the morning, and I don't make eye contact with Theo. I'm still so angry about last night. I don't want to look at him and his perfect haircut and his cute sideburns and his flawlessly cut skinny jeans, because I might just spit on him.

I bury myself in the pages of the music, ignoring the fact that the second-seat cellist is the only person between me and Theo. When it's time to pack up, I see him and Lily Ann having a hushed but heated conversation. I address Lily Ann first. "Hey. So, I'm not going to be at quartet today. Sorry. I need to go to the library to do some research for the volunteer thing I'm doing," I say. It's kind of a lie. I don't need to research anything before this weekend. I honestly just don't know how I can face quartet rehearsal after last night. In fact, I don't think I'll ever be able to. Or I don't want to. "You might want to find another violist to fill in. I've been thinking of switching my independent study anyway, so I can volunteer at the hospital. Like, I'll be researching in the library and stuff." I haven't exactly cleared this with the librarian. But she's been so cool to sponsor Evita's independent study, I'm sure she'll sponsor mine, too.

"Oh no! Really?" Lily Ann asks. It's so fake. I glance briefly at Theo, who is caving in on himself. He can't even bring himself to comment or pretend to be disappointed for my benefit.

"Yeah. Sorry." I turn and go. My stomach burns with acid. Evita, Theo, and I have had some drama in the past. Hurt feelings. Misunderstandings. The couple of weeks after Evita and Theo had their nonbreakup but kept shooting each other stabby looks being the most memorable. The thing is, though, most of that was them. I was always neutral. Switzerland. On the periphery of the drama. I want to shrug this off like I do with most things. It'll be easy enough to take that quartet piece and rearrange it for the Sparrows. But it isn't about that. It's about the fact that Theo didn't stand up for me.

I can't help but wonder if he has some inkling of how I feel. When I was writing the quartet, I kept imagining the way he'd smile and laugh when he got to the syncopation. I'd do anything to make him laugh, to just bask in that attention for a bit. My cheeks burn as I walk through the halls.

I guess it *was* a grand romantic gesture. Lily Ann knows it was. But I can't tell what Theo thinks about any of it. He's so infuriatingly docile when it comes to Lily Ann. He allows himself to be cowed and coddled. He seems happy when she showers him with affection, but other than that, I don't know why he's with her. It sucks, but I'm jealous.

"Lacey!" Evita's grabbing my arm. "Jesus, woman, you're walking like your hair's on fire."

"If my hair were on fire, I'd drop and roll. Only a moron would try to outrun the fire."

"Well. I must be a moron, because if I was on fire, I'd probably just scream and run until the flames consumed me."

"This is why you keep me around," I tell her. A smile creeps back onto my face. "Because I know where the fire blankets are in the chem lab."

"That is just one of the many things I love about you." She crosses her arms. "So, what is up? You look pissed."

"I am."

She shoves me into the nearest girls' room. "Talk."

"We'll be late to bio," I remind her.

"I'll tell Mr. Green I have my period and you had to help me," Evita says. "It's half true anyway. Killer cramps. Now spill."

I tell her about most of it. Like how Theo was acting like he wanted to hang out with me and really it was a pity hangout so he could tell me he wouldn't play the quartet. Evita is suitably angry.

She'd probably be even angrier if I confessed how confused I've been feeling about Theo.

"That little harpy!" She shakes her head furiously, her curly hair going everywhere. "No. We are going to fix this. You are going to play that quartet."

"Thing is, I really don't want to anymore. I actually just kind of quit. We can play the song with the Sparrows."

"Yes! That theme would be killer." She nods. "What are you going to do for independent study?"

"Think there's room for me in the library? I was thinking I could research birth while you work on GSA stuff."

"Ummm. Yes. That would be excellent. We'll go talk to the librarian after government. Don't worry, we'll fix this."

Evita is always so steadfast and loyal. I don't know how anyone goes through high school without an Evita backing them up.

The bell rings. Evita takes my hand and we run to biology.

~

I don't know how I will be able to stand having lunch with Theo and Lily Ann. Fortunately, Evita grabs me by the arm. "You have more girls needing office hours," she says.

"Office hours?"

"You know, in the bathroom. Come on. A couple GSA kids were asking stuff that's out of my depth. Word is getting out that you know your shit."

"That's kind of . . ."

"It's awesome," Evita says, with a smile. "There's obviously a need for this kind of thing and you're a natural."

In the bathroom, there are three girls standing by the sinks looking nervous. Evita pushes all the stall doors open to make sure no one else is here. "I'm going to stand guard by the door," she tells me. "Marie, Amber, and Cam all have questions regarding penises and vaginas and stuff."

"Oh. Uh. Sure," I say.

Marie goes first with questions about the safety of performing oral sex on her girlfriend. I tell her about dental dams and the importance of getting tested for STIs if they plan on forgoing using protection. "In fact, even if you do use protection, that information is good to have." I look up the number of the local women's health clinic on my phone, then give it to her and tell her she can get tested there. Evita chimes in with little aphorisms like "Herpes is for life," and "Friends don't let friends get the clap." She's kind of like the much-needed comedic relief in a serious movie. I find it impossible to be that casual about it. It's easier to keep it informational. Secretly, I can't believe every girl I meet at this school seems to have so much experience while I have none.

Amber also puts the number for the clinic in her phone. When it's her turn, she just blurts out: "So how do you know if a guy comes inside you?"

"Um." I'm so taken aback.

"With a condom?" Evita asks. Oh right, she probably knows more than I do about this. I can't even think about that fact right now.

"Well. No," Amber admits.

"Girl. Condoms. Every time, unless you've both been tested and you're on other birth control . . . ," Evita says. "But without a condom, it should be pretty obvious. Like . . . you know . . . if you're messy afterward."

"But he pulled out and he was still . . . you know . . . hard . . . so . . ."

"Pulling out's not very reliable," I tell her. "There can be sperm present in the pre-ejaculate."

"Oh. Shit."

"Plus, guys stay hard for a little while, you know?" Evita says. Which is exactly the sort of thing I *don't* know.

"How long ago are we talking about?" I ask her. "Do you think you might be pregnant?"

"I am a little late. But I thought that since it was right after my period ended . . ."

I try not to grimace. "Unless you are absolutely following your cycle to a T and you know exactly when you're ovulating, which can be really difficult even if you're totally regular, you can't rely on that."

"Well, that answers my question," Cam chimes in. "Is that true even if you're on your period?"

"Absolutely. I wouldn't rely on that at all," I say.

"You don't have a test or something, do you?" Amber asks. Her face pales.

"Sorry," I say. "But if you go to the health clinic, I don't think you even need an appointment for that."

"Okay."

"Is that it?" Evita asks. "There are two freshmen who think there's a line for the bathroom."

"Yeah. That's it," Amber says. She's out of the bathroom before I can ask her if she's okay.

"Whoa," I say to Evita. "Honestly. How do people not know this stuff?"

"Their mothers don't tell them, I guess. And the school sure as shit doesn't."

"But there's the internet!" I say.

"Not everyone has time to google stuff before they get it on." Evita shrugs. "And then maybe denial takes over? Like, how else do you explain the existence of a TV show devoted entirely to people not knowing they're pregnant until they give birth?"

"I seriously thought my mom was the only person who watched that," I say.

"Duh. We watched it with her, remember?"

"Right." We walk into the cafeteria. Theo and Lily Ann aren't at our table. "Where's Theo?"

"Maybe he's appropriately embarrassed about how he treated you," Evita says.

"Or maybe he and Lily Ann are somewhere talking about how awful I am," I say miserably.

"No way in hell would Theo ever talk shit about you. I don't care how much sex Lily Ann gives him."

"You think?"

"I know."

Evita and I unpack our lunches. I look around the cafeteria, wondering if Theo is just sitting somewhere else. I don't see him, but I do see a couple of the girls I've met with in the bathroom. I get this weird feeling that they are talking about me.

"It's beyond weird that the first time anyone at this school pays attention to me, it's because of condoms," I say.

"The people have questions. You have answers."

"Yeah, I kind of can't wait to hand out the condom pamphlets. I'll print them this weekend."

"You rebel." Evita waggles her eyebrows at me.

I hope Evita can get behind my volunteering at the hospital as enthusiastically as she has about this little public health campaign. She grins at me with her mouth full of hummus and pita.

～

After school, we meet at Evita's locker most days because it's the closest to the parking lot. We leave our backpacks in there. Through the throng of students I can see that Theo and Evita are already there. And Evita looks pissed. I can guess what she's yelling about, and I take my time getting there.

I stop for a drink at the only water fountain in our school that has cold water. I drink until I feel someone standing behind me, waiting for a turn. Glancing down the hall, I see Theo gesturing, and I can tell by the blotchiness forming on his cheeks and neck that he's probably trying not to cry.

As pissed as I am at him, I feel bad for unleashing the full Evita rage on him. Instead of avoiding him, I should probably go to his rescue. We can move past this, hopefully without any of my actual feelings coming to light. I walk up to them with my hands in my back pockets, trying to appear casual.

"Lacey!" Evita says brightly. "I hope you're ready for an epic weekend of rehearsing." She glances at Theo, who is trying to make the fact that he's drying his eyes on the sleeve of his blazer look like he's just tired. "Because we're moving past this quartet nonsense." She looks at her phone. "Guess who's meeting us at my apartment? Alice!"

I can't wait to see Alice again, but I'm honestly so nervous about rehearsing. Even if Theo and I put the quartet behind us, I can't just forget the feelings I've uncovered. I hate that I suddenly don't know how to act around one of my best friends. But the way he's looking at me now with watery blue eyes, I'm wondering if maybe he's this upset because of how he feels about me. As much as I want to shut out those feelings, I know I'm going to spend the rehearsals overanalyzing absolutely everything Theo does and feeling self-conscious about how I act around him.

"Ready to go?" Evita asks.

"Yup," I lie.

Twelve

"Well, that answers that question!" Evita says when Alice steps into her living room.

"Evita!" Janice scolds. She's sitting on the couch, somehow managing to read a book while we make all kinds of noise.

"It's not polite to inquire about the contents of someone's uterus," I tell her.

"This one," Evita says, pointing at me. "Mom, you should have heard Lacey telling the whole world about how to use condoms today. Really eye opening. A lot of people use them wrong. Like put them on too late, or don't leave enough room in the tip. Did you know that?"

"Jesus, Evita," Theo says. "Do you want your *mom* to answer that question?"

"Fair point," Evita says.

"You were telling the whole world about condoms?" Alice asks. "I could have used you last year. Man. I missed so much."

"You've missed *everything*," Evita tells her.

"Evita!" Janice says again.

"I just mean we have to get you caught up! So, there's a person in there?" Evita asks.

"Evita!" Janice and I both say.

"It's okay." Alice laughs. "There is a person in there. A boy. I get to meet him in a couple months."

"Hi, person. You're about to hear some epic music. They can hear in there, right?" Evita asks me.

"Oh. Yeah."

"This guy likes country," Alice says, patting her stomach.

"Oh. No. No, no, no, no. That will not do. Find a place to sit. Actually, should we try to figure out where we'll actually be onstage?" Evita starts moving stuff around.

Theo stands to help her move the keyboard.

"Sit back down, you have bass lines that need to be written down for Bruno," Evita says firmly.

Theo rolls his eyes at me, and I smile. I'm relieved because things actually do feel normal with us this afternoon.

"This is so great!" Alice says to me. "Thanks for inviting me."

Once everything is set, Evita sits by her mixing equipment. "Okay. I'm gonna take main vocals for now, but, Alice, just join in with harmonies as you can, and eventually you can probably sing lead vocals."

"You don't want to be front man?" Theo asks.

"Are you kidding? I'm so busy mixing! We'll share. Let's do 'Super Eighteen.' And, Lacey, start with your viola line and we'll loop that so you can jump on the keys for the build."

I nod. And we're in it. Everything that was right minutes ago is made even better. Alice chimes in when she can, but Theo and Evita and I play as a unit. We're so practiced at listening to one another and glancing at one another for cues. It's the way music is meant to be played.

Our quartet never got this far, and we've been playing for a year. If I can keep playing with the Sparrows, I honestly don't mind if I never play in another string quartet again. At the same time, I can't imagine Theo ever giving it up. He's so good.

We play through our set. It's rough in places, but I know that with only a few more rehearsals, we'll be golden.

I'm grinning as we finish the piece that will be our finale. I'm not the only one. We all just start whooping and laughing. We sound *good*.

"Oh my god, you guys!" Evita says. She practically tackles Theo, knocking him off his chair.

"Watch the cello!" Theo says, but he's laughing, too. He scoops Evita up from his lap, and pretty soon we're all in a group hug.

"You guys are the best," Alice says. "I've missed this."

"We've missed you!" Evita says. "I can't believe you let something as little as being pregnant stop you from going to *school*. There're tons of pregnant girls there all the time, anyway."

"I know. But I always judged them," Alice said. "I didn't want to be one."

"So, how did that happen?" Evita asks, gesturing at her belly.

"Evita!" Theo and Janice and I all say at once.

"Sorry," Evita says.

"Hey. I'm sorry," Theo says, changing the subject for Alice's sake. "I actually gotta jet for a bit."

"Where can you possibly have to go at this hour?" Evita asks, even though we all know.

"I'll be back soon. I'll catch you later, Alice?" he says.

"Yeah. I have to head out anyway," Alice says.

"I'll walk you out," Theo says.

"I let you guys play way too late," Janice says. "But you sounded great. See you at breakfast."

Then it's just me and Evita. I help her organize the pages of notes and music, setting aside stuff that Alice and Bruno might need to look at.

"I'm thinking Bruno's out if he can't come tomorrow. We sounded good enough without him," Evita says.

"Didn't he help get us the gig?"

"Oh, it's fine. Unless *you* want him in the band."

"God. Evita. Let it rest."

"Whatever. I just want you to practice what you preach."

"That line is getting old."

"You okay? You keep looking sort of . . ." Evita looks at me like I'm some puzzle to sort out. And I don't want her sorting me out.

"Oh. Yeah. Just. You think Theo's okay? I mean, you really chewed him out, didn't you?" I ask.

"He can take it. What he can't do is cross you like that ever again."

"He just seemed, like . . ." I don't want to sit here and talk about Theo, but the fear that it'll be obvious how I feel about him is outweighed by my curiosity. "He was just really . . . you know how he's sort of touchy-feely sometimes?"

She laughs. "He always is. It's what defines him. Touchy-feely, nice ass, serious cello skills, and . . . nope . . . that's pretty much it. Oh, good hair."

"Right. He isn't, like, touchier than normal or something?"

"No?" There she goes, looking like she's solving a puzzle.

"Just wondering if there was more going on with him."

"More than a douchey dad, a clingy girlfriend, and us being awesome?"

"No. I guess that accounts for all of it," I say.

"All right then! We totally rocked, right? I'm not just imagining it?" Evita asks as she turns the lights off.

"Not imagining it."

She starts humming one of our songs, and I hum the strings part along with her as we get into our pajamas. We're laughing as she turns off the lights and we get into bed.

Evita snores. So I know she's still sleeping when Theo sneaks back into the room and shoves Evita toward the middle of the queen-size bed.

I toss him a pillow. "Good night, Lacey," he whispers as he slides next to Evita.

"Good night," I say. "Everything good?"

"Meh. Not really. But it'll be fine. I promise," Theo says.

It only takes a few seconds for his breathing to change to the light snores that are nothing next to Evita's. I'm suddenly too amped up to sleep, so I get out my phone and read doula blogs and try not to think about the rise and fall of Theo's chest.

Thirteen

Sunday morning when the radio clicks on, I kick myself for staying up so late last night playing music. I drove home after midnight, because I promised my mom we'd drive to the hospital together. I hit my snooze button for the third time. It's still so dark out, five thirty feels like the middle of the night.

"Fifteen-minute warning!" I hear from upstairs in the kitchen.

"Okay!" I yell back.

Dylan is already awake and cheerful, but Charlie looks as sleepy as I am as he hands Dylan over to me. I give my brother a quick snuggle. "I'm gonna go meet some new babies. But don't worry, you're still my number one," I tell him, even though all he seems to want to do is grab fistfuls of my hair.

My mom throws a bottle of pumped milk in the fridge and looks at me with a dorky grin. "Let's go!"

When we have our fancy coffee drinks and are on our way, she turns the heat up so much that I have to take off my jacket. "You have the heat on a little high for October."

"This is so exciting! We might get to work together today," she says, not making a move to turn down the temperature.

"That'd be cool," I say, even though I'm super nervous. On one hand, it'd be great to have my mom's support. But on the other, if I'm terrible at being a doula, no one will be as disappointed as my mom.

"So, how are you? It feels like ages since we got to talk. And I don't know what you're up to aside from making pamphlets and music. Does that make me sound like a bad mom? It does, doesn't it?"

"You're not a bad mom. Music and pamphlets is pretty much it. Oh, except we sent in our Berklee applications yesterday."

"Exciting. Do I get to hear your audition piece?"

"Sure. And actually, my friend Alice that you met? She's joining our group, too."

"Oh, that's so great. I'm sure she's lucky to have a friend stick with her through that. How are Evita and Theo?"

"I don't know. Good. Absolutely crazed about our gig," I tell her.

"Any boys I should know about? Or girls, for that matter . . ."

"I'm still straight," I inform her.

"You can always talk to me about anything. Really. Ever."

"I know. Thanks."

Commence awkward silence.

"So . . . ?" She looks over at me at a stoplight, sipping her coffee with a grin.

"What?"

"There's obviously a boy."

"There is not. You're full of shit," I say.

"Lacey!"

"Can we please turn down the heat?" I beg.

"Maybe this is my interrogation method. I can make it hotter," she threatens.

"Despite your insistence, you won't get a word about anything out of me," I tell her.

"Ha!" She laughs. "I knew there was something to tell."

"I admit nothing."

"Just as long as you're safe."

"I have still never been kissed, okay? And it's mortifying."

"It should not be mortifying to go at your own speed. So, what? Is it just a crush sort of situation? Or what?"

"Who said there's a situation?" I ask. She will not let this go. And, I guess, in the past, I've told her about my crushes.

"Be a sport. I've got the butt warmers I can still turn on," she presses. "Who is it? Do I know him? Or her?" she asks.

"Seriously? Mom! Are you that disappointed I'm not a lesbian?" I ask.

"You love who you love. I just know that sometimes same-sex crushes happen regardless of sexuality."

I groan. Because, yes, I know this. When discussing sex and attraction and marriage and all that, my mother has always said "him or her." It's equal parts obnoxious and endearing that she's so proudly progressive about such things.

"Won't you tell me who it is? I promise not to look him up in the yearbook or anything," she begs.

"Yeah. Sure. I totally buy that," I tease.

"Someday, I will get all the juicy details out of you and you will allow me to live vicariously through your love life because I'm an old married lady now." She sighs as she makes the last turn into the hospital parking garage.

"Maybe someday. When I'm off at college and you don't know any of my friends." As soon as I say it, I know it's a mistake.

"I know him?"

"No. Maybe peripherally," I lie, my face getting hot. I bite my lip, hoping she doesn't notice my sudden anxiety. If she does, she ignores it as she pulls out her badge and shows it to the parking attendant.

We walk into the hospital together and she looks at me with this wide grin, and I think I'm in for it. But she just says, "I'm proud of you, kid."

"I'm pretty damn proud of you, too, you know," I tell her. In my earliest memories, she's playing with me though she has a textbook in her lap or singing me to sleep even though I know she stayed up studying for hours.

"We're just a good team, aren't we?" she asks.

We enter the elevator, and since we're the only ones in here, she gives me a huge hug. For a moment I want to spill everything about Theo. Because having a crush on him is possibly the worst thing ever. Except I don't want to acknowledge my feelings any more than I already have. Maybe if I never mention them, they'll go away.

When the doors open and we've reached the fourth floor, we let each other go. "Let's go meet some babies." It's basically impossible not to catch a little bit of her enthusiasm.

Kelly is waiting for me on the floor when we get there. "Do you have the paperwork for me?" she asks.

I reach into my bag and hand her the forms that my counselor, the librarian, my mom, and I have all signed. She looks over them. They must be in order, because she looks up at me and smiles. "Ready to dive in?"

"Oh." I thought maybe I'd just resume my old duties and Kelly would call me into a birth if someone came in who needed more help than the nurses could give her. "Yeah."

"Because I have a mom here whose partner isn't coming," Kelly says.

My mom gives my shoulder a squeeze and leaves me there with Kelly. I take a deep breath. "Yeah."

"Okay, drop your bag off at the nurses' station and I'll introduce you. She's a first-time mom. Really lovely."

I follow Kelly down the hall and will my heart to slow down. It's inconveniently racing. I'm supposed to be the calm one in this situation. If this is a big day for me, it's a much, much bigger day for the mom I'm going to help.

"Shana, this is the doula I was telling you about," Kelly says as we enter a standard labor and delivery room. "This is Lacey. I'll let you guys meet each other."

And just like that, I'm left alone. I feel awkward and inept. But Shana smiles warmly at me, as if it's her job to make me feel comfortable and not the other way around. I don't know whether to give her a bit of space or just go right up next to her bed. I try to think about what I'd want if the roles were reversed. But that's the thing: I've never been in labor, I've never been pregnant, I've never had sex, or even kissed anyone.

I've never even been in the hospital as a patient. The closest I can think of to what it must be like to be nervous in a medical setting is when I needed to have a cavity filled a couple years ago. I was practically sick with nerves, and this one hygienist just sat right next to me and chatted with me while I waited for the anesthetic to take effect. It helped a lot.

I pull up the chair that partners normally use. "So, how are feeling?"

"Tired. I was up all night." Shana starts breathing deeply, and I realize she's having a contraction. She's sitting up in the hospital bed, and she puts her arms on either side of her body and sort of braces herself as she closes her eyes and keeps breathing deeply. I can tell it's getting more and more intense as her face scrunches up and she whimpers. Before I can overanalyze everything I'm doing, I reach for her arm and rub it slowly.

"You're doing great," I tell her quietly. "Just keep doing what you're doing."

Her eyes flutter back open when the contraction ends.

"That was a good one," I say. I said the exact same thing when my mom was in labor with Dylan. Every time she had a strong contraction we agreed that it was a "good one."

"They're still not that close together," she says. "I sort of wish it'd hurry up."

"Well, if they're far apart maybe you can rest a little in between. Go ahead and close your eyes. You want anything to get comfortable?" I ask. With each question, I feel less awkward.

"Can I lie on my side?" she asks.

"Yes! Of course! However you want. Do you have an epidural?" I ask. In the workshop I took over the summer, we learned that having an epidural meant it was harder to move, since the mom can't feel her legs very reliably.

"No. Starting to regret that decision, though," she says.

"I'm sure there's still time to change your mind, but you seem like you're doing fine without it. Do you have a birth plan or anything?" I ask.

"I just want to do things naturally," she admits. "Is that stupid? I know it's going to be painful."

"It's up to you. But I think you're doing great. Let's get you comfortable."

I help her onto her side and get her some pillows for between her knees and behind her back. She tries to doze between contractions, and we develop this rhythm of mostly quiet resting and sometimes making small talk. A nurse named Jamie comes in and out every few contractions and asks about her pain and checks her monitors and stuff.

Hours pass like this. I can tell things are intensifying. Shana no longer wants to lie down, and she doesn't get very long between contractions. She's shaky and flushed, and I know that means she's probably getting close to being able to push. Kelly comes in to check on her.

"How are you guys doing?"

Shana doesn't even answer. She's concentrating too hard on what's going on inside of her.

"Might be having some transitional contractions," I say quietly.

"That's great!" Kelly says. "If you start to feel like pushing, let me know."

Shana nods. It's the only outward sign that she even knows we're here. Kelly smiles at me and leaves just as Shana begins having another contraction.

After only a few more contractions, Shana looks at me and quietly says, "I think I might feel it."

"Oh." I hop up. "I'll get Kelly."

I wave her down in the hallway. Kelly and Jamie come in. "Do you check to see if she's at ten centimeters?" I ask Kelly.

"Nope. If she feels like pushing, then she probably is," Kelly says. "If you need to take a five-minute break, this is probably a good time. We'll stay in here for a bit."

"I'll be right back," I tell Shana. Truth is, I'm dying for the bathroom. After I wash my hands, I check my phone, which has been totally silenced. I'm surprised that it's already almost five in the evening. I send a quick text message to Evita, telling her I'll be at her house to rehearse as soon as possible. But I know there's no way I'm leaving Shana until this baby is here.

I get back to the room just as Shana is starting to push. Jamie is sitting in the chair, and the way she's sitting at Shana's bedside, so relaxed, I get the idea she doesn't think this baby is going to be born anytime soon. It's not always like it is in the movies. There isn't a doctor swooping in saying, "It's time to push. Give it all you've got." There's no screaming. The lights are calm and dim. I offer Shana ice chips in between pushes. It doesn't seem like she's getting anywhere. I know first-time moms can push for hours. And she must be so tired from being in labor for so long. I just stay upbeat and offer different positions to try, but nothing seems to help her.

Jamie comes over to where Shana is sitting on a large exercise ball and fiddles with one of the belts for the monitors.

"I'll be right back, darlin'," she says to Shana. She gives me a little pat on the back. Shana looks at the clock and groans.

"This is taking forever," she says. She's despairing and tired.

It's no surprise when Kelly comes in. She checks the baby's progress through the birth canal and tells Shana that hardly any progress has been made.

"And the baby's in a little bit of distress. Nothing dire. The heart rate's just dipping a hair more than we want. If it continues, I'm going to bring in an obstetrician to discuss other options," Kelly says gently.

Shana bursts into tears but nods. I want to cry, too. She has tried so hard. She read up on natural birth. She has come this far without meds. I don't know all the particulars of her situation, but I know she's here, delivering a baby in a hospital, and she doesn't have family with her. I give her a hug and let her cry on my shoulder.

Jamie stands over her and comforts her as well.

"Can I just keep pushing for a little while longer?" she asks. "Will the baby be okay?"

"We're watching the baby, honey. Nothing's an emergency yet. You just keep trying. Give it all you've got and even if you have a C-section, you know you've done amazing," the nurse says.

"I just don't feel like the pushing is working. I am trying and nothing's happening."

I have a lightbulb moment. "We could try something!" I help Shana sit up on the bed. I grab an extra sheet from the closet and twist it around so it makes a kind of rope. "We'll play tug-of-war. I'll pull on one end while you push, and you pull on the other. We'll pull on each other during your contractions. I've heard it can help focus the pushing. It's worth a try, right?" I ask. I read about this recently on a doula blog, and I'd wondered if it would work.

"It's worth a try," Jamie agrees.

When Shana has a contraction and begins pushing, I'm surprised at the strength of her pulling on the sheet. I have to brace myself to pull against her. She groans. Her face turns bright red, but when the contraction ends and she relaxes, she sort of smiles.

"I think I might have felt the baby move or something," she says.

"Let's do that again, then," I say. Somehow with the next push, she is certain she feels something. It still takes a good fifteen minutes until we can see her progress.

"Want a mirror to see your baby?" Jamie asks after a particularly good push.

"You can see the baby?" Shana asks. Her eyes fill with tears.

"I can see the baby enough to know she has a full head of hair," I tell her.

The nurse hands me a mirror to hold for her. "I'm going to get Kelly, because I think we are just a few minutes from meeting your baby." She pats Shana on the knee and gives me a wide smile.

It still takes twenty minutes once Kelly is there. But eventually, that beautiful baby is born and lets out the biggest squall imaginable. And the baby is not the only one crying. Shana is sobbing happy, blubbery tears.

It's well after nine o'clock by the time Shana is settled with the baby and looking ready for a well-deserved nap. "I seriously could not have done that without you," she says.

"You did such an awesome job getting her here." I smile.

I should be tired; I've been on my feet since around six this morning. But I'm on this incredible high.

Once I've said good-bye to Shana, I finally look at my phone. I don't even read the texts I've missed because there are twelve of them. Instead, I dial Evita.

"I know I'm late. I couldn't leave this mom."

"You are late. Very late. But fortunately for you, we've been spending this whole time catching Alice up."

"Okay, I'm gonna get my mom to drive me over there," I say. "You want me to bring anything? Food? Coffee?"

"You know I would never say no to french fries," Evita says. Then I hear her asking Theo and Alice if they want anything. "You're going to want a pen to write this down," she says.

Half an hour later, armed with milkshakes, burgers, and fries, I kick Evita's door because my hands are too full to knock. I can hear that they're in the middle of playing a song, and it sounds really good.

Janice opens the door. "Hey, Lacey. Evita says you were single-handedly delivering a baby or something?"

"I had a little help. But, yeah, I just saw a birth. It was kind of awesome."

"The kids will be happy you're here," Janice says as she helps me juggle the food.

I stand off to the side of the living room while they finish the song. Alice is singing most of the lead vocals. They all look in the zone. Theo smiles at me, but Alice and Evita are way too into singing to acknowledge my presence.

"Wow," I say when they are done. "Alice. You sound so great!"

"She learned all the lyrics. Like. Since yesterday," Evita says. "Are those my fries?"

Even though it's past the time Janice normally makes us stop, we play for another hour. I can't believe we just added Alice this weekend, because everything goes so smoothly.

"We might actually be ready for our gig!" Evita says.

"Did you have any doubts?" Theo asks.

"Honestly? Yes. But I think if we have a good rehearsal tomorrow and Tuesday, we'll be fine. We're really a band!" she squeals.

Theo holds up a milkshake. "To the Sparrows!"

Fourteen

I'm so tired when I arrive at school on Monday morning. After our rehearsal, I spent the night with Evita, but I still had to go home to print out my condom paper and the pamphlets. I meet Evita and Theo at Evita's locker.

"You look awful," Evita says.

"Don't listen to her. You look beautiful," Theo says.

Despite my exhaustion, his words, even if they were said in jest, give me a little thrill. "Will you guys help me fold these?" I ask them. I look over my shoulder to make sure there aren't any teachers around. Because on these sheets there may or may not be drawings of erect penises. Each sheet gets folded in half twice. The sides that face out look innocuous enough. Just a slogan: STAY INFORMED. STAY SAFE. I'm not happy with it as a slogan, but I didn't have anything else. The inside has the instructions on how and when to use condoms. (There's an emphasis on EVERY TIME!)

Theo grabs a stack and starts folding them up against the lockers. "How many did you print?" he asks.

"I don't know. Only thirty or forty copies. I had to use my mom's printer, and it started to run out of ink."

"I'll keep one and make photocopies after school or something," Theo says with a smile.

"I almost forgot!" Evita says. "I have to show you my paper." She opens her backpack.

"Oh god, my paper is awful. I couldn't think of five pages' worth of 'Don't drink and drive.' Like, that statement pretty much says it all," Theo says to her.

Evita hands me her paper, which she balances carefully on both of her hands, and she's singing an *aah* like some sort of angelic choir, as if she's handing me a holy relic.

"Please tell me this is a joke," I tell her.

"Obviously. But what are the chances anyone else knows I'm joking?" she says slyly.

The title of her paper is *Avoiding Date Rape*.

"That is pure genius, Vita," Theo says, looking over her shoulder. "I sort of wish I had thought of it. Although in my case it'd be like: 'Don't assault anyone.' That *definitely* would not be enough material for five pages."

"Well, this is seven pages. Complete with illustrations of appropriate clothing and staying locked in your room on a Friday night."

Sure enough, there's a stick-figure Evita on the last page, sitting in a chair, looking bored. The door in the illustration has a million locks on it, and Evita sips from a cup that is labeled DRINK POURED ONLY BY ME.

"She's gonna know it's a joke when she gets to the pictures," I point out.

"Whatever. I printed an extra copy for your mom," she tells me.

"She'll be delighted."

"How did your paper turn out?" Theo asks me.

"Mine is also seven pages. But the last two pages are my bibliography. She can be angry that I chose to write about condoms, but I think my research is pretty thorough." I hand my paper to Theo, who hands me back a stack of folded pamphlets.

"We should turn them in at the same time, but you should let me put mine on top," Theo says.

"Probably a good idea," Evita says. "Let me hand some of these bad boys out. I need to make sure I get them to our established clients first."

Lily Ann walks over to us. "What are those?"

Theo looks at me as if to ask permission to tell Lily Ann. I shrug. No, I don't want her in on our plans, but I think of all the times I've told Evita to be nice to her, and so I tell her. "I wanted to print up some facts for anyone not lucky enough to see my little condom demonstration. And a lot of people have been asking me questions during lunch and stuff."

"Sex questions?" Lily Ann giggles.

"I'm going to chorus!" Evita announces. I so wish I were going with her.

"Yeah. I mean, I want to make people feel like they can talk about this stuff without feeling shame."

"Oh, I don't feel shame talking about it," Lily Ann says, linking her arm with Theo's.

Theo's arm stiffens, and then he unwraps himself from her. "Actually, Lily Ann, I have to talk to Lacey for a minute. But we'll meet you in orchestra."

Lily Ann pouts and I swear she glares at me, but then she smiles at Theo. "Sure thing. See you guys soon." She spins on her heel and walks down the hall.

"Lacey, I know you probably just want to put it behind us. But I'm still so sorry about the quartet thing. I just hate feeling like I'm not . . . I don't know . . . loyal to you. Or grateful. For the quartet. I don't want her to make you feel weird."

"I'm going to feel weird around her now," I tell him honestly. "I can't really help it."

"I'm really sorry about that. I'm trying to work it out, okay?"

I don't know what he means by that. Is he breaking up with her? But I can't ask him, because there's no way for me to do it in a way that doesn't make it obvious that I'm hoping and wishing they'll break up. I'm just not that good of an actress.

"Sure," I say instead.

"Stuff is just weird right now, right?" Theo asks with a shrug and an easy smile.

"It's a lot less weird when you aren't being weird," I tell him.

"Am I being weird?"

I roll my eyes, making the *pfffff* noise. He elbows me.

"Come on," Theo says. "Let's go give a couple of these to the sexually active band geeks."

Mean Girls quotes always make things less weird.

Fortunately, Mrs. Einhorn doesn't look at our papers when we hand them in. The papers sit on her desk the entire class while she starts a discussion on "ways to stay active." The whole class is supposed to be brainstorming activities that will help keep us fit. She seems especially excited when anyone suggests anything that's not obviously exercise. Like this girl says carrying laundry up the stairs is a good workout, and Mrs. Einhorn wholeheartedly agrees.

"Is it wrong that I hope someone says sex?" Evita whispers.

"I was thinking the same thing," I say.

"Lacey, care to share an idea?" Mrs. Einhorn asks, looking disapproving because I was talking.

"Hiking," I say.

Mrs. Einhorn raises an eyebrow and adds it to the list on the board.

"Lame," Evita whispers.

"Evita?" Mrs. Einhorn calls.

"Bowling," Evita answers.

When Mrs. Einhorn turns her back to write that on the board, I whisper "Chicken" at Evita. She just shrugs.

Once every student has offered some sort of lame form of exercise, Mrs. Einhorn tells us we can work on schoolwork for the rest of class as long as we're quiet. I know it's coming, and I feel totally justified in writing my paper, but I still have a jolt of nerves when she reaches for our papers.

"Don't worry about it," Evita says. "Let's just work on lyrics or something."

Theo turns around. "You seriously didn't do anything wrong writing your paper on that."

"Do I look worried?" I ask.

Theo and Evita exchange a look. "Okay. So. Song lyrics. Like how great would it be if we could write a feminist rage piece, right?" Evita asks.

"Love it," Theo says. "Lacey, do we know anyone who has feminist rage?"

"Guys, always describing feminists as raging does not help feminism. Like feminism is a totally reasonable, equitable thing to be supporting. We don't have to be yelling and burning our bras, you know?"

"Writing a song about moderate, calm feminism just doesn't sound as fun," Evita says.

We whisper and brainstorm for the rest of the class. I keep an eye on the clock, wishing time would go faster so I could get out of here. I'm just waiting for Mrs. Einhorn to call Evita and me up to her desk, and even though I'm mentally prepared to take a stand, I'm not so great at waiting for it to happen.

With only five minutes left in class, Mrs. Einhorn approaches our group with the papers in hand. "Theo, I think you chose an apt topic for your paper. But, honestly, ladies, I'm a bit disappointed you didn't take this chance to turn your attitudes around."

I glance around. Every single student in our class is watching us.

"I don't think there is anything wrong with my attitude. I presented you with a well-researched paper on a topic I am passionate about," I say.

"And I am similarly super serious about not being a victim," Evita says.

"Your paper was farcical and insulting. At least Lacey's is backed up with facts," Mrs. Einhorn says.

"Can't argue with that," Evita says, shrugging.

"But, Lacey, your paper, no matter how well researched, still contains lewd material."

"Lewd?" I say in disbelief. "You know there's nothing lewd about a penis or a vagina, right? Those are just parts of the body."

Victoria, one of the girls who has approached me in the bathroom, chimes in. "That's not lewd!"

Mrs. Einhorn sets her jaw. "I will not be giving either of you girls credit. But I will certainly take your concerns up with the administration."

"That's fine," I say. "I hope you do. Let me know what they say."

Mrs. Einhorn sighs and walks back to her desk as the bell rings. I leave feeling proud of my stand and curious about what the administration will say. But I'm also sweating, and the palms of my hands are indented where I was digging my nails into them.

"You rock, Lacey," Victoria says to me in the hallway as she walks past.

"She has a point," Theo says.

"You guys have to stop trying to make me feel better. It's so transparent. And it ignores the fact that *I'm not actually upset.*"

"Little Lacey just hated being noticed and getting in trouble," Evita says. "Hard to accept our girl is growing up." She mimes wiping tears.

"I like the older, wiser Lacey," Theo says with a grin so goofy, his dimples pop and his ears move. It's incredibly endearing. "You manage to smash the patriarchy with a minimum of raging. It's a thing of beauty."

I get a little jolt when he says this. A jolt of *I want to hear him say nice things about me all the time,* followed by a pang of *How transparent are my feelings at this moment?*

"It occurs to me that, along with advertising condoms, we should maybe be plugging our gig? Like, Lacey, next time Mrs. Einhorn talks with us, try to slip in a casual mention of the Sparrows, okay?" Evita suggests.

Fifteen

Evita's never looked edgier. She's applying more mascara on her false eyelashes. Her eyes are super glammed-up while the rest of her makeup downplays her other features. She'd look like some sort of Disney princess, but she's also wearing patched-up and slashed skinny jeans and a giant knit tunic with a cowl that swallows her whole. She doesn't believe in stilettos, but she's wearing platform sneakers, and her curly hair is teased to epic proportions.

I have no idea what to wear. Janice keeps fluttering by and begging Evita to let her come, but Evita won't hear of it.

"I promise I will send you a video," Theo tells her, trying to usher her out of the room.

"I look so washed out in this," I complain. I've got on a black shirt and black skinny pants. "People will probably think I'm on the stage crew. But I didn't bring anything else. Evita, why haven't we spent more time on our look?"

"A color might make you pop more," Janice says.

"The only other shirt I have here is flannel," I say.

"I might have something for you," Janice tells me. "Be right back." She disappears and reappears with this flowy emerald green tank. The bust is covered in sequins. It is decidedly not me. "Oh, just try it," she says, tossing it at me.

I turn my back to the room, then slip off my T-shirt and put the top on. I don't think there's a thread of natural fiber in this thing, and it feels slippery and cold. But when I turn around, Evita whistles and Theo's eyes go wide and I feel like I might as well be naked. "Guys . . ."

"Shhhhh. You look great." Janice takes my hand and leads me over to the mirror. I hate to admit it, but . . . I do. "Okay. Hair." Before I can protest, she grabs a can of hairspray that she must have been holding the whole time, because it certainly doesn't belong in Evita's room. She sits me on the edge of the bed.

"Oh, Mother, it's your dream come true." Evita giggles. "A daughter-type figure who will let you make her pretty."

"You're a dream come true, darling," Janice says to Evita. "But this will be fun."

She sets to work making my somewhat limp, wavy hair into a sleek ponytail. I look . . . different. But it isn't bad different. So I start playing with makeup, adding more eyeliner than I've ever dared. The self-consciousness is giving way to fun, and Theo whines that he's being left out, so Evita throws him an unopened navy eyeliner.

"I don't know what to do with this," he says.

"What kind of a hipster are you?" Evita asks.

"I'll help you," I offer.

"Make my eyes look like yours," Theo says. "That looks awesome."

I roll my eyes and *pfffff*, but secretly, I agree. My eyes do look awesome, bigger and browner than they've ever been. I sit next to him on the bed and carefully draw some eyeliner on. I get a little thrill when I realize how close our faces are and how I can feel his breath on my wrist and smell that he must have just popped a mint.

"Why don't we do this at all our sleepovers?" Theo asks.

"Because I would never want to go to school like this," I say.

"Why the hell not?" Evita asks. "Nothing wrong with feeling sexy. I mean, if that's your thing. If it's not your thing, you should probably not leave the house like that, sexpot."

"Please shut up," I say brightly. "Is Alice driving with us?"

"She'll meet us there. Bruno will, too." I ignore the pointed look Evita gives me about Bruno.

We are all so excited as we load up Evita's car with our equipment. We're talking about our set list and how many people we hope will show up. Theo and I keep complimenting each other on our eyeliner. Evita's in rare form. She's like a little dictator telling us to be careful and how to stack the cables and stuff. The expensive stuff is placed on blankets in the front seat and buckled in, which I'm pretty sure is Evita just being funny. But it's hard to tell, so Theo and I sit in the backseat and let the important equipment ride shotgun.

The club is half an hour away in a much bigger town, and, of course, Evita has prepared a playlist just for the occasion. Evita demands that I text Alice to make sure she'll be on time. And after I slip my phone back into my pocket, Theo grabs my hand. When

I turn to look at him, I'm expecting a wide, excited grin, but I just get this little half smile. He squeezes my hand, and I squeeze it back. We stay like this, holding hands, for a lot of the drive. Evita is talking nonstop and doesn't seem to notice that Theo is only half here. I don't mention it, because, honestly, I don't want him to let go of my hand.

Evita continues her tyranny and we get things set up as she discusses things with the sound tech. You'd think we were doing some big arena tour, not a forty-minute set at an all-ages night. Still, the excitement is sort of infectious, and when Alice shows up she runs to me squealing.

"Our first gig!" Alice says. "Hey, Theo." Theo gives her a big hug. "Wow. Lacey, you look amazing!"

I almost forgot about the hair and the makeup, and I want to hide, but I just smile and say, "Thanks."

"Alice! Hey!" Evita calls. "Lacey, can you text Bruno? He was supposed to be here by now. I'm letting him sit in for one song."

"I don't have his number," I tell her, so she tosses me her phone. Just as I catch it, it starts buzzing, and I see that—huge coincidence—Bruno is calling. I'm about to toss it back to her, but she and Alice are already deep in discussion, so I answer.

"Hi. Evita's phone," I say.

"Hey. It's Bruno. I'm almost there, had a bit of car trouble. Who is this?" he asks.

"Oh. It's Lacey."

"Right. Lacey. I'm sure Evita's freaking out. I'll be there in ten minutes. Tell her to chill," Bruno says.

"Oh. She's perfectly calm," I joke.

"Yeah. I'll believe that when I see it," he says.

"Okay. See you soon."

I feel a hand on my arm. Theo looks at me conspiratorially. "Let's go find a dark corner to hide in before the despot finds another inane task for us," he says.

And, damn it, I get butterflies when he says "dark corner."

I let out the deep breath I just realized I was holding. I shake my head and roll my shoulders as we walk offstage. Tonight, I will not obsess over Theo. I will *not* let any temporary feelings or weirdness get in the way of what is sure to be a big night in the history of us.

~

When Bruno arrives, Evita makes no secret of trying to force the two of us together. And maybe it's the makeover or the fact that I'm trying to squash my feelings about Theo, but I'm okay with it. More than okay with it. I may actually be flirting. Bruno tunes up his double bass, and I tell him I always wanted to try playing one.

He gives me this little quirky smile that is really endearing. I can almost forgive him for being sort of a setup and for being snobby about music and for being probably too old for me. He offers the neck of the bass.

It's stupid, really. I could play a bass whenever I want. We have two bass players in our orchestra at school. But I take the bass and pluck the strings. Then I do a really out-of-tune, lame attempt at a blues bass line.

"Not half bad," Bruno says, rubbing his beard. "We'll make you a jazz aficionado yet. I can't wait to hear you guys. Evita is allowing me to just play the one song. She told me you composed a lot of the stuff?" His eye contact is really intense. And his long-ish curly hair looks pretty cute pulled back in a ponytail. Maybe Evita is onto something. I hand him his bass back.

"It's all a collaboration," I say.

"She's full of it," Evita calls from where she's adjusting her mic stand for the umpteenth time. "She's the composer of the group."

"Very cool," says Bruno. "I'm all set. See you in the green room."

"Hey, Theo and Lacey, move your spots back a smidge," Evita demands.

"We're not even gonna be in the lights!" Theo complains as he drags his seat and his cello back farther.

"Fine by me," I say.

"Are you kidding? You deserve to be seen," Theo says.

"Sure. Because everyone is always eager to hear the viola part," I say, rolling my eyes.

"Don't do that, Lacey," he says, more forcefully than I'm used to hearing him talk.

"What?"

"Put yourself down. Okay? You rock. I'm sorry that shit with the quartet might have made you feel less awesome." He's blink-ing his lined eyes rapidly.

I cock my head to the side and study him. "What's up with you?"

"What do you mean?"

"You've been quiet."

He shrugs. "Who can get a word in with her?" He nods toward Evita, who keeps running through her prerecorded drum loops.

Then he gives me this decidedly fake smile. All mouth, no dimples.

"You sure? You're not getting stage fright or something?" I ask him. I press my lips together, feeling the lipstick I applied last minute.

"No. It's . . ." He trails off. "Okay. No. It's stupid. We are about to have our first gig. And everything's great."

"You're an awful liar," I tell him.

"To the green room!" Evita calls to us.

Before I can press Theo for more details, he scoops me off my feet and rushes off stage yelling, "To the green room!"

Alice laughs as he gallops past her. We have an entire hour in the green room and backstage before our set starts. After Theo's little burst of energy on the stage, he's quiet, sitting on the couch looking at his phone. Alice paces and sings some vocal warmups and drinks a lot of water.

Bruno tries to strike up a conversation with Theo about reggae. Theo couldn't look less interested. Bruno gets the hint and comes to sit with me and Evita. We're playing a card game that involves a lot of silly rules and slapping the table. It's supposed to be a drinking game, but we've never let that stop us.

Theo stretches and mumbles something about fresh air. He doesn't invite any of us to join him.

"Is he nervous or something?" I ask Evita.

"I suspect something went down with Lily Ann," Evita says with a grin.

"Don't look so happy! He seems miserable," I say.

She shrugs. "He'll be fine once we get onstage in . . . twenty minutes."

"Maybe I should go find him."

"No. Don't. I will. You and Bruno should go check out the crowd and report back how big it is." Evita puts her cards down and replays what she just said. "I mean, the crowd. Report back on how big the crowd is."

It takes me a second. "Oh my god, Evita." I walk away from her before she can keep a string of double entendres going. I have no doubt she can. "Let's check out the crowd," I say to Bruno.

"Sure." He puts a hand on my back as we go through the green room door. Then he grabs my hand to lead me across the floor. It doesn't seem like a big deal to him. But, honestly, at this slight gesture, I feel sort of thrilled. As self-conscious as I was of my whole getup and as nervous as I might be about the gig, all of that disappears and I find that I'm just . . . enjoying myself.

Bruno heads to the bar. "You want something?"

I don't know if he means to buy me alcohol or what. "Cherry Coke," I say. He orders two of them and nods at a bar stool. There's only one free, but he offers it to me.

"This is an excellent crowd. Seriously. Did you all do some advertising or what?"

"I don't think so."

"It doesn't look like it's all high schoolers, either. This is great. I know you all will win them over."

"I hope so." My stomach jumps with preshow nerves.

"To an excellent debut show." Bruno raises his glass.

I clink mine on his and smile. Maybe that's all there is to flirting. Smiling. Talking. A little physical closeness. It's way less intimidating than I thought. Even with this older guy. Even given the fact that other girls are checking him out. "Let's go tell Evita an approximate headcount."

We bring our drinks back to the green room, where Alice is waiting.

"Good crowd?"

"Huge. Amazing. Where's Evita and Theo?" I ask.

"I'll go find them," Alice offers. "Only five more minutes!"

I pick up my viola and bow. I retune it. I loosen and tighten my bow. I take some deep breaths to try to banish the shaky fingers I sometimes get when I perform. Focused on nothing else, I run through a couple trickier phrases of a fast piece. Then I practice the long, round notes of a song that builds layer upon layer with the looping pedals, and if my intonation isn't spot on, it won't sound good.

"You are really good," Bruno says. He sounds surprised but impressed.

Alice, Evita, and Theo walk in. Theo's face is sour, but Alice and Evita look as excited as I am.

"You guys ready? The sound dude says we can go on as soon as we're all set. So, are we set? Let's bring it in." Evita ushers us over to her. "Hold hands, guys."

I put my viola down on the couch and grab Evita's and Theo's hands. Theo gives my hand a little squeeze. When I look at him, he finally smiles.

"Your eyeliner is still on point," I tell him.

"Yours, too."

"Quiet!" Evita says. "Okay. So this is a big moment, but let's just focus on listening to each other. Everything else will go awesome. Just listen to each other and have fun. Right?"

"Absolutely!" Alice says. "Let's do this."

We're all suddenly grinning like idiots as we take the stage. Theo and I take our spots upstage and Alice goes right out front. Evita checks over her sliders, dials, and pedals, then grabs the mic.

"Hi, y'all. Thanks so much. We're the Sparrows, and we hope you enjoy." She looks back at me and mimes screaming in excitement before she faces the crowd and nods the starting beat to our first song. We're starting off with an epic build. Evita snaps a few times into her mic. Alice claps into hers. And then Evita puts the mic right up to her mouth and does this loud "Shhhhhhhhh." Then it's all looped. I start on the keyboard. Just some snappy chords. And Alice starts singing the first song. I stay on the keyboard for the whole first song, which flies by in a blur. The audience claps enthusiastically, and it's only then that I realize how hushed they were during the song. It's possible that we're really good.

I pick up my viola. Evita uses her other keyboard, and we kick into a pop song. She uses a prerecorded beat. Then Theo and I add in the strings. His eyes are locked on mine as we play fast arpeggios and quirky lines here and there. The chorus has us playing epic double stops. And we are grinning at each other.

With each piece, the audience is more and more with us. I didn't know what to expect. I didn't know if people would ignore us and just hang out, treating us like background music. But every person in here is with us on the ride. I'm not self-conscious at all. I let go of the rigidness that normally resides in my spine. I move and flow and dance. I smile at Theo and Evita and Alice whenever they look at me.

We end with the piece we based on the quartet I wrote for Theo. I wasn't even sure we should play it. It's so different from everything else. But it sounds so good with Alice and Evita taking over the lines from the violin parts. Bruno steps in a couple times, and he rounds out our sound on this piece. All eyes are on Theo when he plays his amazing lines. The piece starts and ends with him. He plays with his eyes shut tight. My heart thuds. I really like him. I feel it like a physical pain.

The song ends just when I feel like my heart might burst. The applause and smiles and good feelings are just so overwhelming.

"You guys are amazing. Thanks for welcoming us. We're the Sparrows. Good night!" Evita says. We take a few quick bows and run back to the green room. We all squeal and hug and laugh.

Bruno stands back, rubbing his beard and smiling. "You guys are incredible. Really. You're onto something."

"Yeah?" Evita says. But she knows it. "I feel like I'm going to burst into flames! Does that make sense?"

"Absolutely." Alice laughs.

"And you!" Evita says to Alice. "You are the greatest singer. I could kiss you! And you!" she says to me. "And you!" she says to Theo, whom she actually does kiss squarely on the lips. He just laughs. The funk he was in seems to have disappeared.

Bruno's behind me. His hand is on my lower back again. "Round of sodas on me, guys."

~

Back in the club, a DJ starts spinning benign and uninteresting house music, and the crowd starts dancing. A lot of people come over to congratulate Evita and the rest of us.

"It's crazy hot in here," Evita says over the music. She fishes in her pocket for a hair tie and puts her hair up in a messy bun, then discards her giant sweater. She's wearing just a ribbed tank top with her jeans now, and she looks almost mainstream. She's easily one of the cutest girls in the whole place, and a few people are checking her out for sure. But Theo insists on being the only one to buy her drinks. She downs a Sprite and pulls Theo back onto the floor. Theo reaches for my hand, too.

"You know I don't dance," I tell him. The thought of it mortifies me. I don't even dance when it's just the three of us.

Theo shrugs at me. "You could have fooled me onstage. It's nice to see you let loose, Burke." He and Evita disappear into the crowd. I can feel Bruno hovering behind me.

"You just bared your soul up on that stage and you aren't going to dance even a little?" Bruno asks.

"Dancing to this music is not my thing."

"It's not mine, either. But I'd dance with you," Bruno says, holding out his hand.

Screw it, I think. Maybe it's the top I'm wearing, and the way my bare shoulders make me feel sort of exposed and maybe a little sexy. Or maybe it's the high of performing. But I am so much less concerned with looking stupid while I dance than I've ever been.

"I always feel like a moron." I laugh as I start to move just my shoulders to the beat.

"There's a trick to it, you know," he says. "You have to pretend you're in your bedroom. And, well, barring that, just follow your goofy partner's lead." He starts nodding his head to the beat, and then shaking his hips a little bit.

He starts off fairly goofy, and we're both laughing. But soon we're dancing closer and I'm moving enough that I can feel my ponytail swishing against the exposed skin on my back. He puts his fingertips on my spine and we dance even closer still. We're not grinding. It's not like that. But it does feel sort of sexy, to be touched and to be moving to this music that sounds better by the minute.

After what feels like only a few minutes, though my tired legs would beg to differ, Evita finds us. "I'm totally gonna steal Lacey in a few minutes. I'm tired, and I'm her ride."

"You sober?" Bruno asks her. Perhaps because she's almost impossibly giddy.

"Of course! I know the dangers of drinking and driving because I am in this great senior seminar class," Evita says with a giggle. "Twenty minutes, okay?" she says to me. She disappears back into the crowd, which is much bigger than it was for our set, and I realize I haven't seen Theo.

"It's hot in here," Bruno says, and I follow him outside. It's chilly, even for October, and my jacket is back in the green room, but it feels good for a minute. We walk away from the entrance a little way, to a crowd of smokers, and Bruno pulls a pack of cigarettes out of his pocket.

"You smoke?" I ask him.

"You want one?" he asks.

I shake my head. "I'm pretty sure Evita was trying to set us up so I'd kiss you."

"Oh yeah?" he asks, feeling in his pocket for a lighter. "And?"

"Well. I'm not going to kiss a smoker. No offense," I tell him. The words spill out, and I hope it's not mean.

He considers this for a moment, then puts the cigarette back in the box, which goes back into his pocket. Then he raises his eyebrows at me. And I think, yeah, this could work. Dancing with him was easy, kissing him shouldn't be that weird. But when I realize he's lowering his head to kiss me, I burst out laughing.

I'm such a freak. Who laughs when somebody's about to kiss them? "Sorry. It's too weird."

He shakes his head and laughs, too. "No worries. I'm gonna light this thing, then." Once he locates his lighter, he looks pretty pleased.

"Should I be hurt that it was a toss-up between a cigarette and kissing me?" I ask him.

"Oh, it was not a toss-up. This is a consolation prize," he says slyly.

I roll my eyes and *pfffff*, which now just makes me think about Theo. "Okay. Well. Hopefully I'll see you around. But I guess I should find Evita and Theo."

"Hug?" he asks me. "Another consolation prize?"

I hug him. "Thanks for getting me to dance."

"Your music was killer, by the way," he says with a puff of smoke.

"Thanks." I wave lamely at him and go back inside. That didn't go as planned, but nothing can shake how good I feel right now.

It's easy finding Evita because, even though the music is loud, I can hear her laughing. "You ready to go?" I ask her. She nods and walks back toward the green room.

"Where's Theo?" I ask her when we're backstage where it's marginally quieter.

"Dude. Theo and Alice left a while ago."

"Why did he leave?"

"I don't know. But I am super exhausted, and I can't stand this music. Is it okay that we're leaving now? I mean, you and Bruno . . ."

"Totally fine. I'm tired, too. Maybe you can just take me home, though? I kinda want to sleep in my own bed."

"You and Theo are so not fun." She reaches into her pocket for the keys. She pops the trunk just as someone from the bar carries out some of Evita's equipment. "Careful with that!" she says, grabbing the little mixer from him and laying it tenderly in the trunk as if it were a baby bird.

"So, your show was great," this guy says as I take the keyboard from him. "Any chance you'd want to come back two weeks from Friday and play again?"

Evita looks at me with an enormous grin. "Yeah! Absolutely!"

"Should we check with Theo and Alice?" I ask.

"I'm saying yes. But I'll call you tomorrow to confirm." Evita holds out her hand. When he takes it, she puts her other hand on top of his. It looks almost presidential.

We make a couple of trips back in to load equipment. Evita skips and grins the whole time.

When everything's buckled in and we slam our doors closed, Evita squeals.

"Tonight was the best night ever!" She looks over at me expectantly. "Especially if you got your first kiss?"

"Sorry. Nope. It didn't really work out that way."

"Ah well. Next time."

And I nod. Even though Bruno isn't the one I want to kiss.

Sixteen

It's past midnight when Evita pulls up to my house. It's totally dark and I almost change my mind and go sleep at her place, but without Theo, it doesn't feel like we should continue celebrating. "Good night, rock star," I tell her.

"Back atcha. You have never played better nor looked sexier."

I *pffffff* and roll my eyes. "Getting up for school is going to be terrible."

"I might just stay up all night."

"Have fun with that," I say.

"Love you!" Evita calls once I get out of the car.

"You, too!"

I jog up the steps to my front porch. The house is quiet when I slip the key in the lock.

"Hey," Theo says.

"Holy shit, Theo." I put a hand on my heart, which is currently trying to escape my chest. "That is super creepy. I didn't even see your car."

"Sorry. Yeah, I parked around the corner." Theo's sitting with his legs dangling over the edge of my porch. His hands are shoved in a hoodie that is not nearly warm enough for how cold it is now. "I just had to talk to you."

"Come in. Everyone's asleep, so you have to be quiet." I turn the knob extra carefully and lead him downstairs to the family room. "Why didn't you say hi to Evita? Or, you know, text and warn me you were going to jump out at me?" I tease, but when he sits on the opposite end of the couch from me I see that he's not in a joking mood. "What's wrong?"

"Yeah. It's stupid." His face looks drawn and pale. His eyes are a navy mess of smudged and running eyeliner. "I was already in a shit mood, and then my dad basically told me I had to wash off the eyeliner or I couldn't 'sleep under his roof.'" Theo uses air quotes. "He's convinced everything I do is just to push his buttons. Obviously, I was going to wash it off before bed. But it was the principle of the thing. I told him he was a homophobic asshole, and then I just walked out."

"I'm sorry."

"It's okay. I just wanted to see you. And talk, maybe," he says. His chin quivers, and I'm not sure I'd be able to stand it if he started crying. Not that I haven't seen him cry before. We give him crap because when we watch tearjerkers, he's always the first to grab a tissue. This is different.

I crawl over to him, ignoring the fact that I should maybe be keeping a bit of distance.

"What the hell is wrong, Theo?" I know it isn't just his dad. He's said that kind of thing before to Theo, but it's never made him cry.

"Yeah. So. Lily Ann and I broke up."

My heart pounds. "Oh. Sorry."

"It's okay. I know you guys never liked her. She was always so squarely in my corner and stuff, but that does not make up for how insecure she was about everything."

"She's insecure?" She always seems totally self-possessed. She's the one person I know who doesn't care if Evita hates her. Even the way she plays violin exudes confidence.

"Honestly, she was only insecure about you. But, I mean, you knew that," Theo says.

I shake my head. "Except for the quartet thing."

"Yeah, but it's that, and the fact that you and I spend so much time together, and that you're funny and smart and beautiful."

"Shut up." I laugh—my default reaction to compliments, I guess. "She did not say that."

"Actually, she did."

"Well. That's sweet of her. But totally unfounded." Except that Lily Ann would have every right to worry about my feelings for Theo. I just hope that particular thought isn't written across my face. I swallow and do my best to keep my face neutral. But I'm dying to ask him a million questions. How does he feel about me? How much of his breakup was about me?

"Yeah. It was stupid. I just told her I wanted to play the quartet. I think it's ridiculous not to."

"Really?" I sigh. "I mean, it's great you want to now, but I am not going back to our quartet. I've already switched my independent study to the birth stuff."

"Yeah? God, I'm such an idiot. Sorry I busted it up." He looks like he's about to cry again, and I would do almost anything to keep him from that.

"No, it's good. I like volunteering, and I feel way more into the Sparrows than I ever did about the quartet," I say. "But, honestly, Theo, why didn't you tell us what happened? Before the gig?"

"And ruin the good mood? Nah. It would have sucked to see Evita gloat anyway. You know that's what she'll do. I just wasn't ready to tell her about it yet. Right before we got in the car, I finally texted Lily Ann to tell her to stop texting me. She kept wanting to discuss our feelings and how she thought maybe we could fix it if I was more loyal or some shit like that. But I am so done."

"So. *You* broke up with *her*," I clarify. For some reason, this is important for me to know.

"She threatened to break up with me over the quartet, and I sort of called her on her bluff. And it all just got so messy. Lots of crying and feelings. And then you and Evita were so happy. And Evita was being so pushy about you and Bruno and it just really bugged me."

"Why? I mean, Evita's pushy. You know this." He doesn't answer. I don't tell him that nothing happened with Bruno, because I honestly don't mind that he thinks it's possible that something did. "You wanna watch TV?" Before he can answer, I reach for the remote and turn it on. "I'm gonna get in my pajamas. I still don't feel like myself in this."

"Well, you look amazing. But you always do."

I blink. This is the kind of thing he always says. It just feels different. Maybe because he's finally single. "I'll be right back."

In my room I wipe off the makeup and pull on my PJs. It's only been a minute, but I hear a light rap on my door. I open it and Theo walks in, bringing in this energy that unsettles me.

"I'm actually sort of tired." He smiles sheepishly.

"Me, too. I can't believe we have to be up for school."

He sits on my twin-size bed. "Is this okay?"

Oh god. It's more than okay. But sleepovers when Evita isn't here . . . this is new terrain. "Yeah," I whisper, surprised at how badly I want him to stay here. To leave his smell on my pillow. "You have to be next to the wall, though."

He grins, then kicks off his shoes and unzips his jeans. I look away and blush. He slips into bed, and I turn off the light and crawl in after him.

"My stepdad might not be too keen on this, by the way, so . . ."

"This is why I parked around the corner," he whispers. "My alarm goes off at five. Is that early enough?"

I nod and wiggle until I get comfortable. We sleep next to each other all the time, but I'm trying not to touch him more than necessary. But he closes the space and wraps his arms around me. I wish I knew if this meant anything to him. Judging by how quickly he falls asleep, I doubt there's the same amount of adrenaline running through him as there is for me.

~

It's two o'clock in the morning and I'm not sure I've slept. I just keep staring at the clock and trying not to think about how warm and safe I feel with Theo's arm around my middle. With a frustrated sigh I roll onto my back.

"You're awake," Theo whispers sleepily.

"Yeah. Trouble falling asleep."

"Am I taking up too much space?"

I roll toward him, knowing full well that I'm opening some door that I should probably keep closed. I shake my head.

"Thinking about your big night with the bass player?" There's enough light for me to see his eyebrows waggling at me.

"No. Um . . . not such a big night. Nothing really happened with the bass player," I say, biting my lip.

"Really?"

"Please. He's a smoker. And too old." It's silent for a moment, sort of awkward. "First kiss will just have to wait until I'm thirty, I guess."

Theo doesn't respond right away. When I turn to look at him, I think maybe he's looking at my lips. And now I'm definitely looking at his. I have to pull myself out of this.

"Theo—" I say just as he starts talking.

"I've never been anyone's first kiss," Theo says. He runs his fingers up my arm, and I fight the shiver I feel in my spine.

"Me, neither. Obviously," I say, trying to keep it light.

"I'd like to be, though. Since the position is still available. I mean, if you want."

The butterflies in my stomach multiply and begin flying everywhere. To the tips of my fingers, to my knees. "Well. I just . . ."

"It's weird, right? But it doesn't have to be. I care about you, so I just thought . . . you know, it might be better than some stranger Evita pushes on you, that's all. Totally as friends."

I don't say anything.

"Forget it. I feel stupid for suggesting it." He removes his hand and starts to roll away from me.

"No," I say. "I think that's a good idea." Somehow, I feel brave when I say this, so I reach out for his arm this time. His strong cellist forearm and the curve of his biceps. I've always admired this part of him, but it never seemed okay to just reach out and touch him, as comfortable as he's always been with the reverse.

He turns back toward me, and our noses are about six inches

apart. He's got this smile. It's always been one of my favorite sights. He has deep dimples and crinkly, smiling eyes and expressive eyebrows. I might like his smile even more than his arms.

"Is now okay?" he asks.

"Sure," I say. It sounds so casual. But I have never been more alert in my life. He lays a palm on my cheek and brings his face closer.

I think I was expecting a peck, but he's in no rush. It's warm, feeling his lips against mine, and his nose brushing mine. And he moves slowly, pressing his lips harder against mine, then pulling slightly away and opening his mouth just a bit. At first it feels very technical, but as soon as I begin pushing back, it just becomes about sharing air and pushing and teasing, and when I feel his tongue brush my lip, I respond with my own.

It's as sweet a kiss as I could have imagined, and when he pulls his face back and looks at me with a question, I just breathe out a sigh that embarrasses me immediately, so I cover my face with my hands. He laughs quietly and pulls my head into his chest. I fit so well, curled up into a ball, his legs curved below mine, his arms around me.

"Not bad for a novice," he whispers in my ear.

I punch him playfully on his pecs.

"Shh," he says, exhaling into my hair. "We should probably sleep, right? We have to get up for school."

I nod, but sleeping is even harder than it was before. I just keep staring off into the dark of my room, and squeezing my eyes and my mouth shut tight to keep myself from making some embarrassing, joyful squeal.

Seventeen

"Look who's here," my mom says the next morning. I wake with a start. I glance beside me on the bed, but Theo is long gone. She means me. I'm here.

I don't actually think my mom would be mad that Theo spent the night with me. She knows we sleep over at Evita's. And she'd probably be happy that I had my first kiss and that it was so nice. And respectful. And affectionate. And sexy.

How did he leave without waking me? It all feels like a dream.

A very good dream.

"How was it?"

"Amazing."

"Wish I could have seen it," my mom says. "You are going to be late if you don't get a move on, though."

"Right. You guys should come to the next one. I don't think parents will be banned from that one."

"Oh yeah? You already have one lined up?"

I hop out of bed. "In a couple weeks. A Friday this time! Which is, like, pretty huge because that's a big night."

"That's awesome. I want to hear all the details when you aren't running late. And now I have to shove off for my shift." She gives me a peck on the cheek. "Have a good day."

"You, too. Enjoy meeting the babies."

She nods and smiles, closing the door behind her. Even though I probably don't even have time for a shower, I flop back onto my bed for a second, happy to find that my pillows smell like Theo.

~

It's obvious at school that the three of us are dragging. Theo waits at Evita's locker with coffees. I think maybe he gives me an extra-nice smile, but other than that, there's no indication that anything happened last night. Maybe the kiss was a nice moment between friends and nothing more. Maybe it's something I could tell Evita about and she'd just punch my shoulder and say "Finally!" But I can't find a way to bring it up.

"Hey," Theo says. "I just thought you should both know that Lily Ann and I broke up and I don't really want to talk about it."

"Oh!" Evita says, trying to look surprised, which is exactly what I am also trying to do.

"Sorry, Theo," I say. With this announcement, and using the word *both*, Theo is making it clear that we're not acknowledging that he spent the night with me last night. My stomach gives a little twist. I don't like having secrets from Evita. Keeping the kiss out of it was okay, but pretending like I didn't talk to him at all after the gig? It feels almost like he wishes none of it had happened. *Get it together*, I chide myself.

Evita downs her coffee, then starts talking plans while we walk toward the music wing. "So, I'm already thinking about how we should try to incorporate the Sparrows into as much as possible at school next year. I mean, we're going to have to do music assignments, so just think how awesome it'll be to learn something in school and actually have it matter. Like we'll learn stuff and it'll make our band better. I just feel like we'll have all the opportunities to play. None of this boring class stuff. And, like, when should we move up to Boston? Just think, after June, we don't have to be limited by school anymore. We can tour. We can go straight to Boston. We can go anywhere. Maybe get an opening gig on a tour."

"Evita, that sounds awesome. But this coffee hasn't had enough time to kick in for me to think about all this," I say. Along with not acknowledging the kiss, or the sleepover, I'm not acknowledging just how much volunteering with Shana has made me wonder about nursing school.

"Sorry about Lily Ann, Theo, but this is good. No emotional ties back at home while we tour. Right?" Evita asks.

"Sure," Theo says. "Have fun in choir. Make beautiful music."

When Evita heads to choir, Theo turns to me, eyebrows raised.

"What?" I ask.

"Nothing."

"You left early."

"I thought that was the plan," Theo says as he carries his cello down the hall.

"Yeah. Sure."

Just outside the orchestra room, Theo bends to whisper in my ear. "That kiss, Lacey . . ."

I blush, but as soon as we're through the door, we get death stares from Lily Ann, and the little flutters of desire I was feeling vanish.

~

"This is so much better. I'm sorry you're sad, Theo, but seriously, this whole table for just the three of us. Just the Sparrows." Evita is grinning like a cat with a canary, so happy to have her best friends' attention back where it should be. Only mine isn't. I don't understand how Theo has been so cool all day. Aside from his whispering in my ear, nothing is different. "God. I wish Alice were here. How awful is homeschooling? Like, she isn't keeping the fact that she's pregnant a secret. Some kids from school were at the gig."

"They were?" I ask.

"Yes. Martin McKinley already told me he thought we were great and that you looked really hot," Evita says.

"He did not." I roll my eyes at her.

"Jesus, Lacey, just accept your beauty."

"She has a point," Theo says with a grin.

"Whatever. Did he really like the music?" I ask.

"Duh. And he asked about Alice's baby bump. And I told him to mind his own uterus. I don't think he appreciated it. But anyway, if the secret is out, why doesn't she just come back to school?"

"I kind of think it's her mom's idea. She seemed mostly okay with taking her GED and stuff."

"I don't know if I feel bad for her or jealous. Imagine if we could all just take our GEDs and rehearse all the time," Evita says, and pulls out her phone. "I'm texting her. Coffee after school?"

"I can't," Theo says.

"What?"

"I promised Lily Ann we'd talk about stuff."

"Theo!" Evita exclaims.

"Nope. You don't get to have an opinion on this."

"If you get back together with her . . . ," Evita threatens.

"Do you guys seriously think I have that little conviction?" Theo asks.

"I'm just worried she'll seduce you and you won't be able to resist."

I have nothing to say in this conversation. Because I sort of worry about the same thing Evita does, except if anything like that happened, I'd now actually be pissed, as if I have some claim on Theo.

This is a recurring theme: some girl feels like she has a claim on Theo and he kind of goes along with it. I feel a little sick.

"I'll call you as soon as I'm free. Now, let's go get lectured on how to not be morally bankrupt," Theo says.

～

Mrs. Einhorn isn't the only teacher waiting for us in the classroom. One of the assistant principals, Ms. George, is there looking very stern. This cannot be good.

"Before we get started on our new unit on financial responsibility, Ms. George has a disciplinary matter to discuss," Mrs. Einhorn says.

Then Ms. George pulls out one of our little pamphlets. I probably could have predicted this, but it doesn't stop my pulse from quickening or my palms from getting sweaty. I feel like everyone is looking at me. If they don't know that I made the pamphlets, I'm sure they can guess.

Ms. George wastes no time cutting to the chase. "There are rules regarding the distribution of written materials in our schools. Any flyer, brochure, or informational literature must be approved by the administration before it can be posted or distributed. Let me be totally clear: any literature that contains lewd or pornographic material is not only breaking this rule, it is also offensive and will be treated with serious disciplinary measures. Anyone caught distributing any kind of lewd material will receive an automatic suspension and possible expulsion. Are there any questions?"

A boy that we know from GSA, Paul, raises his hand. "Can you explain what in that particular brochure is so offensive? We've had pretty frank discussions of that type of thing in this class, and I'm wondering if you can clarify what constitutes lewd material?"

I appreciate his question. I think maybe he's standing up for me. Then he glances quickly in my direction. It's totally not subtle.

"You know what, if you are ever planning to distribute something and you aren't sure if it's lewd or not, bring it by the office," Ms. George says. "Because I think all of you know, instinctively, if something is school-appropriate or not."

Theo raises his hand, and I want to kick his chair to stop him from engaging in this discussion. Why am I the only one of us who wants to keep a low profile? "How does the administration feel about lessons that teach their students to be ashamed of their bodies?"

"Theo, if you have an issue with a lesson, you are free to come talk to me anytime," Ms. George says tiredly. Theo got in frequent trouble for fighting during freshman and sophomore years, so he and Ms. George have spent some time together. I think she understood that he didn't start the fights. He was just quick to return anything that was thrown at him. His fuse has gotten longer since then. Or maybe people don't mess with him now that he's taller than most people. Theo has told us that he likes Ms. George.

"I honestly think some of the policies at this school are a little outdated," Theo says.

"That's not up to me, Theo. But I want to be totally clear: whether or not you think something is appropriate isn't up for debate. You are not to distribute any material without administration approval. Does everybody understand?" Ms. George asks.

Most of the class nods.

"Thank you, Mrs. Einhorn," Ms. George says.

"Are you talking to all of the classes about this?" Paul asks.

"I will, if it becomes a more widespread problem," she answers, and she looks right at me.

My cheeks burn, and I find it hard to swallow. Still, I know that I'm lucky to have had a warning. I want to do things to help people. But there have to be ways to help that don't involve getting suspended.

Ms. George leaves, and Mrs. Einhorn starts a lecture on credit cards and debt. It's super boring, and my eyelids feel heavy from lack of sleep. I make eye contact with Paul at one point, and he smiles at me and gives me a sly thumbs-up.

~

"Are you okay, Lace?" Evita asks me as we drive to my house. I told her I wanted to hang out there instead of her place today. I just feel on edge. About the pamphlets. About the school policies. But mostly about Theo.

"Tired, why?"

"You've seemed quiet. Is this about the brochures? Because I think we'll find another act of resistance. And no one's been suspended yet."

"No. It's not that. I really am just tired." I want to tell her why I couldn't sleep. I want to be able to let out the giddy squeal I had trouble holding in. I want to tell her everything, like I always do. But it really didn't seem like a big thing to Theo. Aside from that one comment, he acted like nothing had happened. I'm not willing to hurt Evita over something that didn't even matter to Theo. "Honestly, I'm pretty surprised Theo is going to hang out with Lily Ann." That's not the whole truth, but it is true.

"Right? What the hell? He broke up with her *last night* and they need to talk about it already? Like, give it a minute." She puts her feet up on the dashboard until she notices me glaring. "We do not want him to get back together with Lily Ann. Maybe we need to find another girl for Theo."

"What? Why? I didn't think you'd want him to be with anyone."

"I don't know. Yeah. Well. Maybe just a rebound. Someone

who makes him feel like he doesn't need Lily Ann. There are more fish in the sea. That kind of thing."

I know this is my chance to say something. If not about the kiss, then maybe about my feelings for him. How I've been jealous of Lily Ann, and how it goes so much deeper than just being jealous of the time Theo spent with her.

"So . . . you wouldn't . . . I don't know . . . want to try being with him again?" I ask. The lump in my throat is back.

"No. I thought about that. But I think he's definitely, totally moved on from me, and I don't feel like going through that again. We're good, him and me, right now. I would not trade that for anything, even though he's adorable in tight pants, right?"

"Okay." Even agreeing that he looks good in tight pants would feel like an admission. I feel like the moment where I could ask if she'd be okay if I liked Theo is slipping away.

"I'm texting Alice your address, is that okay?"

"That's fine," I say. She starts talking about Alice and the band and I kind of just let her chatter away. I listen for an in, a way to get her to talk more about Theo. Maybe I'm hoping she'll create that moment. Like somehow she'll say, *Well, Lacey, if you still need your first kiss and Theo is single* . . . But she doesn't, so I bite my lip, hoping for another chance to tell her.

Eighteen

Once we're at my house and have described Ms. George's announcement, my mom starts fixing us snacks. "I'm proud of you for taking a stand, anyway," she says as she rummages through the fridge and produces a bag of baby carrots.

"I want to take a stand, but I don't want to be *expelled*," I say to my mom.

"No one would expel you. For telling your friends how to protect themselves? That's absurd." My mom plops the carrots down on the dining room table and sits with me and Evita. She flips the one pamphlet I have left over and over. "I don't know. I think these are great."

"Right, but I can't keep handing them out," I say.

"So, you keep talking to kids in the bathroom," Evita says. "Besides, even if the pamphlet was short-lived, I think it firmly established you as the school's sex-ed guru. Like, people know to ask you stuff now. We can just let word spread naturally and make the office hours in the bathroom a regular thing."

"Yeah. That's true," I say.

There's a knock on the door, and I'm not sure who's happier to see Alice: Evita or my mom.

"Alice, you remember my mom." I give my mom a look that says *Try to look a little less excited to see her.*

"Hi, Ms. Burke," Alice says.

Evita jumps up from her chair. "I missed you," she says as she squeezes Alice just a little too tightly.

"It's been, what, like fifteen hours since you saw me?" Alice says, laughing.

"So much has happened. First, we booked another gig. Second, Theo broke up with Lily Ann. Third, Theo ditched us for Lily Ann anyway. Am I missing any big developments?" Evita asks me.

I just shake my head.

"Another gig! When?" Alice asks.

"Two weeks, a Friday night! Should be a big crowd."

"Two weeks should be fine," Alice says. She presses her lips tightly together.

"What?" Evita asks.

"At some point this baby is going to be born. Like, two weeks is fine. But in two months? Who knows."

"Then you get a babysitter," Evita says.

Alice looks grim. It's the same way she looked when she was sitting all alone in the waiting room. "Things are gonna change, you know? I'll probably need to get a job as soon as I can, so I can afford a place to live."

"You aren't going to live at home?" I ask.

"Only if I put the baby up for adoption. But I honestly haven't even considered it. It's not what I want."

"Honey, you'll figure it out," my mom says.

"Wait, your mom is going to kick you out?" I ask.

"I don't know if she actually will. That's what she's said all along, but she hasn't brought it up recently, and she let me put a bassinet in my room. It'll be okay, plus Eric says he'll pay child support or whatever," Alice says. "Sorry, I didn't mean to put a whole damper on everything. It's just starting to get more real. There's a lot I need to figure out. For so long it was me wondering if I was pregnant, and then just trying to get through the days with morning sickness, and then about hiding the fact that I was pregnant from people at school because I was so embarrassed. But those worries, they were nothing in the grand scheme of things."

"You just take each obstacle as it comes. They will all become less daunting," my mom says.

"Wow," Evita says. She reaches across the table and grabs Alice's hand. "You know we've got your back, right?"

I nod. "Definitely."

"And Theo, too."

Alice blinks back tears. "You guys are the best."

"You're a Sparrow. We've got your back no matter what," Evita says.

"Can you believe all this shit is because I didn't know how to get on birth control? Evita was telling me about the advice you were giving people," Alice tells me. "I wish I could be in the bathroom so I could grip these girls by the shoulders and tell them to run, don't walk, to get on the pill."

"Or condoms, Jesus," I say. "Like, I want to just hand them out to everyone I meet. Like those attendants in bathrooms at the fancy places in the movies. 'Hi. How are you? Breath mint? Hand towel? Condom? Tampon? Pregnancy test? Toothpick?'"

"Ha. That'd be awesome. Forget a new stadium. That's what the school board should pay for next," Alice says.

"Yeah, oh I'm sure. They are *so* progressive," Evita says.

It is a good idea, though. I mean, getting condoms isn't actually that difficult, but it seems like a lot of people are just too nervous to buy them or go to the clinic. "What if we did give out condoms?" I ask Evita. "Like when we have office hours. Everyone who asks a question gets a condom."

"That is a great idea!" my mom says. "Then your classmates could get them without even having the hurdle of asking for them or buying them."

"Let's do it. Where will we get all of them?" Evita asks.

"I'll chip in a few boxes," my mom says. "Then, I bet the clinic would give us some. And I think there are organizations that'd probably send us some. I think they do that for colleges. They should do it for small mountain towns, too."

"I bet if everyone walked around with condoms, no one would feel so embarrassed about having them. Or about asking to use them. I always felt so sheepish suggesting condoms. Even though, hello, I should have insisted. That's why I wanted to be on the pill," Alice says.

"Maybe get some pregnancy tests, too?" Evita suggests. "Or are those expensive? Like, same deal—if they were readily available, maybe it wouldn't feel like such a big deal to take one if you weren't sure. People would just feel so much less embarrassed about what was going on in their bodies."

"You can actually get cheap test strips online. I took about twenty before I finally let it sink in that I was pregnant. I would have gone broke if I hadn't found those," Alice says.

"Absolutely, that's what they use at the hospital," my mom says.

"Can I borrow your notebook?" I ask Evita.

I write CONDOM PROJECT at the top. We brainstorm and doodle. We think about ways to package them and hand them out. Evita grabs the notebook and draws a cartoon little condom guy. She draws him with a frown and a speech bubble that says, "Don't make me sad. Use me!"

My mom answers the door when there's a knock. The three of us are at the kitchen table, too busy laughing to get up.

"But the real question is: What do we name our cartoon condom?" Evita asks.

"Dicky? Peter?" Theo says from behind us. "What is all this?"

"We are going to get prophylactics for everyone!" Evita says.

"Trying to figure out a distribution scheme," Alice tells him as he squeezes a chair in between mine and Evita's.

"It would be great if people could just help themselves. Obviously, we can give them out at office hours, but that sort of leaves the male contingent out . . . ," I say, tapping my pencil against the table.

"Wait. We don't need all three of our lockers, do we?" I ask. "Like, we can keep our stuff in two of them and then just stock the third one full of condoms and pamphlets and pregnancy tests or whatever. And tampons and pads, because it's also stupid that they don't have those in the bathroom. We can still give some out in the bathroom and stuff. But we can store them there."

"You guys shouldn't risk that. Maybe my old locker is still empty," Alice suggests.

"Do you remember your combo?" Theo asks.

"Yeah. I'll write it down for you."

"But how will we get all this in there?" I ask.

"I can hide boxes upon boxes in my oversize sweaters!" Evita says. "I'll be like a condom mule! Theo will be of no use here. He can only cram one in his tight pants. And who knows if he'll even need to do that anymore, provided he didn't get back with Lily Ann today."

"I'm sitting right here," Theo says. "We did not get back together. I did get my ukulele back. And I think I could probably manage four condoms, one in each pocket." He stands up and sticks his hands in all the pockets of his faux-moto skinny jeans. The pants are ridiculously cute on him.

"So that's three boxes of condoms for me, and four condoms for Theo. How many can you smuggle in, Lacey?" Evita asks.

We are all so into this little covert operation. "I could add some into my viola case and my backpack."

"Who knew condoms could be so fun?" Alice laughs.

"Oh. I did," Theo deadpans.

"Gross," Evita says. "But, don't worry, we'll find you another willing participant again sometime."

"I think you mean an 'enthusiastically consenting participant,'" I say with a giggle.

"Naturally," Evita says. "I was never that enthusiastic, was I?"

"You were fine," Theo mumbles, glancing at my mom, his ears turning as red as mine feel.

"Sorry," Evita says, realizing how uncomfortable most of the room is at this moment.

"Should I go buy some?" my mom asks.

"Get the best variety you can," I tell her.

"I'd offer to go with you, but I'm not sure how that would look," Theo says.

"Eww!" Alice giggles.

I wouldn't mind a moment alone with Theo. For lots of reasons, though mostly to talk. I wonder if I can somehow suggest Alice and Evita go with my mom, but my mind draws a blank.

~

By the time my mom comes back from the store, we've got a system set up. Evita found simple condom instructions on my computer, and we printed them out as small as we could legibly make them. We're all sitting on the floor of my room and cutting them out when my mom tosses boxes of condoms at us.

"Don't have too much fun," my mom says, closing my door.

"Who knew there was such a wide variety of products," I say.

"Right? Look at all these colors and textures and *flavors*!" Evita laughs as she opens a box of flavored condoms. "Theo, banana flavor. *Banana!*"

She tosses him a few in yellow wrappers.

"Banana flavor is the worst fake flavor. Like, banana candy is always gross," Alice says. "Blech."

"We'll set aside all the vanilla ones for you," I say.

Evita nudges Theo with her foot. "What's your deal?" she asks him. He does not seem to find any of this nearly as fun as Alice, Evita, and I do.

Maybe he's feeling as weird about sorting condoms with me as I do with him. But I doubt it. I feel this extra weight with each

of our interactions, wondering what it means and what he's thinking. I cannot get that kiss out of my head. But Theo mostly seems
mopey. He might be sad about his breakup, and that possibility
is more than I can handle.

"Maybe he's just sad he doesn't need condoms anymore," I
blurt out. As soon as the words fly out, I want to shove them
back in.

"Whoa. Lacey. You just went there," Theo says.

"My girl speaks her mind now. It's a whole thing," Evita says.
"Apparently she told Bruno that smoking was gross."

"I did. He told you that?" I ask her.

"Yeah. Oh, Bruno and I are super tight. He told me he thought
you were maybe into him and that you were hot, but that you
were not into kissing a smoker. Ah well, Lacey, we will get you
kissed by a nonsmoker one of these days."

"You did seem pretty into him," Theo says, one of his eyebrows raised. I want to ask him right now if that bothers him.
"Okay, honestly, I think I feel weird about this whole thing
because I am the only person here who would . . . you know . . .
wear one of these." He holds up a condom.

"Darling. Give yourself more credit." Evita grabs the condom
from him and hands him one that's branded for bigger men.

"Yeah. Gee. Why would I feel weird about any of this?" Theo
says, a smile finally creeping onto his face.

"You shouldn't feel weird," I tell him. "That's the whole problem at school, right? Like. You have a penis. If you're gonna use
it, you should wrap it up."

"Wow, Lacey." Theo shakes his head. But he's definitely
smiling.

"Sock it before you rock it," I say as deadpan as I can.

"I'm writing that down on the instructions. Is it too late for us to print out new ones?" Evita asks, grabbing a stack of already-cut pages. "Is that 'rock it' two words or 'rocket' like the ship?"

"Well, I meant two words, but you should definitely have the condom in place before any blasting off occurs." I giggle.

"Oh, Jesus. I'm gonna go raid your fridge while you ladies come up with innuendos. This is mortifying," Theo says with a chipper smile.

"Either he is embarrassed because I know he's chickenshit about buying his own condoms, or he's hiding a boner," Evita whispers. "It does not take much for him."

"Evita! Stop!" Alice says, laughing.

"What? It's just so strange, right? Boys just think it and then . . . you know . . . like . . . that's it. That's all it takes. Is that all it takes for you?" Evita asks.

"Takes for what? I don't get boners," Alice says. We're all getting giddy, but seeing Alice laughing so much is nice. Except for when she's singing, she's looked serious or anxious whenever I see her.

"Yeah. That's all pretty awkward . . . ," I say.

"You think it's awkward now, wait until you encounter one . . ." Alice searches for the right word.

"Socially?" Evita offers.

"Yes, socially. Social boner interactions." She laughs. "Like, maybe it's just me, but I don't find social vaginas nearly this hilarious."

"Vaginas are so serious," Evita says. "I've never encountered one . . . socially . . . but . . . I'm open to the possibility." Evita giggles.

"Yeah?" Alice asks. "I thought the ace thing sort of meant you didn't."

"No way. It just means that I don't want to, like, jump people that I just met. And I could take it or leave it, between you and me. Some ace people are sex-repulsed, and that's fine, but I'm not. I just think dating girls would be nice."

"We will find you a nice girl then!" Alice says. "Are there any other bi girls in the GSA?"

"None that hold a candle to you." Evita grins. "None that I would want to see . . . socially." Evita and Alice both start giggling. They are so punchy.

"You guys are nuts," I say.

"Okay, okay," Evita says, trying to get the laughter back under control. "Don't make a big thing. But speaking of nuts—"

Alice snorts.

"I might have gotten asked out on a date by that guy Paul."

"Senior seminar Paul?" I ask.

"Dude. He came to the last GSA meeting because he is totally gray-A, and he's cute."

"GSA is an excellent place to meet people who don't mind talking about gender and sexuality and are generally enlightened," Alice says. "Or at least it was before my mother made me quit. Too enlightened for her."

"Dude. I haven't met your mom, but she sucks," Evita says.

"What did I miss?" Theo asks when he comes back in with soda and pretzels. "There were no bananas, or I would have suggested that as a snack."

"Cucumbers?" Evita asks with a sly grin.

"I think my mom might have bought an eggplant," I say.

"An eggplant!" Evita laughs. "When you aren't feeling uptight about your lack of experience, you are hilarious."

"Evita, she is not uptight," Theo says. Maybe he noticed my shoulders stiffen at the word. "You told me yourself she was giving blow job advice."

"Yeah, not on technique or whatever. But, yeah," Evita says. "Sorry, Lacey."

"You gotta stop giving me crap for not having a sordid history like you two."

"You're right. But that's not gonna stop me from helping you create your own sordid history, now that I know that you want one," Evita says. "Now where are the glow-in-the-dark condoms? We need to make these packs as fun as possible."

I'm digging around in the shopping bag when I feel Theo's hand on my leg, giving me a reassuring squeeze. The squeeze seems to say, *We have a history she doesn't know about*, and for the millionth time I wonder if there was more to our kiss than a favor between friends. I hand Evita the box she asked for and dare to glance at him. He gives me the slightest possible smile and begins bundling the condoms into groups of three.

~

When Alice tells us she's tired and wants to go home, she asks me to walk her out to her car.

"What's up?" I ask her outside.

"I have a question. And you can totally say no." Alice bites her lip.

"Sure," I say.

"I know you're serious about the doula thing and about

coming to my appointments, but I realized I hadn't asked you about maybe being . . . *my* doula." She gives me a nervous smile.

"Oh my god, Alice, of *course*." I grin. "I would love to!"

"Really?" she asks.

"Yes!"

"I don't know why I was nervous to ask you."

"It's all a pretty big deal. I get it," I say.

"I had so much fun today," Alice says. "Seriously. What would I do without you guys?" She gives me a big hug. "Thanks, Lacey."

She gets in her car and drives off. I practically skip inside, so excited to tell my mom and Evita and Theo that I'm officially Alice's doula! And I didn't think anything could possibly be more exciting today than condoms.

Nineteen

All three of us walk into school with our backpacks full of condoms. It feels decidedly badass. What doesn't feel badass is how I keep obsessing over when I can get Theo alone to ask him what the hell is going on between us, because his silence is *killing me*.

"Locker four-twelve," I read from the sticky notes Alice gave us. We stop in front of Alice's old locker, and I spin the combination, trying not to look conspicuous. Of course, the harder I try, the more nervous I get, and I keep glancing around.

"Let us stand guard and you just focus on the task at hand," Theo says reassuringly. Maybe they can hear my heart pounding. I'm exhilarated, but I also can't stop picturing Ms. George standing in front of our class talking about suspension and expulsion.

"We need a spy movie theme song playing or something," Evita says. "Like, some real walking-away-from-something-exploding-in-slow-motion jams."

The locker opens, and it's empty. At least I don't have to worry that we'll get caught breaking into a locker that belongs to someone.

I unzip my backpack and start shoving the "fun packs" and a few individually wrapped pads and tampons onto the shelf. When my backpack is empty, I step aside and stand guard as Evita unpacks hers.

"We need bins or something. This one shelf isn't going to cut it," Evita says.

"I'll add it to the shopping list," I tell her. "And if possible, just tell people the locker number and combo. Like, don't write it down. I don't think this project will last very long if there are notes with that info all over the floor. We'll just tell people who ask our advice. Or maybe, Theo, if you hear guys bragging about sex or whatever."

"I don't actually hang out with any guys, let alone ones who brag about sex," he says.

"Whatever. Just keep an ear out."

The guy with the locker next to this one arrives and gives us a questioning look. Then he glances into the locker and his eyes get a little wider. "Are those . . ."

"Take a couple, if you want," I offer.

"Oh. Sure."

Evita hands him some with a huge grin. "Better safe than sorry."

"Guys, hurry up," I say, shifting my weight from one foot to the other.

"You don't break the rules much, do you?" Theo asks.

"Like you do?"

"Only all the time. My dad has forbidden me from wearing makeup, remember?" Theo has decided to make eyeliner part of his morning routine. "But honestly, that is one of the main reasons I find it so appealing."

"I'm sure the looks you get from girls have nothing to do with that choice," Evita says, zipping up her backpack. "I think people have heard you're single again."

"Oh. Yeah. Lily Ann is going around saying lovely things, I'm sure," Theo says. He fills the bottom of the locker with the condoms he has in his bag.

"Screw her. I'm not talking about that. I'm talking about how much other girls are flirting with you," Evita says.

"They are not," I tell her.

"Yeah, no way," Theo says, slamming the locker shut.

"You're just not observant. Everyone is smiling at him more. Everyone."

I look around. The hallway is crowded, because we only have a couple minutes until first period starts. And sure enough, a lot of girls glance at Theo. Maybe it's more than usual. Or maybe I just care more. I get this churning feeling in my stomach that someone is going to snatch him up now that he's single.

"Maybe you better take some of these," Evita says, slipping a bag into his back pocket. Even that bothers me. It's not the first time Evita has reached into his pocket, fishing around for a wallet or his keys, but it's the first time I really wish I had that closeness with him.

I slam the locker shut, way harder than I mean to. But how does anyone do this? How does anyone realize they like someone and then somehow find a way to be with that person, without clamming up or being anxious? How am I supposed to be around Theo and not want to touch him? Or shoot nasty looks at girls who flirt with him?

I hand Evita and Theo sticky notes with the locker number and combo. "Maybe don't tell too many people today. I want to change the world but also not get caught," I say.

"Roger that," Evita says as we head to the music wing. When we get to the choir room, Evita gives us high fives. "Go team!"

I smile when we high five, but it feels forced. I'm mad that the anxiety I'm feeling over Theo, and over being caught, is overshadowing what should be a triumphant moment.

As soon as Evita's in the choir room and Theo and I finally have a few moments without her, I give him a little shove.

"What's that for?" Theo says.

"It's super shitty that we haven't had a chance to talk," I say.

"Oh. Do we need to talk?" Theo asks.

"Are you kidding?" I ask. "Speaking to you without Evita around is impossible."

"I know, I know. I'm sorry." He pauses right outside the orchestra room door. He glances around, checking for Lily Ann, I'm sure. "I've honestly been all over the place. I'm sorry."

His eye contact is intense. These moments where it's just him and me make everything else seem less important.

"I keep thinking about it, and I feel like you don't, and it sucks," I say, breaking eye contact.

"That's nuts. I've been thinking about it. I've been thinking nonstop about kissing you and about how cool you are," Theo says.

"Did you think at all how I might feel about it?" I ask him.

"Like maybe you were only interested in kissing me because you thought I had kissed someone else. Or maybe you're too embarrassed to admit that you did kiss me."

"Embarrassed? Why would I be embarrassed?"

"Because it's me. Boring, average me."

"I don't think that at all," he says quietly.

I give him a second to tell me what he *does* think. But he's staring at his shoes, that nice moment gone. Our orchestra teacher comes to the door as the bell rings.

"You joining us?" she asks.

"Yeah," I say. I give Theo four beats—a measure—of silence before sighing and walking into class.

～

Five minutes into lunch, and Theo won't look at me. It's not in a mean or even obvious way—he just seems to find reasons to talk nonstop to Evita about anything and everything. But I notice.

"I'm gonna head to the bathroom and see if anyone's waiting for office hours," I say, shoving the crust of my sandwich in my mouth and washing it down with my water.

"Should I come with?" Evita asks.

"I'll text you if I need backup," I tell her.

I shove the bathroom door open. I don't even want to answer people's sex questions, I just need a break from the "Theo mindfuck," as I have now dubbed it. What if he doesn't like me like that at all and just doesn't know how to tell me? I'm not as pretty as Evita. And she and Lily Ann both totally have those elven looks: small features, big eyes. I'm probably not even his type.

Inside the bathroom, a girl I talked to before, Cam, is leaning on a sink. She's with a friend. Cam nods toward me. "Lacey. This is Janie. She's a freshman."

"Hi, Janie," I say.

"Hi," she says.

"What's up?"

Janie looks nervously at Cam.

"I won't talk about anything you ask me. Confidentiality. And nothing embarrasses me. *Nothing*," I emphasize. *Except the fact that I kissed my best friend and he's maybe not into me that way.*

"My . . . boyfriend . . . he doesn't go here," Janie says. She looks so nervous.

"That's okay," I say, unsure what else to say.

"You want me to wait outside?" Cam asks.

Janie nods.

"So. He wants to do . . . stuff . . . ," Janie says.

"Do you? Want to?" I ask.

"Yeah. No. Totally. But, like, I'm so nervous about . . . it . . ."

"Well, it's totally okay to be nervous. But you should communicate with him about your comfort level with everything and make sure you're on the same page."

"No. Specifically. Nervous about *it*."

"Listen. I'm not going to judge you. But you have to tell me which 'it' we're talking about here," I say. "I could guess. But there are just so many guesses."

"My vagina," she practically whispers. Even though we're alone in here, she glances around nervously.

"Okay. Like . . ."

"What if it smells?" she says suddenly.

"I totally get feeling self-conscious about that. But every

person has their own smell. And as long as you aren't noticing any new or concerning smells, which could be a sign of an infection, your smell is likely totally healthy. You can shower beforehand, but you don't need to do anything special."

"Like, what about good-smelling soap or spray or whatever?"

My mom has for sure covered this topic. Anytime there's an ad on TV for feminine sprays, she positively loses her mind.

"Anything that has a strong scent can actually irritate your skin. Your vagina doesn't need to be cleaned. Some warm water is fine, but that's kind of all you need. Vaginas are pretty great at keeping their pH balanced and all that. And anyone who tells you that you need to smell a certain way is just trying to sell you something."

"Just water?" she asks. "Really?"

"It's that simple," I tell her. "Is there anything else you're worried about? Or have questions about?"

She just shakes her head.

"Well, if anything else comes up, you can talk to me. And if you or anyone you know ever needs condoms, there are a bunch for free in locker four-twelve and I can give you the combo to put in your phone."

"Thanks," she mumbles, pulling out her phone.

I tell her the combo. "Feel free to share the combo with your friends, but try not to write it down so we don't get caught," I tell her.

"I will," she says, and she leaves.

I stand by the sink and look at myself in the mirror. I might as well wait here to see if anyone else needs advice or condoms. I don't need to engage anymore with the Theo mindfuck.

I blink a couple times looking in the mirror. I always feel oddly self-conscious looking at myself in school bathrooms, like I don't want people to think I'm vain if they come in here. Meanwhile, every other girl seems not even to think twice before primping. I tuck a few wisps of hair behind my ears and sigh loudly, just as the door swings open.

"You coming back?" Evita calls, her voice bouncing off the tiled walls.

"Sure," I say.

"Because we have band business to discuss," she says.

"Should we have band meetings without Alice?" I ask.

"Mostly we're discussing how we need to have an epic all-weekend rehearsal," she says.

"You're not a little tired after Wednesday night?"

"When has being a little tired ever stopped me?" Evita says. She comes and stands next to me, pouting in the mirror. "I look good," she says. She makes a series of poses and faces in the mirror, admiring herself.

I sigh. Here's Evita, proving we are so unlike each other that there's no way Theo could like her and then me. She turns and looks at me quizzically. She can almost definitely tell something is bothering me.

"Come on. Did anyone need advice? Did you give out the locker combo?" Evita asks.

"Only to one person today so far."

"That's one less baby or new case of chlamydia," Evita says, offering her hand for a high five.

"That's true," I say, slapping her hand with a minimum of enthusiasm.

"For the rest of the day, I'm going to make it my personal mission to tell everyone I know the locker combination," Evita says.

"Everyone?" I ask. I love her enthusiasm, but subtlety is not her strong suit.

"Quietly. I won't write it down. You're not nervous about getting caught or something, are you?" Evita says.

"No, not really."

"Okay, well, let's get to senior seminar early, just in case we can pass the locker combo off to some new kids. Plus . . . I kind of want to say hi to Paul and nail down plans for our date tonight."

"Sure," I say. "You're pretty excited about this date, huh?"

"Uh, yeah. Paul is cute and pro-safe-sex and he gets my identity," she says. "I'm totally writing a song about that. Right? Like how sexy respect and consent are." She starts singing, "You had me from the moment/you pulled it from your pocket/slide it on and I'll be ready to rock it."

"Oh my god." I laugh. She knows exactly how to make me smile.

"Yeah. We'll work on that one at rehearsal this afternoon. I'm totally serious."

"I think it's great," I say.

She takes me by the hand. "Let's go sing it to Paul."

Twenty

At our Saturday-morning rehearsal, we are totally off. Evita is a little bummed because her date with Paul turned out to be kind of boring and uninspiring. ("He likes terrible music. Total dealbreaker.") Somehow, she shoves that disappointment aside and is all business. But Theo and I are both a mess, and I think it's affecting Alice, too, who keeps forgetting the lyrics. When Theo misses his entrance on a piece we've been playing for months, Evita just stops singing.

"Theo!" she says into the mic.

"God. Sorry," he says, setting his bow on his music stand.

Evita shuts off the drum loop and looks at Alice. "You sounded great, though."

"Thanks," Alice says.

"Let's take five. I'm gonna make some coffee and the two of you should get your heads out of your rears," Evita says.

Evita goes into the kitchen. Theo looks at me sheepishly. "That was totally my fault. I just kept spacing out."

"Oh! Are we talking to each other?" I ask him. Because it's the first time he's made eye contact with me since orchestra class yesterday morning.

"We weren't not talking," Theo says defensively.

Alice looks between me and Theo but doesn't say anything.

"You're being weird," I tell him.

He nods his head toward the kitchen and gives me a warning glance. I roll my eyes at him. Sometimes it's easier to be annoyed than hurt. I put my viola down and walk into the kitchen.

"I don't get it," Evita says. She's leaning on the counter, watching the coffeemaker drip. "It sounds like we never practice. Like we haven't been playing the same fucking pieces for weeks."

"I know. We could work on that new piece," I say. "I actually have a new riff we could try it with."

"Which new piece?" Evita asks.

"The sexy one. Rocket. Or . . . rock. It. Two words. Did we ever decide?"

"Lacey Burke! You minx! I didn't think you'd actually want to do that song!"

"Are you kidding? It was hilarious."

"Alice!" Evita calls. When Alice joins us in the kitchen, Evita says, "Weigh in on these lyrics and if you would sing them."

Evita sings it again, and Alice laughs. "That's filthy."

"We need some lines about consent," Evita says.

"Enthusiastic consent," I add.

"You are a broken record." Evita laughs.

I can feel myself shedding layers of annoyance and confusion and stress, standing in this kitchen listening to coffee brew. Then Theo pokes his head around the doorframe of the kitchen.

"Guys, I think maybe I'm not feeling that great," he says apologetically.

"Will coffee help?" Evita asks.

"I just don't think I'm going to be that useful rehearsing when I feel like this," he says. He's back to not looking at me.

"That's fine. We can work on writing new stuff," I say, daring him to make eye contact. "Feel better."

"Okay. I'll see y'all later," he says.

Evita looks like someone just smacked her. "Wait. Seriously? You guys, we have gig in exactly two weeks. I'm sorry you're not feeling good, but . . ."

"Evita, it's fine," Alice says. "Maybe I can finally get all the lyrics down and we can work on a new song."

"Can we please pick up tomorrow first thing?" Evita asks.

"I'm volunteering tomorrow," I say.

"Seriously, guys?" Evita looks pissed. "If we don't rehearse today or tomorrow, we wasted a whole weekend. Let's just get it together and keep rehearsing."

"I really gotta go. You guys keep working. I'm just not going to be actually helpful," Theo says.

"You're the backbone of the Sparrows!" Evita wails. "And Lacey, I thought you were just trying out volunteering last weekend, and you're going again?"

"Yeah. Well, I changed my independent study to focus on being a doula so I can volunteer regularly. Last week was pretty amazing. And I want to be experienced when it's time for Eli to be born," I say.

"Come on! You know I'll sound like a jerk if I argue with that." Then Evita glares at Theo. "Bye, Theo. Just go," she says, shooing him out.

"Don't be mad," he says.

"I'll be mad if I want to. But feel better or whatever," she says as he leaves. "Honestly. What is going on with him?" she asks. "Did he tell you anything?"

I shake my head.

"I hope this isn't Lily Ann stuff. I will be so mad if she keeps interfering with the Sparrows from beyond the girlfriend grave."

"He did seem kind of bummed," Alice says.

"Let's record some percussion tracks for this song," Evita says. "Let's fuel up. It's half-caf," she tells Alice. She hands us mugs and we all sit around with coffee and brainstorm lyrics. The song might have started out as a joke, but now the three of us are taking it seriously. When we have a couple verses, Evita wants to record all kinds of noises to make the beat.

I'm participating and recording the things she asks me to, but I only feel partially here. Between concentrating on clapping beats into a microphone, I try to guess what Theo is thinking. Maybe he left because he can tell I'm mad at him, and he doesn't want to let me down. I'm so distracted by the idea that he might not actually like me like that. He might be acting awkward just because he doesn't know how to say that. My hands feel heavy and lazy, and I have to give each pass I'm recording a few tries before I get it right. If Evita's frustrated, she's not showing it.

"Try that one again," she says. "I'd rather have a single recording that's a few measures long so any looping isn't as obvious, and you keep falling behind the beat at the end."

"Alice could try it," I suggest.

Alice studies me for only a split second before nodding. "Sure. I can try it."

"Lacey has the sharpest clap, though," Evita says.

"Oh, let me try," Alice argues.

"I'm gonna grab more coffee," I say.

I shake my head, hoping to dislodge the worries. If anything that happened between me and Theo ruins our band, I will never forgive myself.

After Alice claps the beat (perfectly on her first try), Evita calls in to me. "Hey, Lacey, since Theo left his cello here, I don't suppose you'd be able to pluck a little bass line for us, would you?" she asks.

I put the mug down on the counter and pop back into the living room. "Cello and viola aren't the same thing. I'm not sure Theo would be super happy about it."

"This is so pointless," Evita says.

"Why don't I just play it on the viola and teach it to him later?" I suggest.

"Okay. Or! Why don't you try percussing on your viola some. Would putting fingers on the strings change the tones it makes when you tap on it?"

"I'll play around," I say.

When we pack it in for the night, I'm exhausted, emotionally more than anything. My eyes are starting to glaze over. Even after Alice leaves, Evita and I huddle around her laptop, layering parts together to build the track for the new song.

"I need to sleep," I tell her, taking off my headphones.

"Yeah. You need to be up early, huh?" she asks.

I nod.

"I'm sorry if I was cranky about you volunteering," she says.

"I get it. It doesn't mean I don't want to play music with you, though," I tell her.

She leans her head on my shoulder. "I'm just a little worried you won't want to be in the band when we graduate."

"Are you kidding? I'll always want to be in the band."

"I don't know. Maybe not if you go to nursing school, or if all your weekends are spent at hospitals. I get wanting to help Alice. I want to help Alice. I'd catch a thousand of her babies if I thought it would help her."

"She'd be touched to hear that," I say.

"It's just that it's like on the opposite side of the spectrum from music. Like, nursing is so sciencey and music is so artsy."

"I don't know if I agree with that," I say. "Both are sort of about caring for people and wanting to connect with them."

"That's so cheesy and I love it," Evita says.

Twenty-one

I'm helping a fourth-time mom named Jessica. She's rocking the drug-free labor thing. The only reason she needs me is because her babysitter is sick and her husband is on childcare duty. I feel bad that her husband is out in the waiting room with three kids under the age of five. I offered to switch with him and watch the kids, but he told me that they were too much of a handful. And whenever I walk through the halls and hear the ruckus they're making, I'm glad he didn't take me up on the offer.

My mom is working today, and she's Jessica's nurse. I felt nervous at first, every time Mom walked in the door. I want to be good at this so she'll be proud, but pretty soon, I'm too busy focusing on Jessica to even give my mom a second thought.

Jessica looks at me after a particularly intense contraction. Her forehead is sweating. Her arms are shaky. "Are you thirsty?" I ask her. She gives me a little nod, and I put the drinking straw to her lips. Even when she doesn't want a back rub or anything, I'm just here, being present.

When Jessica's labor becomes intense, I give her counter-pressure on her lower back as she leans over; I breathe with her; I give her ice packs for her head. And even though she's doing the hardest work imaginable, she smiles and thanks me. After a contraction finishes, Kelly comes in and smiles.

"How are you feeling?" she asks Jessica.

Jessica says, "I think I might be ready."

"Oh! That's great; let's meet this baby!" Kelly ducks her head out the door and calls my mom in. Then she washes her hands and puts on gloves. She tells my mom and me that Jessica delivered her last baby in two quick pushes. I feel special to be included in this little conversation, but then I realize that Jessica's husband should be here.

So I tell Jessica that and duck out. Her husband jumps up when he sees me.

"She's getting ready to push, so, really, let me watch the kids. We won't leave the waiting room. It'll be fine," I tell him.

He looks flushed and excited, and it melts my heart. I'm sad to miss the birth, but I know my mom will fill me in on all the details.

"You sure?" he asks.

"Of course." The youngest is asleep lying across two cushioned chairs and the older two are coloring.

As soon as the dad has gone down the hall, the youngest is awakened by howling from the oldest when the middle child bites him. "No biting!" I'm suddenly out of my depth. I fancy myself good with kids, but I don't know these three, so I pull out the big guns. "Who wants to watch a movie on my phone?" This works as long as I'm holding the phone, which means I'm sitting on the floor cross-legged and holding it to my chest as they sit in three waiting room chairs, slack jawed and transfixed. I ignore my phone when it buzzes, because I don't want to break the spell the kids are under.

Then it buzzes again. And again. Someone is sending me rapid-fire texts. And they just have to wait. Even though it could maybe be Theo breaking his silence, telling me how he actually feels instead of dodging me. I'm afraid I won't like what he has to say, though, so I focus on the kids.

The movie is more than half over when my mom finds us in the waiting room. "Your mom and dad say you can come meet your new sibling," she says with a smile.

"After this part?" the oldest boy asks, pointing to my phone.

"Movie's going off. Follow the nurse," I order them, and somehow they fall into line. "I'm just gonna wait here," I tell my mom.

"Sure," she says. And then she mouths *It's a girl* and winks at me. I climb onto one of the waiting room chairs, suddenly feeling exhausted.

My phone reveals seven messages from Theo.

Lacey! We should talk. What are
you up to?

Shit. You're totally volunteering
right now.

Sorry.

I hope this isn't dinging while
some poor lady is pushing with
all her might.

Ding Ding Ding.

Sorry. I dunno. Call me when you
get a chance. I'm crawling out of
my skin.

Not literally.

He's joking. Relief washes over me. If he's joking, that must
mean good things. At least it should mean talking.

I let myself smile as I type a response.

> I'm volunteering. But I'm on a
> sort of break. What's up? You
> still have all your skin?

As soon as I hit send, I cringe. Because I'm picturing all his
skin. And I've seen a lot of it. I mean, not in sexual situations.
Obviously. But just getting dressed and stuff. I'd be lying to
myself if I didn't admit to noticing his skin. And his muscles,
which always surprise me because of how thin he looks with
clothes on. And . . .

Oh my god. I need to stop thinking about this. What if we
never talk about that kiss again? Except I'm not about to let that
happen.

A lull, like, you could have a
visitor? Because I don't want to
have just wasted that five bucks
to park . . .

My heart jumps.

Um. You're here?

Dude. I fucking love hospitals.
Being here reminds me of that
time my grandfather had
open-heart surgery that didn't
save him. Good times.

Seriously. Where are you?

The question, Burke, is: Where
are YOU?

I smile.

Labor and Delivery. Fourth
floor. I'm in the waiting room.

The elevator dings, and I stand with anticipation. But then I
feel overeager and stupid, so I sit back down and try to look busy
on my phone. It's like I don't even recognize myself, getting frazzled over my best friend, who—yes—I am massively attracted to,

but who has known me since before puberty, and who knew when I had that first crush on a kid named Jake, which, looking back, was a horrible choice for me, since we had nothing in common and he is now a known marijuana distributor. Theo hung out with me that time I had bronchitis and had to keep spitting out phlegm because it made me want to vomit. He was the first person I ever played an original composition for. If I wasn't nervous then, why am I now?

And yet, when he rounds the corner with a somewhat dinky bouquet of flowers, I can't keep the smile off my face nor my butt in the chair.

"Hey!" I say.

"Hey there." He crosses the waiting room in only a few long strides and sits next to me. Right next to me.

"Umm. You bought flowers?" He looks good. Happy.

"No. I was just wandering around on the main floor for so long, I took an awkwardly long time in the gift shop, so I didn't want to *not* buy something, you know?" Then he shakes his head. "That's probably stupid. I bet lots of people wander around the gift shop when they have time to kill."

"Yeah. That's basically what the gift shop is for."

"Well. They're for you." He hands them over, like he's glad to be rid of them.

"Thanks." They are sort of pretty. But I don't know what to do with them. They aren't explicitly a romantic gesture. Right? "Maybe we can put them at the nurses' station to brighten things up a bit."

"This whole floor is bright. Compared to the morgue."

"Were you ever in the morgue?" I ask, shocked.

"Well. No. But I'd imagine it isn't as nice as this." He slides down in his chair and puts his head on my shoulder. I think about resting my cheek on his head when he suddenly straightens back up. "Oh. God. I'm sorry. You probably have stuff to do, right? Yeah. I'll go. Unless you want me to wait till you're done so we can . . . talk? Maybe?"

"Yes!" I say, probably way too eagerly. We're going to talk. And he looks happy. Not at all like he's preparing to let me down gently. Unless *that's* what the flowers were for. "I mean, I'd like to wrap things up with this one mom. And my mom is here, but she probably won't mind me cutting out a little early . . ."

He brightens considerably. "Yeah. Finish, and we can talk."

"Where's Evita?"

"She and Alice are practicing vocal stuff and working on lyrics until we can get there."

"What time did you tell them you'd meet up?"

"Eight?"

I look at the clock. It isn't even five yet. But I don't think I'm going to get to another birth before seven. Theo and I will have three hours, just the two of us. The thought, honestly, makes me a little tingly.

"I'll go wrap up," I say. I can't hide my dorky grin.

As I turn to leave with the flowers, Theo reaches out and grabs my arm. He stands, grasps a carnation whose stem is already a bit mangled, breaks it off, tucks it behind my ear, and nods approval. He's grinning, too. I roll my eyes at him, even though I'm really thinking about how nice it feels when he tickles my ear.

I give the flowers to Jessica and her family. I admire her new baby girl. Jessica gets teary-eyed when she says good-bye to me.

It's really special, being with a woman during labor. I've only known her half a day, but we're close somehow.

I stop at the nurses' station and tell my mom that I'm leaving with Theo.

Kelly stops me right outside the waiting room.

"You did a great job in there. I mean it—you should start booking summer clients now if you think you want to attend births when school lets out. I know it feels far away, but you might want to try out the on-call lifestyle. And you could probably charge a decent amount with your experience now."

I consider that. I hadn't thought so far ahead as a summer job. There are a million other decisions I'll have to make this year. Namely: college. Even though a summer job as a doula would be great, I'm just not ready to admit that the end of senior year is going to be here before I know it.

"I will definitely think about it." I glance over at Theo. He and Evita, no matter how they might try, don't really understand why I like being here. They'd probably be disappointed if I made summer plans without even talking to them about it. My heart speeds up when he ambles over to us.

"Hi, I'm Theo," he says pleasantly.

"Kelly." She offers her hand. "Your girlfriend's pretty great."

I start to set the record straight, but Theo beats me to it.

"Yeah. She is," he says, throwing his arm around my shoulders.

I elbow him. Hard.

"Nice to meet you. Have a great week," Kelly tells me, then waves and turns to walk back to the nurses' station.

"I'll actually see you this week. I'm coming with Alice for her appointment."

"Awesome. I'll see you then!"

"Ouch," Theo says, dropping his arm and rubbing his ribs.

"Baby," I tease him. "Come on, let's get out of here." My palms start sweating, and my heart is racing, but it's not unpleasant. Quite the opposite.

Twenty-two

Once we're in Theo's car, he just starts talking. Rapidly.

"I super didn't do things right when we kissed, Lacey. Like, if I had known that maybe it meant something to you . . . I wouldn't have acted like it wasn't a big deal. I just didn't want to make it a big deal because I thought that might be uncool."

"Uncool how?"

"You're a tough nut to crack. You know? Like you don't want to make big deals about things you haven't done, or whatever. And I've heard you say so often that you think virginity is just this patriarchal construct—"

"Okay, well, it is, but—"

"And I thought maybe if I made a thing about your first kiss, like, it'd be all bad feminist of me."

"That's dumb. It felt like it meant something to me and not to you, and I was kind of pissed. And embarrassed."

"Please don't be embarrassed! I screwed things up. And I have a long history of screwing things up. I really, *really* don't want to do the wrong thing here."

"Possibly, Theo, the wrong thing was ignoring me and trying not to look me in the eye," I say.

"That's fair. I was nervous. I just really like you. You know? And I didn't know how you felt or what Evita would think, and I didn't know how to act. But I was a shitty friend."

"Theo, this is fairly impossible for me to say out loud . . . ," I start. I remind myself again that this is one of my best friends. I shouldn't be nervous to talk to him. Though it's never felt like so much was on the line.

"Yeah?" he asks.

"I really like you. And I really wanted to kiss you. And I really wanted the kiss to mean something." I look at my hands, my fingers folding and unfolding, trying to keep my nerves at bay.

"Well. This is me saying that I *wanted* to kiss you. And I've been wanting to kiss you and I still want to kiss you and it's making me nuts that I don't know what you want."

"Okay. But you're not allowed to be intimidated by feminism!" I laugh, because, oh my god, I'm so relieved.

"It is scary! It's hard to be a dude."

"It is actually not hard to be a dude."

"Maybe not comparatively, but still! I want to respect you and be allowed to want you."

I blink. "You just used the words *want you*. About me."

"Well. Yeah. Is that okay?"

"Absolutely."

We get to my house, and I'm bummed that Charlie's car is there. I'm not sure where I hoped he'd be, or what exactly I hoped would happen next . . . but hanging out with Charlie and Dylan was not it.

"Before we go in, just let me text my mom," I tell him.

> You should invite Charlie and
> Dylan to dinner.

And why is that?

> Remember how you wanted
> to live vicariously through me?
> Well . . .

I'm getting details?

> Maybe.

Lacey!!!!!!

"You're texting your mom about me?" Theo asks.

"Not directly. Come on, we can watch TV while we wait for Charlie and Dylan to leave."

"That is beyond weird."

"If you want to kiss me again, you'll play along."

"We could drive somewhere."

"I want to change out of hospital-smelling clothes and then . . . whatever."

"Whatever?" Theo laughs.

"Let's just go in." I'm getting so nervous and excited and practically giddy. I don't even recognize myself.

Sure enough, when we get inside, Charlie is packing a diaper bag for Dylan. "Hey, guys, I'm meeting your mom for pizza. You wanna come?"

"Oh, we have band rehearsal later. But thanks," I say. "We're just going to watch TV for a little bit." I am trying so hard to act normal, but nothing about this is normal.

"Okay," Charlie says.

I lead Theo downstairs and instruct him to wait on the couch so I can change. In my room, I try to take deep breaths. What do you wear when you're going to for sure make out with your best friend and the boy you actually truly love and care about? Do I try to look good? Do I aim for comfort? Do I aim for easy to discard? Will we even be discarding clothes? Am I ready for that kind of thing? Oh my god.

I end up going for comfortable but still cute. Clothes I would wear to rehearsal anyway. And I brush my teeth. That step seems obvious. When I go back to the family room, I sit near, but not next to, Theo. He smiles at me. A half smile that shows one perfectly formed dimple.

"Later, guys!" Charlie calls down.

When the front door slams shut and we are finally alone, we look at each other, not sure what to say, and we finally laugh.

"I don't want to be awkward!" I say.

"I don't mind awkward," Theo says.

I just look at him, because the last twenty minutes have been so strange. All I wanted was to be alone with him, and now I am.

"Should we . . . watch a movie or something?" I ask.

"Could we watch it in your room? Even with Charlie gone, I feel like he'll walk back in with a shotgun."

I laugh. "My mother would never be with a guy who had that kind of stance on his stepdaughter kissing."

"What if we do more than kissing?"

Yeah. That definitely gives me some butterflies, and not the stomach kind. The ones that make you want to take your clothes off. "Okay, yeah, let's go in my room."

I fire up my computer and put on a mindless comedy that I know won't be overly engrossing and holds little chance of setting off Theo's waterworks. I sit down on the edge of the bed and Theo scoots over so his back is pressed against my leg. He tilts his head back and smiles at me.

"Just sit next to me," I say, nudging him with my knee.

He leaps up, shuts off my light for the movie-theater effect, and sits next to me. He puts his arm around me, and I angle myself so I can lean back into him. He smells good. And his nose is bumping into my ear.

"Lacey," he whispers.

"I'm trying to watch," I object, even though it's just the opening credits.

"Do you really not want to kiss me right this second?"

My heart, quite predictably, starts to speed up, and I get this hyper-focus on every sensation. His fingers trailing up my arm.

His breath on my neck. How warm he is when he's this close. "I actually really do," I whisper.

When we kiss, it feels like it'd be easy just to give myself over to sensation. My body does sort of know what it's doing. But my brain doesn't shut off like I was always afraid it would. It's incredibly empowering, realizing that I'm still in control.

We bump teeth because we're both smiling so hard. Instead of being awkward, it makes us both laugh. We've shifted back so his weight is on me and he's surrounding me and it feels safe and good. His hands are on my stomach and he starts tugging at the bottom of my shirt.

"Is this okay?" he asks breathlessly.

I nod and arch my back so he can lift my shirt over my head. This is a first. I'm in a bra, underneath him, on my bed. We stop kissing and he looks at me. He's checking in, making sure it's okay. So I speak up.

"Theo . . . ," I say. We should discuss our expectations. I should let him know what I'm comfortable with and what's off the table. "This is nice, but I want to keep underwear on, okay?"

"Sure thing, Lace." He kisses my shoulder, playing with the strap of my bra.

"It's simply not fair for me to be this unclothed while you still have a jacket on," I joke.

"Fair enough," he says. In no time flat he's shrugging out of his jacket and yanking his faded T-shirt over his head. Just like that, we're back to kissing. He tugs the elastic from the bottom of my braid, and I, in turn, ruffle his carefully combed hair. It's all so teasing and fun, and we're both smiling and winded as we kiss and keep kissing. It's way more fun than I thought it could be.

~

When Theo unbuttons his jeans, I help him tug them down. And I lift my hips so he can pull my leggings down. He stops kissing me to check in. He raises his eyebrows to ask if it's okay.

"It's cold in here," I whisper, even though there's no one else to hear.

He smiles, then pulls the comforter out from under me and throws it over both of us.

"Are we seriously in my bed in our underwear?" I giggle.

He takes the moment to look me up and down very seriously. "Yes, yes we are." He puts his weight on me and kisses my cheek and my ear. He runs his fingers through my hair. I wrap my arms and legs around him. He starts to move against me, and I moan softly.

"Oh my god, Lacey, I would do anything to get you to make that sound more," he says. He's all smiles. And I think, yes, he is the perfect person to do these things with. I trust him. He always makes sure I'm consenting. He cares about me. I care about him. I always feel safe. I kiss his jaw and the spot right underneath his jaw, all these places I've admired but never really touched when I wanted to.

His weight still covers me and I have that feeling of wanting more, so when he leans his hips against mine, I push back. I have honestly never felt like this. Beyond feeling close and having fun, I want to keep doing this. "I want to keep going, but . . ."

"Hmm?" he asks.

"If you think . . ." It doesn't matter how comfortable I am discussing this with people I barely know; it's difficult for me to say these words now. "If you think you might come, at any point, it's fine, so long as the underwear rule still applies."

"Yeah, okay." He nods with a dorky smile on his face. "Does the underwear rule apply to your bra?"

"What?" I ask. "No, that really doesn't matter."

"So . . . ?"

I blush. You'd think that being intimate enough that no part of his arousal is hidden, I'd be fine with this, but I'm suddenly nervous.

"It's okay," he says.

But I squirm to reach both hands behind my back and, after fumbling for a moment, unclasp my bra. Nothing quite prepares me for the feeling of cold air on my skin.

He looks for a moment, grinning devilishly. "You look incredible."

I smack his shoulder and giggle. Nervousness gone. And we're back to kissing and wandering hands and increasing pressure. And I'm also back to ignoring everything but this.

Until he slows and rolls so that he's next to me, and I turn toward him and our legs stack and our arms tangle and we're still so close.

"So . . . I, uh . . ." Theo blushes.

"Finished?" I offer.

"Yeah," he says. "So . . ." He pushes some hair off my forehead. "Like . . . I could help you finish?"

"Uh. I don't know about that," I say. "I can handle that on my own."

"It's only fair," he says.

"Honestly. This is all great, but I'm not sure I'm ready for that," I say. Even though I'm incredibly turned on still, I'm not ready to be that vulnerable with him. I'm happy right now.

"You sure?"

"I am sure."

He looks worried. "Just say the word and I'll return that favor," he says, kissing me again.

"Seriously. Don't worry. I am super happy with how things are going."

"But you'll tell me if you ever want anything else?"

"You'll be the first to know." I giggle. And he gives me this smile that I've never seen from him. Like he can't keep it off his face. He blinks at me. We're both just grinning at each other.

This really, really feels like falling in love, and it's way faster and more intense than I imagined.

"Theo . . . ," I start.

"Yeah?"

"I mean, technically. It's all just . . . You were single for five minutes," I point out. "And you have never felt, like, actually available . . . because of . . ." Evita. I can't say her name.

"You know I want to be with you," Theo says, and he sounds sincere.

"There's no 'want' about it. You are with me. You have now left your DNA on my bedsheets."

"Truth." Theo kisses my shoulder. "So, listen, I really like this and want to be together. I hope that's clear."

"Got it. Me, too," I say, the grin returning. "But I sort of want to get out of here before my folks come home." Though, really, I could curl up with him and never move.

"Yeah. Sure. Should we go hang out with Evita and Alice?" Theo asks.

"She's gonna know," I say.

"I really don't think she will. We'll just endeavor to keep our clothes on."

"Okay. I can handle that," I say. "But should I really spend the night there?"

"We'll make Evita sleep in the middle, so it won't be weird."

I scrunch up my nose.

He laughs. "Or not. Let's get out of here, though. I'd much rather Evita know something's up than Charlie."

"I wouldn't," I grumble.

"So we're keeping this under wraps?" Theo asks.

"Yes. Just until we figure out if we're really doing this. And then we can tell Evita?" I ask.

"You aren't sure you want to be with me?" Theo asks.

"It's definitely not that I don't want to. Just that it'll take me half a minute to fully believe that you like me like that."

"Despite all the evidence?" He gestures to the entire scene around us. The sheets are rumpled, my hair is messy, he's gotta change out of his boxers . . .

"Yeah. Despite that."

"I get it. Okay. Come on, get up," he says, jumping off the bed.

We get dressed and are out the door as quickly as we can manage.

"I'm starving," I realize as soon as we drive off in his car.

"Me, too! Fast food it is. And this is our alibi. I've been

189

getting food. With you. For an hour. Nothing funny," Theo says seriously. He thinks for a minute. "This is perhaps the best day I've ever had . . . because the sounds you made . . ." He looks slyly over at me.

"Please don't mention that ever again," I say, hiding my face.

"What? Don't be embarrassed!"

"I'm going to try not to be."

"You shouldn't be embarrassed about being sexy as hell. Like, feminism and stuff," he says.

"Okay. I will try not to blush when you say that, because of feminism. But . . . you're blushing."

"I am not," he says, his ears getting pinker by the second.

We pull up to the drive-through and order meals for ourselves and enough fries to feed a whole army. Because maybe if we shove food at our friends, they won't ask questions.

When we pull up to Evita's apartment building, I'm suddenly struck with the thought that I don't want to share Theo with anyone else. I think maybe he has the same thought, because he looks at me and sighs. We walk up the stairs to her apartment without holding hands. When we get to her door, he glances over his shoulder to make sure no one is around. Then he gives me one last slow kiss before he knocks on Evita's door.

Twenty-three

I can't stop thinking about Theo. It's honestly ridiculous. Walking into school between Theo and Evita, I have to keep myself from smiling. All the time. The corners of my mouth just threaten to give away how excited I am about us. I fight the urge to glance over at him, constantly. He moves to my other side, so he can be between Evita and me. He flings his arms over both of us. It's something he would normally do. But what's new is now I keep getting flashbacks to the way he felt in my bed.

We check Alice's old locker first thing in the morning, and I am surprised to see a noticeable dent in the number of condoms. Inside the locker, I put a flyer about a new part of our locker project we came up with last night, a Tumblr called "locker412," where people can submit anonymous questions they have about sexual health. I only printed one of these, attempting to follow the rules as closely as I can.

"So, tell people about the locker and the Tumblr, but try not to write any of it down," I remind them.

"I'm on it," Evita says.

"I actually got some Facebook messages about the locker, so I feel like word is getting out without us needing to tell everyone," I say. "And I got a question about herpes on Facebook Messenger at five a.m., and the notification woke me up, so the Tumblr is preferable."

"You know you can turn notifications off, right?" Evita says.

"It's never been an issue before the herpes wake-up call this morning." I shrug. "Partially because I couldn't not look up herpes once I saw it, you know?"

"Check you out, making a big difference," Theo says. He might have the same problem I have with smiling. At least I don't have ridiculous dimples like he does.

"Go team," Evita says. Then she sings a line from our new song.

I shush her. "We're going for under the radar here."

"I'm not great at under the radar," Evita says. Then she busts out a dance move.

I close the locker before we attract any faculty attention.

When we go our separate ways for first period, Theo whispers in my ear, "When can we hang out again?"

"I'm going with Alice to an appointment tomorrow afternoon, so I don't think we'll rehearse. After the appointment?"

"I'll meet you at your house," Theo says. He reaches over and holds my hand for a split second before we go into orchestra.

∿

I'm disappointed after first and second period when the Tumblr inbox is still empty.

"No one is thinking about sex this early," Evita says. "It doesn't mean it's a bad idea."

"Are you forgetting the five a.m. herpes wake-up call?" Theo asks.

"True."

But then at lunch, Evita walks from table to table, casually talking about the Tumblr to anyone who will listen.

"She is so much more extroverted than I am," I tell Theo, watching Evita pull up a chair at a table full of popular kids.

"She's much more extroverted than everybody," he says. "You look cute today," he adds.

My mouth does that obnoxious over-the-top smiling thing again.

~

After school, at Evita's, I get my first Tumblr question. "You guys!" I say, putting down my viola. "This question is *amazing*."

> *is it true you can't consent when you're drunk?*
> *what if you're buzzed?*

Evita looks over my shoulder. "Did you tell your mom about the Tumblr? That's obviously her question."

"I've been training for this moment," I say.

"What's the question?" Alice asks.

I read it aloud.

"I . . . don't know the answer to that," Alice admits.

"Okay, so, legally, you can't consent when you're under the influence, so the short answer is no," I tell her. "But the long answer is that we should all be examining what consent is all the time, and if there is any question, even a slight doubt, you stop and check in. And hopefully, these conversations happen before you're hooking up. Especially when drinking is involved. I hate it when people demonize sex or blame alcohol for bad decisions, but the truth is we all need to be really careful mixing sex with anything other than complete sobriety and total honesty. Yeah, you might want to have sex when you're buzzed, but we should all want to have consensual sex. Consent is the sexiest thing in the world."

Alice smiles at me. "Wow. You really are a badass."

"I just need to write all these thoughts down. Evita, can I use your laptop?" I ask.

"Sure. The Sparrows will take five so you can enlighten the world and so I can get water," Evita says.

Theo sits behind me while I type. He starts rubbing my shoulders. I have this knee-jerk reaction that he's being obvious, so I swat his hands away.

"Sorry," he mumbles.

"Honestly, you should always get consent even for that," I say. "Not everyone wants their shoulders rubbed."

"Umm. Except for me," Alice says.

"Gladly," Theo says. He sits behind her. "Would you like me to rub your shoulders?" he asks.

"Please do," Alice says with a laugh. "I'm totally asking Kelly about my back pain. Like, I know some is normal. But this is, like, my entire back and rib cage hurt all the time."

"Only a few more weeks," I say.

"I just read that babies at this point gain half a pound a week!" Alice says. "He already feels huge."

I finish typing my answer, then post it. I get a wave of nerves about it. Even if the Tumblr is anonymous, most of the people posting on here probably know it's me. I'm not used to feeling visible. With the band, and with this project, and with volunteering, I'm getting a lot more spotlight than I'm used to.

Twenty-four

"Sorry I'm a little late," I tell Alice when I see her in the waiting room on Tuesday. "I've never actually tried to get out of the school parking lot right after dismissal, and I don't think I'll try to again."

"It's fine. I think they're running pretty far behind, like usual. I feel like all I do is sit in this waiting room and practice at Evita's."

"I feel the same way. Except with school and Evita's." I shrug off my coat.

"Really? Nothing else going on with you?" Alice asks, looking innocent.

"What do you mean?"

"What I mean is that I'm not stupid. And you and Theo . . ."

"What?" I swallow a lump.

"You're not into each other?" she asks.

"Into each other?" I repeat.

"You're not a great liar, Lacey. You're blushing."

I sigh. I wish I weren't so transparent. "Yeah. I don't know. We kissed. But only because Evita kept trying to get me kissed, because I hadn't kissed anyone and here I was giving everyone sex advice and hearing way too much about what people do with each other—"

"Sorry about that," Alice says.

"No. It's fine. She just kept giving me a hard time. So Theo offered to kiss me." In this moment, I don't know how much I should tell her.

"Of course he did. He broke up with his girlfriend for you."

"No, he didn't. We just kissed the night of the gig."

"And that was it?" Alice asks, sounding skeptical. It must be obvious that that wasn't it. There must be some part of me that is giving away the fact that Theo and I are both really into each other. In fact, I can't help smiling just thinking of it.

"I mean. I don't know." I shrug. I am so busted. I keep giving people partial truths. Not just Alice. I told my mom Theo and I had maybe made out Sunday night. I didn't tell her about the fact that I *really* like him and feel surprisingly ready for sex with him. I don't want my friends to know that I'm becoming more interested in the possibility of nursing school. I don't want my mom to know, either, or she'll get her hopes up. I don't want the kids at school who have started coming to me for sex advice to know I'm still as inexperienced as I am. It's all a little tiring.

Alice isn't quite my best friend, but we're getting closer every day. I know some pretty intimate things about her. We don't have much of a history, but maybe that's why it's so easy to talk to her.

"That wasn't really it," I tell her.

"Oh yeah?" She laughs. Probably because it is obvious.

"After I volunteered on Sunday . . . we kind of got together."

"You guys had sex?" Alice's eyes are wide.

"Well. No. I mean, over the clothes. Some clothes. Underwear. Just underwear. Or whatever."

"Wow."

I'm suddenly defensive. Is it so surprising that I could be attractive to someone? "What do you mean?"

"No. Nothing. I actually think it's pretty awesome. You guys make a really cute couple. Like, you make each other smile a lot. And you'd treat each other well, you know?"

"Really?" I smile.

"Totally. But I take it Evita does not know any of this?"

"No way."

"Yeah. That's tough."

"Sorry. I didn't mean to make you keep a secret for me," I say, feeling suddenly very guilty.

"It's fine. How many secrets are you keeping for other people? Like, from all the sex advice you're giving. And my pregnancy, even though it took exactly ten seconds into our gig for everyone to know. But I will say, I feel better now that my pregnancy isn't a secret. It felt good to be open about it." She raises her eyebrows at me. "Food for thought."

"I bet. I just have to figure out how to tell her."

"Better to tell her imperfectly than not tell her at all," Alice says.

"That sounds like sage advice."

"Good. I'm practicing, because I'm going to be someone's mom pretty soon," she says, smiling.

"Alice!" a nurse calls out.

"Come on," Alice says. "Maybe Kelly can write you a prescription for birth control."

"I've had prescriptions written for me since I was fifteen," I tell her. "I've just never filled them."

"Well, don't be like me. Fill it before you know you need it. Let's go see how much weight I've gained."

"Thanks for the talk," I say.

"Anytime. Thanks for distracting me from the fact that I'm going to ruin my vagina in a month and a half."

"It won't be ruined."

"Well, it won't be the same."

"No. That's probably true. But nothing will be."

"Amen to that. I'm still trying to wrap my brain around it," Alice says.

It makes me want to stop obsessing over the fact that I don't know what I'm doing with myself. Because at least my future is my own.

As promised, Theo is waiting for me at my house. I sort of assumed he'd be creepy about it, parking around the corner and hiding in the bushes like he did the other night. But he's in my kitchen, feeding Dylan some combination of blended fruits and veggies that doesn't look remotely appetizing. He's laughing easily with my mom.

"Is any of this making it into his mouth?" Theo asks.

"The key is to scoop up the stuff on his chin rather than going back in the jar for more," my mom says. "Hi, Lacey. How's Alice?"

"Everything's looking good. Can I steal this guy?" I ask, looking at Theo.

"Actually, Lacey, can I have a word?" Mom asks. "Theo, just give him as much food as he wants, if you don't mind."

"My pleasure," Theo says.

I follow my mom into her room. "Hey," she says quietly. "So, we haven't really had a chance to talk about things."

"What do you want to discuss?"

"You're being careful?"

"Mom. I'm not going to go into details about things. But rest assured, I know absolutely everything there is to know about sex and how to be safe."

"Oh, Lacey, I know you know about birth control and things, but there's more to it, isn't there? I mean, your feelings, for one. And your friendships. I just wanted to make sure you were doing all right and making good choices."

"I don't know, Mom. I think that's what Theo and I have to talk about today. I mean, Evita doesn't know anything. But we really like each other, I think. And Theo is Theo. I trust him one hundred percent."

"He is a wonderful friend. And that's what I wish for you in a partner. But Evita's your friend, too."

"Mom. I know." It comes out so exasperated. I just don't want to hear from my mom how I'm being a terrible friend.

"I'm here if you need a chat is all, okay?"

"Okay. Sorry."

My mom hugs me. We're about the same height now, so our heads rest on each other's shoulders. "Remember that oral sex is still sex," she whispers.

"Oh my god, Mom." I roll my eyes. I've heard that a million times. But maybe I'm lucky. I probably won't end up like Alice. I won't end up like *my mom*, which is what she's afraid of. But being my mom can't be too terrible, can it? I look at her life now, and it seems pretty great. "I love you," I tell her before I walk out of her bedroom.

"You, too." She follows me down the stairs. "Theo, I'll clean him up. Then we're gonna get bundled up and go to the park."

She gives me a look that I know means *I'm letting you guys be alone, but be responsible.* I roll my eyes at her. She grabs Dylan from his high chair.

Theo and I start downstairs. "You have baby food in your hair," I tell him.

"I'm trying it out as a deep conditioning treatment. I really think I'm onto something," he says.

Once we're in my room, he takes a flying leap and tackles me onto the bed. No matter how much I know we have talk through things, this makes me giggle.

"Shh," he whispers. My mom is still here, probably. Theo smiles easily. He moves next to me and pulls the covers up over both of us. "I've put some thought into how we can sort of . . . ease into being a couple. I've got a plan."

"Oh yeah?"

"Okay. So. We make the topic of your first kiss come up again. Right? With Evita, I mean. And we somehow make her think that having the two of us kiss is her idea. Then she can take all the credit for us being together, and then maybe we can skip the whole bad-feelings thing."

"That sounds reasonable," I say. "And it isn't hard to get her to bug me about that."

"Exactly. It's all gonna be perfect." He puts his face right next to mine. Our noses are touching, and the air I'm breathing is warm. "Tell me if I shouldn't say this. But. Lacey, I, like, really, devotedly like you. Like, a lot. It just hit me. I was sitting there with Dylan, waiting for you to come home, and I just couldn't wait to see you. I've always wanted to be around you, but, like, I *really* like you. Is that okay?"

"Why do we keep asking each other that? It's okay if you like me. I really like you. But I have for, like, an embarrassingly long time, I think."

"That's cute." Then he puts his nose right next to my ear and whispers so softly. "Can I keep kissing you?"

I nod. I'm nodding and we're kissing. We just keep kissing. I want more. I really do. It isn't like losing control. I'm in total command of choosing to do things that feel good.

I remember why I like being with him in the first place. I never, not in a million years, thought I would ever be comfortable with this. But I'm unzipping my jeans, and once they're off, I'm tugging at his shirt and enjoying putting my hands on the parts of him I like, his pecs and the little dimple above his triceps that sticks out when he's hovering above me. And I let him do the same to me, except he's kissing me in all these places. He even kisses my belly.

"So . . . ," I say.

"Hmm?" he asks, working his way back up and kissing my shoulder.

"Well. I think I would like . . ." I sort of grimace at how awkward I'm being.

"Lacey. I definitely want to hear what you would like. So, you know, feel free to let me know."

I nod. I've thought about this. I've thought about it a lot. And I'm ready to try something new. As ready as I am, though, it doesn't take the nerves away. I hop out of bed.

"This is just a suggestion," I say, walking to my closet. My closet, which is, at this moment, full of condoms and all things safe sex. I open up the closet and go right for the box of dental dams. "But, you know that if you use your mouth, I mean, we'll be sharing, you know, fluids and stuff."

He looks flustered. "Oh. Didn't I tell you I got tested for everything? Shit. I meant to show you my labs. And, I mean, you don't have anything."

On paper, he's right. He's been tested, and there's almost no chance I've contracted anything. But there's still some part of my brain that's holding a neon sign over the fact that we're going to share fluids. "I know . . . Like, this is the way it's supposed to go. You get tested and I assure you that I have never had any other sexual contact, but . . ."

"Okay, but I want to make you comfortable," Theo says.

God, I'm so nervous.

"So, let's just use one. For research's sake, if nothing else," he says, nodding.

"Yeah," I say, instantly relieved. I blush as I dig through the options in the closet. "Strawberry or vanilla?" I ask him.

"Lacey, you look super serious. Like a lot rides on my decision," Theo says.

"I could never be serious about a vanilla guy," I joke.

"Better choose strawberry, then."

So I toss the small package at him and kick the rest of my collection back into the closet. Theo holds his hand out to me, and I climb back into bed.

"So, provided I use this," he says, holding it up, "you would like me to go down on you?"

"Yeah. Like. Maybe in a minute. I'm . . . sort of nervous," I tell him.

"Got it." He nods solemnly. And I kiss him.

"Are you . . . ? I mean, you have to tell me that that's what you want, too," I say between kisses.

"Oh. Yes. We are completely on the same page there," he says with a devilish grin.

I nod. And we're kissing again. And then he's kissing down my body like he was before.

"You good so far?" Theo asks quietly.

I just nod. He puts a hand on each of my thighs, and this really is what I want. Then he slides his hands under my butt and hooks his thumbs under the opening of my underwear.

I mean, I know this is what he meant, but suddenly I'm nervous again. He looks up at me. And I nod again. When the cold air hits me, I feel so vulnerable and uncertain. But then he puts a finger on me. Which is good, because I really think I might have exploded from frustration if he hadn't. I let out a breath I didn't know I was holding. It's embarrassingly shaky. But Theo's breath is shaky, too.

He moves his hand. And this new sound escapes me. Just a little moan.

"Oh my god, Lacey," he says. But it's a good "Oh my god," and I think he's enjoying this, too.

I want him to keep going, so I sort of shift my weight against his hand. He starts to lower his head.

His hands are on my thighs again, and he looks up at me. I sort of wish he'd stop doing that. "You look nervous," he says.

"I am, a little."

"I'm going to kiss you until you're not nervous, okay? Just say the word and we'll move on. Or if we don't move on, that's fine, too, okay?" He climbs back up and kisses me. It doesn't take long for the nerves to disappear.

Twenty-five

Word about the Tumblr must have spread quickly, because by lunchtime the next day, there are a dozen questions to be answered. We also had to restock the locker, this time adding pregnancy tests, dental dams, and little samples of personal lubricant. The questions and comments I get are pretty varied.

How do you make it hurt less the first time?
(I point out that foreplay and lubricant will help.)

You rock!
(Not a question, but appreciated just the same.)

If you need condoms for oral, what about hand jobs?
(I reply with a frank discussion about exchange of bodily fluids and how you still need to be aware of this even if it isn't as obvious.)

Are you still going to do bathroom office hours?

(It's a little late today, but I will tomorrow.)

"So, you basically know everything about everything at this point, huh?" Evita asks from across the table.

I look up from where I'm typing on my phone. "Well. No. I still have to research some stuff."

"Still. I'm impressed. It wasn't that long ago that you got all embarrassed when people talked about this stuff."

"Give her some credit," Theo says. "She knows her stuff."

"But you're still not, like, curious about firsthand knowledge?" Evita asks. "I mean, every allosexual person made it sound like such a big deal, and I wanted to know what it was like."

"Evita, this again?" I say. But Theo catches my eye and raises his eyebrow, and I remember we want this to come up. We want Evita to suggest that I kiss Theo.

"I am curious," I say carefully. "But I'm really not into the idea of trying to hook up with some random dude for experience."

"Okay, hear me out. I speak from some experience here, and— no offense, Theo—but someone random guy might actually be preferable. That way, if things are awkward, which I think they always are, you don't have to talk to him again. Or if, you know, you don't like hooking up with that person, they won't take it personally. No offense, Theo."

"I think I might be a little shy to communicate openly with some random person."

"See, I think it'll be easier for you. You won't worry so much about what he'll think."

Theo is having a hard time keeping a straight face, but from where he is sitting next to Evita, I'm the only one who is seeing his goofy grin, and I really don't appreciate it.

"I mean, why don't I just use a vibrator and call it a day," I say. "Oh, wait . . ."

"Come on, Lacey. It's not all about the orgasm."

Theo can't help it. He starts laughing.

"What is your problem?" Evita asks him.

"No problem. Lacey is just so not into your idea of a random hookup. Why don't you offer to kiss her again?" Theo says.

"I do have excellent oral hygiene." Evita smiles.

"I love you," I say, "but you're not my type."

"Maybe you need to narrow down your type for me," Evita says.

I have to fight the urge not to look over at Theo. "Well. Guys."

"Yeah. That's not that specific," Evita says. "You'll tell me if you want me to find you someone."

"Okay, thanks," I say, unsure how to make this conversation fit the plan. I am honestly not sure how Evita could miss the fact that there is someone right next to her who I might want to kiss.

Theo and I only manage to be alone for a minute after school. Somehow, he convinced Evita that she should buy all of us coffee and we should wait in my car so it could stay warm.

"Our plan failed," Theo says from the passenger seat.

"Spectacularly," I say. "We really need to figure out a way to tell her."

"You want me to?" Theo offers.

"No. I really think I should tell her. Because . . ." I can't finish that sentence. Because she still loves Theo, and this should come from me because we can actually talk about how she feels about it.

"Okay. That's fine." He takes a deep breath. "I love you," he whispers.

I want to say it back. I know we only just got together. But I've loved him in some capacity or another for years. It's that this particular way is new. I just can't say it until Evita knows.

Twenty-six

The next morning, locker 412 is empty. Totally cleared out, and not by us. I let out a little yelp when I open the locker, and I slam it shut again.

"What?" Evita asks.

"Someone cleared it out," I whisper. I look over my shoulder, suddenly paranoid that I'll see Ms. George on a stakeout, ready to pounce and catch us.

"Everything?" Evita asks. "Whoa. Like . . . students who needed condoms, or . . ."

I start walking down the hall. "No, like the flyer was gone, too. And no way that many kids took things since Monday morning."

"Slow down," Theo says. "I mean, some kid could be a jerk and just decided he would take all the freebies. Right? I mean, that's totally a dick move, don't get me wrong, but it doesn't mean anyone is onto us."

"I don't know. I really don't know why someone would do that."

"People are jerks," Evita says with a shrug.

"But if I were a teacher, and I heard about the locker, that's what I'd do. I'd empty it," I say.

"Yeah. Except they didn't change the combination or anything," Theo says.

"That's true."

"And if we're not already in trouble, then we probably won't be," Evita says.

"Maybe," I say. Still, I can't help feeling like we got caught. Or if it was another student who emptied it, that they're laughing at me right now. It's a sinking feeling. I've been so excited about making a difference and sticking it to the man, but I'm not actually cut out for rule breaking. "I should post on the Tumblr. If it was a teacher, I don't want anyone getting in trouble for breaking into an empty locker."

I pull out my phone and write a post announcing that locker 412 is empty.

"I still have enough fun packs of condoms in my bag for a decent orgy," Evita says. "We should just hand them out to anyone who asks, or whatever."

"Yeah."

"Listen, even if the locker was only open for a few days, it made people feel less weird about condoms. That was the whole point, right?" Theo says. "You definitely made me feel less weird about them." The tips of his ears turn pink.

"That's something, I guess," I say.

~

At lunch, I tell Theo and Evita that I am going to hang out in the bathroom.

"I'm coming with you," Evita says.

"Guys. That's not fair," Theo says.

"You can't come in the girls' room. No one will want to discuss their menstrual cramps with you there," Evita says.

"I can't just sit at this table alone," he says, dismayed.

"Then sit in the hall," Evita says.

"Good idea. I'll stand guard."

"Uh. Sure," I say.

Theo salutes us as we enter the bathroom. "I'll be out here if you need a male perspective on anything."

Inside, there are two girls standing by the sinks. "Hey, guys. What's up?" I ask. It takes me exactly two seconds to get into professional-sex-advisor mode.

"I made Ashley come talk to you," the shorter girl says.

"Ashley," I say, "what's going on?"

"Okay. So . . . maybe this is gross . . . ," Ashley starts.

"Get over it," the other girl says. "Lacey is the one who told me about peeing after sex, okay? She probably totally saved my life."

I guess that was her on Tumblr last night. She had recurrent, very painful UTIs, and she was afraid to keep going to the doctor for them.

"Okay, well, I've been with my boyfriend for, like, a year and half. So . . . you know . . . we've been . . ." Ashley turns red.

"Sexually active?" I ask.

"Yeah. We've been having sex."

"Using protection?" I ask.

"Yeah. Well. Yeah. So . . . I'm on the pill now. But my boyfriend feels like that means he shouldn't use a condom."

"Well, the pill won't protect you from sexually transmitted infections," I tell her.

"No. I know. He actually got tested and stuff. And I did, too. But . . ." She looks so embarrassed.

"Girl, you got tested and everything?" Evita says. "You rock."

"Yeah. That is pretty awesome," I tell her.

"The thing is, I sort of hate doing it. Without. It grosses me out. You know?" She looks at me. And I nod. Even though, well, I haven't experienced that.

"Like, I hate it. It's messy. Should I just get over it? He thinks I'm being crazy when I suggest using condoms. He says none of his friends use them."

"Okay. Regardless of whether or not that's true, what other people are doing *does not matter*. And just because you're being fairly safe without condoms, the added protection is never a bad idea. But the most important thing is, you don't like it. That matters. He needs to respect what you like and what you don't like." I used a dental dam when it wasn't "necessary," but it isn't always about that. I'm speaking from experience, but not an experience I can acknowledge.

"But I don't want to be some prude about it," Ashley says. "I mean, he says it's not as good with condoms."

"Seriously, even if nobody else on the planet used condoms, if that's what you're comfortable with, that's what you should do. Besides, how does he know that his friends don't use condoms? I'd ask him if he's in the room with his friends when they aren't using condoms. You know?"

She sighs with relief. "Yeah. Okay."

"Don't be afraid to tell him what you need," I say. And, oh my god, I sound exactly like my mother.

"Thanks, Lacey," Ashley says.

"Oh. Don't forget your party favors!" Evita says. She plops her backpack on the shelf near the mirror and opens it. Bags of condoms spill out.

"You weren't kidding that you had a ton." I laugh.

"Condoms for everyone," Evita says. "In fact, take some for your friends."

"Thanks," the shorter girl says. She blushes as she grabs a couple bags.

There's a knock on the bathroom door. "Theo! We're almost done!" I yell.

"Ladies?"

It's not Theo. Ms. George is standing just inside the doorway, and she does not look pleased.

Twenty-seven

Ms. George pulls a box out from under her desk. I don't even have to look inside to know that it's full of condoms and lube and pregnancy tests and dental dams and brochures for the local sexual health clinic and instructions for how to use a condom (drawings of penises included, because duh). She even has the flyer for the Tumblr.

Theo, Evita, and I are sitting in hard plastic chairs opposite Ms. George's desk, and I'm shaking.

"Who does all this belong to?" Ms. George asks.

"Those belong to me. It's a hobby. And I'm not sure what's wrong with having these items. It isn't a weapon or drugs or whatever," Evita says.

"What exactly is your hobby?" Ms. George asks.

Evita grins like the Cheshire Cat.

"Don't answer that," Ms. George says. "Evita says this belongs to her. So, what do you two have to say? Lacey, you were clearly distributing these materials with Evita, and Theo, you were assisting."

"Yeah," Theo says. "That stuff is as much mine as hers."

"Mine, too," I manage, even though my throat feels like it's full of cotton.

"Most of these items were found in what is supposed to be an unoccupied locker. Are you aware that distributing sexual paraphernalia falls under the category of distributing lewd material?"

"Paraphernalia." Evita laughs. "Pretty sure there are rules against drug paraphernalia, and I don't use the condoms as a bong or whatever. In fact, I know so little about smoking marijuana that I don't know anything about bongs other than the fact that people make them and use them to smoke. This is just a health tool. Just like tampons. Or aren't we allowed those? I know some people think using tampons means you aren't a virgin. Is that what you're asserting? Because I will defend my right to use a tampon with my dying breath. Even if I've got a shaky track record with them. Did you know they can actually sort of hide in your vagina and get stuck? Freaky stuff."

"Evita," I say. "Stop."

"No." She leans back in her chair. "Listen. I want my lawyer. Or my mom. Really, either will do. Bring our moms in, if we're in trouble. Because you still haven't told us what rule we're breaking."

Ms. George doesn't look at all amused. In fact, I'm pretty sure she's giving Evita a chance to dig herself deeper into a hole. Or all of us. Or however that analogy would apply to this situation. She opens her desk drawer and pulls out the latest booklet of our tiny school district's regulations. She flips through until she finds the page she's looking for. She turns the book around on her desk, her fingernail pointing to a rule about distributing printed material.

We're not supposed to at all unless we've been given pre-approval by the administration. Furthermore, distributing violent, lewd, or otherwise harmful material is grounds for suspension or expulsion.

Expulsion. Oh my god.

Ms. George waits until all three of us have read that part.

"I know you were all in class the day I addressed my concern with distributing lewd material. Mrs. Einhorn believed the three of you were distributing those brochures. I thought I was very clear about the consequences. If you are found to be distributing lewd materials, you will be suspended. That's what I told you last week, and that still stands."

"We weren't distributing anything! We were just . . . storing them," Theo says.

"I saw Evita and Lacey distributing condoms," Ms. George says.

"Okay, but that doesn't really fit the rule against distributing flyers or whatever," Theo says.

"There was a flyer posted in the locker about a website," Ms. George says. "Furthermore, it is clear you were behind the brochures. Overall, you have been spreading lewd information throughout the school, whether it was on fliers or through contraband."

"I'm sorry," I cut in. "I'm confused. How is this lewd or harmful?"

"How is it lewd?" Ms. George repeats.

"Yeah. It's not pornographic. It's not objectifying. It's not suggestive."

"There are diagrams of penises in here."

"Yes. Penises. Because that's where you put a condom. There are also vaginas. Because that's where you put tampons."

"We are not equating tampons and condoms," Ms. George argues.

"Why not? They are both sanitary health products," I say.

"You don't use tampons for sex."

This is another one of those moments I feel like I've been training for my whole life. "Distributing literature on safe sex isn't *harmful*. Making us sit in classes that demonize sex *is*. The ramifications are endless. Shame for normal sexuality. Which contributes to all sorts of shitty things, especially for women. Like slut shaming. And rape. Denying that the students in this school are having sex is ridiculous. They are. Whether or not you make them feel bad about it. Whether or not you prepare them for healthy decisions in that area. Whether or not you give them condoms. Telling us that only virgins are pure is bullshit. All of this is bullshit. It's all bananas. We're doing something *good* for the school. Everyone is walking around a little more prepared, and maybe a little more respectful. Because everyone at this school is damaged by puritanical attitudes and the bullshit you guys teach here."

Theo is gripping my arm.

"The school's health curriculum is not up for review here. But the consequences of your actions are," Ms. George says. "I've heard what you've said. I'm going to talk to Mr. Crawley about this. You three wait here."

She gets up stiffly. Once the door closes behind her, I let out a giant breath I was holding.

"Holy shit, Lacey," Evita says. "You might have just told her she was responsible for people being raped. I mean, I'm not sure I followed it entirely, but . . . damn."

"That's not what I meant, exactly. Did I just get us suspended or expelled?" I ask, looking between both of them.

Evita shakes her head. "Even if we get suspended, I'm sure it'll be fine. We're in this together, and, I mean, you did have a chance to get some of that frustration off your chest, right?"

I let out another breath. "I'm sorry if I just got us in more trouble."

"Hey. If we get suspended, that just means some epic rehearsals," Evita says.

"All we were doing was helping people!" I say.

The door opens again, and Ms. George and the principal, Mr. Crawley, enter.

"Guys," Mr. Crawley says. He already looks fed up with us. "You knew you were breaking the rules. And you were disrespectful to Ms. George."

"We were just giving her our opinion that none of this is lewd," Evita says.

Mr. Crawley holds up a hand to stop her. "I'm taking disciplinary action, because we are very serious about putting an end to this. It's not up to you to decide what is and is not lewd or unhealthy or harmful. You were warned about distributing lewd materials. In following the guidelines, you are getting two days' suspension, starting with today. We'll see you guys again on Monday."

My heart starts racing. I don't even know what that means. Will I fail assignments for those two days? That could affect all my grades. What happens when colleges get our final transcripts?

Will we lose our spots in orchestra? Theo grips my knee because it's starting to shake.

"I see that all three of you have independent studies," Mr. Crawley says.

I jerk my head up when he says that. What does that have to do with anything?

"Yeah. We do," Theo says.

"Having an independent study is a privilege for students with clean records."

I can feel the blood draining from my face. "My independent study is tied to an internship," I say.

"I'm sorry to say that you're going to need to replace your internship with another class. There are openings in driver's ed and hospitality, that I know of." Mr. Crawley says this like it isn't a huge deal. Just changing a course. But the idea of not volunteering at the hospital takes my breath away. I hadn't realized how important it was to me. I was counting on showing up this weekend. On meeting new moms and babies.

I really need to figure out if nursing is for me. Because it feels like it just might be.

Evita must see how gutted this news makes me. "That is so unfair!" she wails. "Her internship is important. Isn't a suspension enough?"

"Those are the rules. We take these things seriously," Ms. George says. "I wish you had heeded my warning."

"Ms. George will accompany you to your lockers while I notify your parents. Do you have transportation, or do you need to wait for rides?" Mr. Crawley asks.

"We can drive ourselves," Theo says.

"You can gather your things," Mr. Crawley says. "I hope this is the last time I see the three of you."

"We hope so, too," Evita says cheerfully.

Ms. George leads us out of her office. The halls are empty. Everyone's in their after-lunch classes. I'm so glad no one can see us marched through the halls with our heads hanging low.

"Our suspension starts with missing senior seminar," Evita says. "So that's something."

We stop at Theo's locker, then Evita's, and then mine. I'm self-conscious when I unzip my backpack, because I also have condoms in mine. I try to cram every textbook into my bag. I don't want to get behind in any classes. With my now-heavy backpack on my shoulders, Evita grabs my hand. I must look shocked or upset, because Theo grabs my other hand.

We have to walk past our senior seminar classroom on our way to the main entrance. The door is open, and I can hear Mrs. Einhorn talking about credit scores. She pauses her lecture when she sees us walking past her door. I swear she has a smug, satisfied look when she turns back to her class.

I catch a couple of our classmates looking at us with wide eyes. I'm so far from invisible right now, and instead of making me feel proud to have taken a stand, it just makes me feel small. I want out of this particular spotlight. Especially when I see one of my classmates raise her phone and snap a picture.

Twenty-eight

We pile into my car. I get into the driver's seat and just kind of process everything for a second. I'm a jumble. I'm shocked. I'm exhilarated. I'm embarrassed. I'm beyond pissed about the internship. Evita slides into the passenger seat and turns to face me.

"Lacey, you still with us, babe?" Evita asks.

"Babe?" I say, turning to her. I don't know what possesses me to make a joke, but in true Evita style, I mime vomiting.

Evita laughs and then so do I, all my tenseness just bubbling out in laughter.

"What is so funny?" Theo says.

"We just got suspended!" I say. "But do you think maybe they'll change their minds about our independent studies?"

"Honestly, I'm okay with switching to hospitality. Or whatever. The quartet—or trio or whatever—is so over."

"But I really like mine," I say.

"Listen. We'll figure that out. But right now, we need some music!" Evita says.

My phone vibrates in my pocket. "Hold the music for a second."

"Hello?" I answer.

"Lacey Elizabeth Burke," my mom says.

"Yes?" I say.

"Put her on speaker," Theo says.

"Get your butt home right now. You are in big trouble. And I am so freaking proud of you. Was it just you?"

"We got suspended, too!" Evita says.

"Okay, well, we need to discuss everything," my mom says. "Are you coming home?"

"My mom's calling me, too," Evita says, reaching for her phone.

"Yeah. I'm coming home."

"Tell Janice she's welcome here. And Theo's folks."

"Thanks," Theo says loudly from the backseat. He shakes his head at me. No way will his parents be as supportive as mine.

Theo's mom and Janice go way back. They were friends in high school. It kind of baffles me that anyone who has been lifelong friends with Janice wouldn't be more supportive.

"See you in a bit," I say.

Evita wraps up her conversation with her mom. When I fire up the car, Evita turns to Theo. "Do you need to call your folks? Or are we ready for some music?"

"I'll just text them," he says.

Evita wastes no time putting on one of her favorite singers.

I keep glancing at Theo in the rearview mirror. I thought he'd be more excited, like Evita, who is dancing and singing. But he's just tapping furiously on his phone.

"Everything okay?" I ask him. The look on his face. I just want to climb back there and hug him.

"Yeah. My dad is not too happy," Theo says. "I thought maybe having a son caught with loads of condoms would make him proud. What could be manlier?"

"Your dad is a jerk. It isn't like you were doing the condom project to get his approval," Evita says. "So, what? Are you grounded?"

"I'm in 'big trouble,'" Theo says, using air quotes. "But I'm the fourth kid, so they probably won't even remember to follow through on that. They were so hard on my oldest sister. Then my middle two sisters just got away with more and more. So I'm lucky, really."

"My mom will be happy to smother you with extra parental attention if you want," I say.

"And you know my mom will," Evita says.

"Anyway, we love you," I say. This makes him smile. It's a small smile. And since Evita is back to dancing, it's a smile just for me. And I realize what I just said and that even though it's in a different context, it's the first time I've told him I love him since he said it to me.

～

"We support you," my mom says.

"Absolutely," Charlie chimes in.

"And I'll raise hell about the independent study thing," my mom says.

"You don't think I'll actually have to stop volunteering, do you?"

"The hospital was pretty clear that it has to be through the school," my mom says sympathetically. "You might want to give Kelly a heads-up, but I'm going to meet with Ms. George about all of this."

"Can we maybe not fight the suspension as hard? I kind of want a day off," Evita says.

"I never thought I'd be okay with you getting suspended," says Janice. "But I have to say, I love the sound of everything you've been doing."

We've been sitting at my dining room table, going through every aspect of our project, filling Janice in on the details she didn't know. She and my mom have been scrolling through the Tumblr.

"So, what are you guys going to do now?" Charlie asks. "I mean, it's not that I agree with the school about you distributing lewd content, but you can't just go back in there and keep it going."

The baby monitor on the counter crackles as Dylan wakes up. Charlie gives me a smile and excuses himself to take care of the baby.

"I know we can't keep handing things out," I say. "But what can we do? I mean, I'll keep the Tumblr going. Ms. George obviously knows about it now, but I don't see what she can do about it."

"But getting the kids condoms is so important," my mom says. "Or at least creating an atmosphere of respect and responsibility instead of shame and deviance."

"I don't know if we did all that," I say.

"You absolutely have," Theo says. "Don't sell yourself short. You made me feel less stupid asking about things or talking about it."

"That just makes me want to keep going, then," I say. "But if we are going to be banging our heads against the stupid 'lewd material' rule, then maybe the rule needs to change. Or at least *lewd* has to be better defined so it doesn't include vital information about health and sexuality."

"I don't know if this backward town can get on board with that," Evita says. "But, yeah, what you've said about abstinence-only education being ineffective . . . It seems pretty clear that more needs to be taught."

"So maybe we need to make a case with the people at the top," I say.

"I support this one hundred percent," my mom says.

"Will they listen to statistics?" I ask my mom.

"Statistics are important," Evita says. "But what they should be listening to is their students. Like what if Alice gave her perspective? Like how stupid is it that she didn't feel like she could keep coming to school the minute she got pregnant? And not that you should share confidential stuff people ask you, but maybe some of those kids would share."

"I don't know. That's a bit of a leap. To go from being too nervous to ask anyone about sex, to getting the courage to ask me, to then stand in front of the school board . . ."

"You don't know until you ask," Evita says. "I think you could make a kickass argument. Just look at that shit you said to Ms. George. I mean, Lacey, all of this is, like, your superpower."

"You're making me blush," I say. "We're going to do this, right? I know we're leaving this school in . . . seven months . . . not that I'm counting. I want to leave it swinging."

"Agreed. Me, too," Theo says.

"I hate to be a dissenting voice . . . ," Janice says.

"What?" Evita asks.

"I don't want you guys risking anything in the future. I mean, I have no doubt that music schools won't be as strict as other colleges, but I don't want y'all to get into a fight you can't win that might hurt your prospects."

Evita bites her lip. "Okay. If Berklee doesn't want a bunch of talented-as-fuck—sorry, Mom—kids just because they didn't want their classmates to get syphilis, then I don't want them."

"Agreed," Theo says.

"I understand that, sweetheart. Let's just maybe avoid any more suspensions. One seems like one thing, but more and it could sound a little like you don't respect institutions," Janice says. "I know that's probably not what y'all want to hear."

"I *don't* respect this particular institution," Evita says. "I'm not about to keep that quiet."

"I'm sure Janice just wants you guys to be thoughtful and not do anything rash. But I think presenting things civilly and informatively to the school board is doing it the right way," my mom says. "And, yeah, suspensions don't look great, but you guys should write letters to your colleges now. Tell them what's up. Tell them you'll fight for what's right and what's best for your friends. Lacey, from what you told me about UMass Amherst, they'll be in total support of that."

"Yeah," I say. I turn to Theo and Evita. "They even highlighted the work an alum did with Planned Parenthood. Like, right on their nursing school home page. It was pretty inspiring. It really made me realize the stupid ideals we have here aren't universal. I can really see us in Massachusetts, where things are much more liberal. And, honestly, nursing school could be really awesome."

"Wait . . . ," Theo says.

"I'm not saying I've decided to go to nursing school," I say quickly.

"But you're thinking about it?" Theo asks. "Like, seriously considering it? Amherst is *two hours* from Boston."

His question takes me by surprise. Mostly because . . . I *am* considering it. I can see myself there. I can see arming myself with knowledge that will really help people.

"I don't know yet," I say.

"We were all going to get an apartment in the city! When were you going to tell us you were seriously considering this?" Theo says, his voice getting louder.

"Theo. Relax. She just said she's thinking about it," Evita says. "Although, for sure we will be discussing this," she says to me sternly.

I never thought Evita would be the one to be cooler about this. Theo looks totally stricken.

He goes really quiet. Arms crossed over his stomach, slumped in the chair, fiddling with the sleeve of his shirt.

"You guys. We'll figure this out, right?" Evita fills the silence. "And right now we have a ton of time on our hands. So, we should make a plan, practice some music, write some letters to colleges, discuss college choices ad nauseum and stuff. But I'm actually sort of hungry right now. Right?"

"I'll make some lunch," my mom offers.

"I should call my folks," Theo says quietly. He gets up from the table and goes outside.

"Okay," Evita says. "Do we know when the next school board meeting is?"

"I'll check," Janice says.

"We should write a Tumblr post. Right, Lacey?" Evita asks.

"Yeah. You can. I'm just gonna check on Theo," I say.

I grab the first jacket I can find hanging by the door, even though it's Charlie's and it swallows me whole. It's getting colder and bleaker outside every day. Theo sits on the far end of my porch, just watching the trees drop their leaves.

I slide down next to him. "Hey."

He's quiet for a moment. "You know, I think I got ahead of myself," he says.

"What do you mean?" I ask.

"I sort of let myself really fall for you," he says. He has a wobbly sort of smile. His eyeliner is smudged.

I hold my breath and wait for him to finish his thought. But I want to make him feel better.

"You didn't tell me you were seriously considering nursing school. I'm totally and completely falling for you, and now I'm not even sure we'll be together next year."

I shake my head. "I don't know when I started actually considering it. I only applied to make my mom happy. But I think nursing school could actually be great. Amherst isn't that far from Boston. I applied there so we could still be in the Sparrows. Like, see each other every single weekend."

He nods and sniffs some snot back into his nose. He dabs at his eyes with his sleeve.

"I'm sorry we haven't talked about this. But when we're together, it's not like we've been . . . talking," I tease.

He lets out a little laugh that's maybe more of a sob. I would do anything in this moment to make him feel better.

"I do this, though. All the time," he says. "I'm destined to be more serious about girls than they are about me. And this felt different. With you. Like it's just so right and you wanted to be with me."

"I do want to be with you!" I say forcefully. "In fact, I basically would rather us never be apart. If you must know."

"I kind of want to kiss you. All the time. But now especially."

I glance around. No one can see us from inside the house. I put a hand on either side of his cheeks where they're scratchy. I lean in. His breath is warm and sweet. I kiss him slowly. It's perfect. Kissing him makes every other part of this day seem unimportant.

He leans his forehead and nose against mine. "I was so excited about being together next year," he says. "We'd be able to kiss all the time!" He pulls me close and I lay my head on his shoulder. "Please tell me when you know what you're going to do. Not knowing how next year will be really sucks."

"I don't like not knowing, either," I say. "I'm sorry I didn't tell you I was actually thinking about Amherst. It's only just recently, thinking about the stuff we've been doing at school, and about volunteering. I know I could do music forever. And I will. I just might want to give this a shot, maybe. I mean, that's what the internship was for. If I still have the internship . . . I just think I could be really good at it."

"I know you could. You definitely could. But I just had this picture of us being together, and I don't want to lose that. I think about it all the time."

"I'm sorry," I say. And I am. *So* sorry. I don't want to give that up, either. But I can't reassure him about something that is still so unknown to me.

His eyes are watering so much, the tears are starting to drip down his cheeks. That sight, maybe even more than his smile or his dimples, makes me want to kiss him more. So I do. I put both hands back on his scruffy cheeks and kiss him.

Kissing him makes me want to forget about Amherst. I want to forget about everything except the way this feels. But my mind is still spinning. Today's been a lot. I don't know how to feel about being suspended, about losing my volunteer job, about the fact that going to Amherst would make Theo this upset. I shiver involuntarily.

"You cold?" Theo asks me.

I shake my head, because right now I feel almost too warm. "We should probably go back in."

He backs up a step. "Yeah. Probably should not be making out on your front porch. Except if we aren't going to be together next year, I'm not sure I'll want to do anything *but* kiss you as much as possible before then."

"God. Theo. I wouldn't break up with you. We could still kiss every weekend. All weekend. Music and kissing."

He sighs. "Okay. But that's not the same as sleeping in the same bed every night."

"I know," I say. "Believe me, I'm factoring that into my decision."

He hops back onto the porch. "Let's go in."

We go back inside, even though, I agree, we could just keep kissing from now until next year.

My mom is setting sandwiches on the table. "Okay. I'm going to call Ms. George and ask about internship stuff. You guys eat up."

"So . . . ," Evita says. "Just to be clear . . . if you went to Amherst, you'd—what?—come to Boston every weekend?"

"Yeah. I think so. But I honestly don't know what I'm doing. I do know that the Sparrows will stay together, okay?" I tell her.

She's staring at me. At first, I think she's studying me to figure out which way I'm leaning between music and nursing school. But her eyes narrow.

"Why are you so red?" she asks.

I put down the sandwich I was about to eat.

"It's just cold outside," Theo says quickly. Probably too quickly.

Evita looks between us. I put a hand on my cheek. It's burning, still warm from where Theo's stubble rubbed against me. I move my fingers to my lips.

"Oh my god!" Evita says, her eyes widening. "You guys were . . . kissing? Is that a rash from kissing? Is *that* why you're upset about Amherst?" she yells at Theo.

Janice comes up behind Evita and lays a hand on her shoulder, but Evita shrugs it off.

"What's going on with you two? Tell me!" Evita yells.

"Evita. It's sort of . . ." Theo looks at me and shrugs. "We were going to tell you."

"Tell me what?" Evita's eyes burn right into mine.

"Evita, I'm sorry," I say. "I really like him."

"Apparently," she says. She shoves her plate away from her. "This is bullshit. I tell you *everything*." She stands up from the table.

"I know," I say.

"Evita. We didn't want you to be hurt," Theo says.

She scoffs and starts pacing. "We? You're, like, totally an 'us' and I'm not part of that. That's fucking awful."

"What? No!" I say. "This doesn't change anything."

"You and I both know that's bullshit," she spits. "I was just about to tell you that I have your back. That I support you and your college decision and that I don't mind getting suspended. *I have your back*. And you clearly don't have mine."

"Come on, Evita," Theo says. "That is *not* true."

She points at me. "I told you *everything*!" She grabs her backpack and starts for the front door. "Mom. We're leaving. I'll meet you in the car."

She stomps out the front door, slamming it behind her.

"Should we talk to her? Or maybe I should?" I ask him.

"I think you should let her cool down first. She'll probably be ready to talk soon," he says.

"Janice . . . ," I say, watching her grab her coat. "I'm so sorry." She waves us off, but I can tell this is a shock to her, too.

"I'll see y'all a little later, okay?" She follows Evita out the door.

"This is bad," I say. "This is awful."

"Well. I don't think it was ever going to go that well. To be honest," Theo says.

He doesn't know the half of it. And he can't know. Evita told me she still loves him romantically. And if it wasn't clear before that our being together would be like a knife in the back, it certainly is now. I can't tell him this, but we just broke Evita's heart. And hers is the last heart I'd ever want to break.

"Listen. She's our best friend. She'll come around. She's just going to be angry for a while first," Theo says.

My mom comes down the stairs. "Is everything okay?" she asks. "I was on the phone. But there was yelling. Where's Evita?"

"She and Janice left. Sort of dropped a bomb on her," I say.

My mom presses her lips together. "That was probably hard for her."

"Dropping a lot of bombs all over the place," Theo says quietly.

"Seriously?" I turn to him. "Are you just trying to make me feel worse?"

"I just mean that we didn't tell Evita yet. But you also didn't tell me about the college thing." He shrugs.

"There isn't actually anything to tell there! I wasn't keeping anything from you!" I say. "Can we maybe table the whole you-being-upset thing? I've disappointed enough people today!"

"Sorry," Theo says.

"Honey, he's allowed to feel how he feels," my mom says.

"Mom!" I yell. "I really don't want to talk about any of this right now!"

They both look shocked. I never yell. Never snap. But all of this is too much.

"Do you want me to stay? Should I go?" Theo asks.

"Maybe. I kind of want to be alone," I tell him.

He looks so dejected. Even that makes me bristle. It isn't like

I was trying to hurt anyone. Both he and Evita always assumed I would do what they wanted. And it sucks realizing that I am potentially letting them both down. But I also have a right to make my own decisions.

"I'll drive you home, sweetheart," my mom says to Theo.

"Lacey?" Theo says. I can tell he wishes I would ask him to stay.

"I'll call you. Okay? I need a minute to feel bad about all of this." He looks so upset, I feel a little guilty for snapping. I offer him a hug. "Just, tell me if Evita talks to you?" I ask.

He nods.

"I'll be back soon," Mom says.

~

Once Dylan is up and changed, I sit on the living room floor with him, handing him blocks to drool on. Charlie's at the sink doing dishes. He doesn't try to talk to me, which is nice. It's calm in here. At least it is until Mom blows in the door.

"You all right?" Mom asks me the moment she's in the door. She throws her coat on the coatrack and sits next to me on the floor.

"Sorry I yelled," I say.

She shakes her head at me. "Are you kidding? That was a totally appropriate reaction."

"Evita probably hates us. And Theo was pretty upset about the college thing. And, honestly, that just sort of pisses me off. I get where he's coming from, but, like, I'm not making any choices just so I don't hurt his feelings. At first, I was just applying to Amherst as, like, a distant possibility. But I actually think I might want to go there, and it's scary. It changes all of our plans. And the band. I'm totally Yoko-ing this whole situation," I say.

"I actually think that blaming Yoko for the breakup of the Beatles was sort of misogynistic. It's problematic to blame her for being an influence on John's life, casting the woman as a villain automatically."

"Maybe this isn't the time to be analyzing Yoko Ono and misogyny," Charlie says from his spot at the sink.

"I just need to figure out what I'm going to say to Evita to make this okay," I say.

"Honey, maybe there isn't some magical 'right thing' you can say to Evita, you know?" my mom says. "Maybe you both need to figure how to be okay with this and still support each other. I'm not saying it's going to be easy, but I bet you can do it. I think it's time to start being totally honest with her."

I nod sadly. My mom wants to say more. I can pretty much say exactly what she would tell me about sisterhood and the importance of supporting women in their choices and viewing them as just as capable and complex as men. I can already hear her saying that society has conditioned us all to sow seeds of discord between women, and that I need to be an unfaltering ally to all women and so on. I wait for her to launch into it.

Instead she says, "I'm fixing us tea."

I give Dylan a kiss and head downstairs to flip through the channels on the TV. When my mom brings the tea down, I turn it off.

"You're not going to lecture me on sisterhood and honesty?" I ask her.

"No. I'm not. Those things are great in theory. And we should always aim for them. We should always aim to lift each other up and not put each other down. But maybe you thought you were sparing her. Maybe you were trying to protect her."

"I don't think it was as noble as that. Part of me wanted things with Theo to be just for Theo and me. At least for a little while. I didn't know how we'd all adjust. I didn't know how to be his girlfriend and how to make it okay with everyone."

My mom reaches over and puts a hand on my shoulder. "You can't always make things okay for everybody. No one can. Do you know that I was scared out of my mind for you to meet Charlie?"

"Really? You were so cool about it, though. You were just like, 'Hey, I've been spending a lot of time with this guy and I'd like you two to get to know each other.'"

She laughs. "Maybe I seemed cool, but, oh my gosh, Lacey, I was so scared. Charlie was, too, but he just wanted you to like him—I don't think he ever doubted for a second that we'd work things out, no matter how you two got along. I knew differently, though. I knew that I would give up absolutely everything if I thought it was best for you."

"I guess it's good that I liked him."

"You can say that again. But I think I know how you're feeling. You're in a space where everything is up in the air and you have stronger hopes and wishes than you've ever had, but things are also out of your hands. It's scary."

I nod, my eyes prickling.

"Oh, sweetie." She leans over and hugs me. "You are a beautiful, thoughtful, strong young woman. You wouldn't hurt anyone unnecessarily, ever. It's just not in your nature. So, I know it must be extra hard to know you've caused pain. That doesn't mean you don't get to feel your own pain, though."

"Mom. Stop. Seriously. It's like you're trying to make me cry." I sniff, wipe my nose on my sleeve, and take a sip of my tea.

"My last word on the subject: don't be afraid or feel guilty if you're happy during this. When I was pregnant with you, I spent so much time being scared out of my mind. I used to feel so guilty feeling joy. I remember laughing out loud when you started really moving in there. It tickled. It was a ridiculous, bizarre feeling, and it made me so deliriously happy. As soon as the laugh escaped, I felt awful. Like I should only be serious and anxious and unhappy about being pregnant at sixteen. I wish I could have just laughed. That memory will always be as sad as it is happy. But it's still happy. You can enjoy being in love."

I nod. *In love*. It sounds so huge. Maybe it is. Because my feelings for Theo have exploded. From a crush, to infatuation, to discovering he's this whole other person when we are together. In a way, the making out and the sex with him has been about meeting this new person. I'm noticing all new things. I'm having to reconcile this sweet, naked, funny boy with the one I've known half my life.

I nod at my mom. She gets it. I am feeling happier and sadder today than I can ever remember feeling.

My mom puts her arm around me. "It's a lot," she says, leaning her head against mine. "You don't need to have a baby to have your whole world change in a matter of weeks."

She's right. I didn't think I'd be considering nursing school.

But that's not even the biggest change. Suddenly, sex isn't an abstract thing. It's not about discovering how my own body works, although that has happened, too; it's about allowing myself to be vulnerable, to ask for the things I want. These past few weeks have been enormous, and I haven't felt the weight of that until now.

"I love you, Mom."

~

Before I completely collapse from exhaustion, I pull the Tumblr back up. There are notes of encouragement and a few more questions in the inbox. Almost all of them are anonymous, but I see one from "HelloCello25" and click on it. There's a picture of Theo, looking goofy with his tongue out and eyes rimmed in midnight-blue eyeliner, his hair spiked up and messy the way it is before he combs it. It's perhaps the cutest Tumblr avatar I've ever seen. His comment: *Locker 412 forever! Keep sticking it to the man!*

I know what he's doing. He probably wanted to call or text, but also wanted to give me space. I pull out my phone.

> **Your avi is the cutest thing ever.**

Yeah?

I kind of want to see you. I feel
bad that I got on your case about
college.

> **I need a night to myself.**

Fine. But I reserve the right to
think of my girlfriend all night

Did you just refer to me as your
girlfriend?

Uh . . . yes? Is that okay?

This is acceptable.

<3

He just texted me a heart. So I text him a kissy face back. Oh
god, we are that couple. My eyes feel gritty from how exhaust-
ing today has been. I have every intention of falling asleep, but I
keep checking my phone whenever I feel myself drifting off. I'm
just waiting for Evita to tell me everything is okay. But she never
does.

Twenty-nine

My alarm goes off, even though I don't need to be at school today. I slept in my clothes and my teeth feel furry. Evita didn't call or text me last night. The triumph of our suspension yesterday feels significantly less triumphant without Evita. I start feeling all this doubt. Doubt that I've made a difference. Doubt that I'll make the right choice about college. Doubt that Evita will ever forgive me.

I slam the off button. I should have at least turned off the radio alarm, because the morning DJ is the worst. My throat is dry, and I'm hungry. If I go back to sleep now, I'll probably sleep all day and fall deeper and deeper into self-pity.

I grab my phone to find a distraction. I open Instagram first. I mostly follow musicians and a few random people from school. Expecting to scroll through images of concerts and music equipment and general musician shenanigans, I'm surprised to see that I have notifications. And I rarely post.

I've been tagged in a picture. I tap on it, and it's the worst picture of me ever taken. Posted by a kid I've never even heard of. It's me, walking half a step behind Ms. George, flanked by Evita and Theo. I have a stupid look on my face and I'm slumped over. But someone added something to the picture. A superhero cape. I glance at the caption. *The administration *tried* to bust up the condom project. Lacey, real American hero. #condomsforeveryone #locker412*

I click on the tags. #locker412 is everywhere. So many kids have taken pictures with . . . condoms. A lot of them are kind of hilarious. There's one of a condom being passed between two hands in a science classroom of our school, just like how you'd expect a note to be passed. There's another of someone's butt in tight jeans, condoms in each pocket. There's more than one banana with the added tag #practicemakesperfect. I knew people were taking condoms. I knew word must have gotten out, but how had I missed all of this?

We're clearly onto something. Just a few weeks ago, girls were embarrassed to even talk about condoms. Now so many of the same girls are posing for Instagram pics with them. It's beyond awesome. I don't care if I'm suspended; I have to find a way to keep this going.

I get out of bed and open my closet, where I now have boxes and boxes of condoms and "sexual paraphernalia," as Ms. George called it. I dump the condoms on my floor. I throw some dental dams and pamphlets on the pile for good measure. I sit on the floor with all of them surrounding me. And I do the unthinkable: I take a selfie with them. Historically, I've thought selfies are inane. I never look good in them. I pose with an encouraging face and a thumbs-up. I write the caption *We might have gotten suspended for #locker412 #condomsforeveryone but I am coming up with a plan. In the meantime: #besafe #sockitbeforeyourockit* It occurs to me that Evita would probably be able to come up with amazing hashtags for this.

I look at the image. I have bedhead. My nose is red. It's far from a cute picture, but I kind of love it. I hit post before I can think better of it. I could sit here and see if anyone likes it. Or I could go upstairs and try to forget about the fact that people from school might be looking at me and judging me.

I head upstairs. My mom is up and rushing around; she's working today. She flits around the kitchen finding butter before her toast gets cold, pouring herself coffee. She almost drops her mug when she realizes I'm there, creeping in the doorway.

She rushes over and wraps me in a big hug that's way too much this early in the morning. "Oh, bear, are you okay? I wanted to go and wake you up about a dozen times, but Charlie wouldn't let me. He thought you needed space. But I wasn't entirely sure that having your mother wasn't better than having space. Or if maybe that's what you needed even if you wanted to be alone. Like maybe we just need to talk things through more."

"Mom. I'm okay. Seriously. I just need to talk to Evita. And figure out the college thing. Jesus. I feel like no matter what I decide, I'm going to disappoint someone."

"Nothing would disappoint me. Well. Maybe if you took up smoking. Or dropped out of high school. Okay, honestly, I'd be disappointed if you got pregnant. But, like, supportive-disappointed. Unlike if you started smoking. You don't smoke, right?"

I shake my head and laugh.

"Well then. I want you to be happy. So, don't give me a second thought. If that's the only reason you applied to Amherst . . ."

"It was at first, honestly. But now . . . I've loved volunteering. It feels amazing to help people take charge of their health. But it also feels amazing to make music with my friends. I just need to make decisions, maybe. I have made so few in my life so far, you know?"

"Plenty of time for that. College is the first of many huge decisions in life."

"Great," I say, rolling my eyes.

"It is great. Think of all the possibilities." My mom smiles. What she isn't saying is *way more possibilities than I had*. That's a heavy weight to carry. "In fact, I think you have a possibility walking up the front walk right now."

"I do?" I assume it's Theo, and I feel my heart rate pick up. But it isn't Theo. It's Evita. It's Evita, and she doesn't look mad.

She doesn't even knock; she just comes right in the front door. "Oh good, I'm not waking you up," she says. "I thought you might be sleeping in, since we don't have school today. Thanks for that, by the way."

"I don't take all the credit. You were the one caught red-handed with condoms," I say.

"Yes, but it was your rude and profane and *lewd* tirade that probably got us this little vacation." Evita holds up a tray of coffees and a bag of baked goods. "I brought so many pastries."

"I'll leave you girls to it. I have to get ready for work. But I will take one of those." My mom takes one of the offered pastries and then shoots me a meaningful glance behind Evita's back.

"Let's go to the family room," I suggest. Evita puts the bag on the coffee table. She takes a muffin out, thinks better of it, and puts it back. I know she's about to launch into a speech, and I just hope that her chipperness this morning means it will be gentle.

"Lacey. I love you." She takes a deep breath. "Your not telling me about Theo is total bullshit."

I nod.

"You *lied* to me. Like, since when do we keep secrets from each other? I mean, I showed you when I got burned in that bullshit bikini wax."

"You sure did," I say, recalling that particular shock to the system.

"So, the point is, I don't keep anything from you. Not even the most intimate, embarrassing stuff. I kind of thought it was a two-way street. I thought we had this link. Like I knew what you were thinking. Like how I knew you were worried your strapless dress was going to fall during your mom's wedding. Or how you were always nervous in ninth-grade English because you thought our teacher was cute and there was sex in *Romeo and Juliet* and he kept talking about it. Or how that one car commercial gives you goosebumps. I mean, how can I know that you don't like maraschino cherries—like a freak—and not realize you were in love with our best friend?"

I open my mouth to explain, and maybe she's not ready to hear it because she shoves a coffee drink at me.

"This is for you. It's apparently some sort of berry chocolate something-or-other. Utterly ridiculous."

"Thanks." I pause for a moment, gathering all the thoughts

I loosely organized when I couldn't sleep. "Evita. I can't believe I didn't tell you. I mean, I can, because obviously I didn't tell you, but it's an awful feeling."

"Let me stop you right there. This can go one of two ways," Evita says. "You can spew a bunch of things rehashing why you didn't tell me and trying to make yourself feel better about the deception, or we can set that aside, and you can actually tell me what happened. And when you seem happy about something, I will endeavor to feel similarly on your behalf."

"So . . . you want to hear about Theo and stuff?"

"It's not that I want to hear about Theo. In fact, I *don't* want to hear about Theo. But I want you to talk to me about it. I want to hear about *you*. I want to know all the things I wish I had known all along. If that makes sense."

"Okay. Um. Sure." I take a sip of my drink. "Holy shit. That's like pure sugar."

"Yes. Yes it is. To loosen your tongue."

"Does that work?"

"You tell me."

I take a deep breath. "So, he sort of just offered to kiss me. After I didn't kiss Bruno. Like, I guess it kind of bugged him that you wanted me to kiss Bruno. So I guess maybe he liked me?"

"Lacey. Of *course* he likes you."

"Please don't say something about how he'd screw any girl who flirted with him," I say bitterly. I've heard that before.

"No. I mean, duh, he likes you. Because he has always liked you. Not always in the kissing way. But, yeah, now that I see that about you guys, it does feel kind of obvious. You are both sort of amazing, so it makes sense."

"Sure. Right."

"I just don't want to start this conversation off with you not giving yourself a little credit."

"Well. Thanks. That means a lot."

"Continue."

"So, he wanted to kiss me. And I really wanted to kiss him. So we did."

"Where?"

"My house. My bed. We've spent the night together a couple of times."

"That's what feels kind of sneaky about it, by the way."

"What? Like you would have wanted an invitation to come over and watch us fool around?"

"No. Probably not. Sorry. We aren't discussing the deception. Did you like the kissing?"

"Uh. Yeah. That's why it kept happening."

"I don't know. I kissed Theo a lot. And I thought it was fun. But it never changed anything about what I wanted to do with him. Like, it was never, 'Yeah, we're kissing, you should put your hand in my shirt now.'"

"Oh. Okay. Well, losing clothes has happened. For sure. But I don't totally want to go into that."

"Fair enough. Continue."

"I don't know what else to tell you. I think maybe I was attracted to him for, like, a long time. But he was never available, so I just kind of felt jealous of you or Lily Ann and dealt with it. But suddenly it was this possibility, and he felt the same way about me, and I honestly felt like I couldn't believe my luck."

"Okay. So, you can understand how I'm feeling," Evita says.

"You haven't told me how you're feeling."

"Insanely, ridiculously, physically, viscerally jealous."

"I guess that's what I figured. And I don't want you to feel that way."

"Well, tough cookies. I can't help feeling that way. But I also know I don't want to be with him like that. Not in a physical way. I'm just not interested. And, at the time, it felt easier to kind of break up with him, or whatever. Like how do you say to someone who you're with that you'd rather cuddle and maybe make out? How do you tell a guy you don't like having sex with them and expect things to work out? I mean, what makes being asexual difficult in our society is that we're all taught that sexual relationships are sort of the most important relationships. Like, totally negating all of the other things that might be important to the people in the relationship. And I just don't see it that way."

I shrug. Truth is, I'm obviously glad she and Theo didn't work out, and that adds a layer of guilt to what I'm already feeling.

"So, short story: I'm asexual. Like, totally. Totally happy with that. I don't feel like I'm missing out. I'm maybe curious about how other people experience things because it's so different from how I do. But, obviously, Theo is allosexual. Like, there is this whole spectrum of sexuality from asexual to allosexual. I am on one end. He's on the other. And his sexual attraction bothered me. And my asexuality bothered him, even though I hadn't totally worked out the terms yet. We didn't agree about how to be together. That's about as incompatible as you can be, right?"

"He could be tone-deaf," I say. "You've already made it clear that musical taste is sort of a factor in your romantic feelings."

"Oh, right. I'm actually giving Paul another chance, by the way. I think he just needs a musical education. We might have been texting when I was upset yesterday."

"That's great!" I say.

"I know you're probably hoping I'll fall for Paul so you're off the hook," Evita says, looking at me with a raised eyebrow.

"Well . . . or I could also want you to be happy?" I say.

"Right. So, regardless of my possible crush on Paul. You and Theo? It's probably going to be incredibly painful for a while. And I'm still pretty pissed. But, here's the thing: believe it or not, I actually really want you and him to be happy. For real. You like kissing him. He likes kissing you. You probably find each other attractive in a way that makes literally no sense to me. But if it makes you happy, I'll try to understand and be supportive and all that. The bit that makes me murderous is that you wouldn't tell me something so important. Like, now I feel like a moron for not seeing it, because seeing you talk about it now, it's like you have this little extra something to your smile. I mostly feel stupid. I hate feeling stupid. And I'm jealous that the two of you have something that I will never have with either of you. And society is just so fucking amatonormative. You know? Like, we're told that what you and Theo have—romantically and sexually—is more important than what I could have with either of you."

"I mean, you and I, and you and him, we'll all have other things with each other."

"Are you inviting me to be your celibate sister-wife? Because that is something I could squarely get behind."

I laugh. "I don't know about that. But you and Theo were always like my prime example of how best friends should be. I don't think I'll ever be as close to him as you are. In a way."

"Now you have all these things that are just between the two of you. And it sucks."

"I can understand that."

"So stop keeping things from me. Being on the outside is the worst thing in the world, at least when it comes to you."

"Got it."

"I want every detail."

"Sure."

"Like . . . well . . . did you guys . . ."—she leans in—"have actual sex?"

"Evita, what does actual sex mean?" I ask, lowering my voice. Charlie is a sound sleeper so long as Dylan's also asleep, but I'm not cool with him being privy to this conversation.

"Duh."

"We've done enough things that, yes, probably. But I haven't, you know . . ."

"No home run, but you're definitely on third."

"I'm really not sure why you'd want to hear this."

"I told you! I don't want to be on the outside. I mean, I told you everything we did."

"I wish you hadn't sometimes, though."

"Okay. But aren't friends supposed to discuss this? Like *Sex and the City* or whatever."

"I don't like just doing what people are 'supposed' to do."

"Fair enough. But if I've learned anything from you and our locker project, it's that we shouldn't shy away from talking about all things sex just because we've been told to be ashamed of it all our lives."

"True, but I also think it's personal and we should only share what we want."

"Fine. Okay. But I'm telling you now: I'd rather you keep me in the loop than worry about hurting my feelings, okay?"

"I'm honestly so surprised that you're kind of okay with us."

"Lacey. I want you to be happy. I also want to live in Boston and have a band and be your sister-wife, but I think you know that."

"Yeah. And I will keep you in the loop about that also."

"Any thoughts on college?"

"I'm on the fence. More on the fence than I even realized. And I hate being on the fence, but I will tell you as soon as I start to wobble one way or the other."

"And I will try not to be a strong breeze knocking you off that fence, but it's hard for me."

"I know."

"I love you. And Theo. And I am not going to dwell on the deception more than necessary, but that sucked yesterday, Lacey."

"I know."

"So, what are we doing with the rest of the day?"

"There is a certain boy who would probably really like to know that you don't hate him."

"Ah. That boy. Yes. Call your boyfriend and tell him to get his tight-pantsed butt over here."

"I am so not used to that word," I tell her, taking another sip of my cup full of chocolate syrup.

"Boyfriend. He's your boyfriend."

"Shut up. I know."

"And sometimes, your boyfriend is sort of an asshole," she says.

"You do not pull your punches," I tell her.

"I do sometimes, actually."

"Yeah. Thanks for that."

I sigh. The weight of that secret was heavier than I realized.

I glance over at Evita. Her hair is wild and teased up in the messiest, biggest bun ever. She's wearing a jacket so large she can draw her legs up into it.

"You're kind of the best," I tell her.

"I know." She pauses. "Oh! I forgot to tell you, maybe I shouldn't ask you to keep secrets from your boyfriend, but you'll still keep the whole 'me loving him' thing from him? Like, I'm not pro-secret generally, as you well know, but I gotta play that one close to the chest."

"Got it. I would never."

"And, look, I might be a little miserable about all of this, but can we not make a big thing of it? I want to be cool. I will be cool. It just might take me a hot second."

"Absolutely."

"You're pretty great, too, you know."

Thirty

Even with everything out in the open, Theo and I still aren't sure how to act in front of Evita and Alice. We're taking a break from playing music to make school board plans. Evita proudly shows off the Instagram posts I found. And we've received dozens of messages of support on Tumblr.

"If even half these people show up to a school board meeting, it will be great. I mean, I've never been to a school board meeting, and I don't know anyone else who has," Evita says.

Theo and I are careful to sit on either side of Evita, not wanting to look too cozy together. But we keep stealing glances at each other, and we're always smiling.

"I think we should set up an email account and ask people to email us if they want to join our presentation. Or we can keep anything they want us to read anonymous," I suggest.

"You might want to do an online petition as well. Show how many students would welcome the change. Adults like numbers, right?" Alice says.

"When is the next school board meeting, anyway?" Theo asks.

"It's soon. A week from Wednesday," I say.

"Okay, well, that interferes a little bit with the amount of rehearsal we need before our gig next Friday, but I'll allow it," Evita says.

"Oh, well, only if you'll allow it." Theo laughs.

"I'm serious. We need to rehearse. A lot. And I don't want to show up to this school board meeting looking anything but super prepared," Evita says.

"Don't worry," I tell her. "I've got this. The three of us will talk. And, Alice?"

"You want me to talk?" Alice asks.

"Only if you want to. You do sort of have a unique viewpoint on all this," I say.

"Because the system failed me?" Alice says.

"I didn't mean it like that," I say. "It's just that you said yourself that—"

She smiles. "I'm teasing. Of course I'll share my experiences."

"Bonus points if you can bring it around to how girls often lose the most with abstinence-only education," I tell her. "I'll dig up some statistics for you on that."

"Post the info on Tumblr, and then we need to rehearse," Evita says.

~

Our suspension plus the weekend is spent at Evita's house either preparing for the school board meeting or rehearsing. By the time Monday rolls around, we have perfected our set list and also recruited a dozen other students to speak at the school board meeting.

When I walk into school, I am floored by all the smiles I get. I even get a high five from some kid I don't know.

"Someone is finally getting the attention she deserves," Theo says when we drop our stuff in Evita's locker before our music classes.

"I'm not entirely sure how I feel about it," I say.

"Oh, come on, you like the spotlight, admit it," Evita says. "Next you'll be begging me to let you front the band."

"That will never happen," I tell her.

Evita looks between me and Theo. "Yeah. I'm gonna get to choir a little early this morning," she says as she turns on her heel and walks down the hall.

It's nice of her. Theo and I haven't had a single second with just the two of us since the day we got suspended.

"Hi," I say, suddenly feeling shy.

"Hey yourself," Theo says, brushing a hair off my face in the way he always does these days. "Now that we're quasi-alone in this crowded hall, I have a big question for you." He turns to look at me. "Would you maybe want to have an official date?"

"Do we need an official date? I thought dates were so you could get to know someone."

"Hear me out. I know it's November."

"Yes . . ."

"It's November, and it'll probably be cold, but maybe we could try camping?"

"Camping?" We live near so many campgrounds, and my mom and I would occasionally go when I was younger, but only in the summer, when the days were hot and the nights were perfectly cool.

"I know. It's okay if you don't want to. It's just . . . we never get to be actually alone. My dad has awesome gear. Plenty of warm sleeping bags. And if we hate it, we can just leave, you know? But I might actually surprise you with my campfire-building skills."

"Do your skills involve lighter fluid?"

"No. Come on. Give me some credit. Building fires and camping are, like, the only manly things I do."

"Cello is manly."

"Ha. Yeah. Okay. Seriously, though, let's go camping."

"When?"

"Thursday."

"A school night? The night before a gig? Are you crazy?"

"Probably. But I thought we could just skip school on Friday. More time to rehearse anyway."

"Skip school? Have you met me?"

"Well, now that you've been suspended . . . I bet your mom would call you out," he says. He looks a little crestfallen that I'm not jumping at the chance.

"I don't think my mom will call me out of school to have sex."

"Oh. No. This isn't some kind of tactic to get you to have sex with me," Theo says, horrified.

"No. I know. But, seriously, my mom is cool, but I'm not sure she's *that* cool."

"Well, think about it," he says.

It is a totally nuts idea. But I want to. "I'll work it out. I would love to go camping with you in the mountains in November."

Maybe love does make you do crazy things. The moment I have the thought, it just feels right to say it. "I love you," I say.

"I really love you," he says, without even thinking about it. I couldn't keep the smile off my face even if I tried.

~

At lunch Evita gives us her blessing for our date. It probably helps that we had an amazing rehearsal yesterday. "I think you guys are crazy, but the band will not suffer if we don't rehearse after school Thursday as long as we rehearse all day Friday. But, Theo, darling, go get me a pretzel or something in the lunch line, I need a word with Lacey."

Theo rolls his eyes. "You just expect everyone to do everything you say, don't you?"

"Basically." She shoos him away. She turns to me once he's out of earshot. "This is, like, it, right?"

"What do you mean?" I ask. I know what she means.

"You're going to go all the way."

"'All the way'? What a dumb expression."

"Okay. Enough with your pickiness about sex terms. Will you allow his penis to enter your vagina?"

"Shh," I say, blushing.

"Sorry. It seemed like you wanted me to be specific."

"I don't know, Evita. Like, I'm trying not to make that be a big thing."

She smirks. "A big thing."

"Oh my god."

"I just want to know these things. I told you before we did it."

"Yeah. Again, you did *not* need to do that."

"But friends talk about this stuff," Evita says, with a pout.

"I'm so grateful you are being cool about all this. But I feel like I need to draw the line somewhere. You can't know every detail of that. Not because I don't love you. I'm just not into talking about things before I've had a chance to sort of keep them to myself."

"I do not understand the impulse to keep anything to yourself. But I guess I respect it."

"Thanks. And . . . maybe . . . could you not, like, call or text us too much while we're camping?"

"Why?" she says way too loudly.

"For Christ's sake, Evita, because we might be . . ."—I drop my voice—"doing it for the first time, okay?"

"Say no more. I shall not disturb you and your first experience of sexual intercourse."

"Thank you."

Theo comes back with a pretzel. "What did I miss?"

Evita snorts.

"Evita thinks I should wear wool socks," I say.

"And I think Theo should wear something else," Evita mumbles.

"Oh Jesus!" I say loudly, not caring when people turn in their seats at my outburst.

Thirty-one

My stomach is full of butterflies when I get into Theo's car after school on Thursday. I have a duffel bag full of warm clothes and blankets, a toothbrush, and condoms, which I might be using today. Oh my god. I did not think I would be nervous. I have to let out a shaky breath before turning to him and smiling.

Theo's backseat is full of various nylon drawstring bags I guess are a tent and sleeping bags. There are a few grocery bags of snacks. He has the biggest grin on his face. "I have surprises for you."

"Oh yeah?"

He looks devilish. "Big surprises."

"Well, that's a little cocky," I tell him. A feeble attempt at a penis joke. And I'm not sure it'll even come across.

It does, because he gives me this shocked look. "Are you saying my cockiness isn't deserved?"

I shrug. "Not much to compare it to."

"Well. Yeah. But I figure, a tall guy like me . . . big feet . . . all that." He smirks. "No, but seriously. We can discuss that in great detail later. Check it out." He reaches past the pillows and the sleeping bags and pulls out a large gift bag.

"You got me a present? For our date? I didn't get you anything."

"Open it." He grins. "I've been holding on to this for a long time."

"I can tell." The big bag is crinkled and scuffed. Who knows how long it's been floating around his messy backseat.

"Open it!" he demands.

I dig through the layers of mismatched tissue paper and put my hand on something plush. "A teddy bear?" I ask him. It's not the kind of thing he'd buy me. We haven't been a couple long, but I know we aren't a chocolate-and-flowers kind of pair. So I pull out the yellow stuffed toy. It's like a cross between a flying saucer and a fried egg. It has two cute eyes on the top of its round middle.

"There's more," he says gleefully.

I pull out a blue peanut-shaped stuffed toy, with the same adorable eyes. Then a purple creature shaped like a spiral. There are half a dozen in all.

"These are . . . cute," I say.

"Do you know what they are?" he asks.

"No."

"I'm a bit disappointed in you, Burke," he says. He points to the yellow one. "This is herpes. And I also gave you HPV, syphilis, and gonorrhea. Oh, and an egg and a sperm. Those ones have to stay separated."

"Oh yeah!" I say. "That is a sperm! I was thinking tadpole." I laugh.

"Who knew sperm were so cute?"

"I mean, these are awesome. What's the occasion?"

"So. I bought these when I got my clean bill of health from the clinic. And the plan was, once we, you know, had sex, I'd give them to you all apologetic, like, 'I have to tell you something: I gave you HPV.' Then I'd pull this out and we'd have a good laugh about it. And then later I'd give you syphilis. And we'd laugh about it. But, well, I realized that it might not be terribly politically correct to give you a gift just because you had sex with me. So I'm giving them to you just for being awesome and for being willing to go camping in November." He grins.

"You know me so well."

"Really, they're educational tools."

"Right. A girl did ask me about syphilis the other day."

"See! This could come in handy."

I nod.

"So, you ready to go camping?" he asks. He's so giddy. He rubs his hands together and puts the car in reverse.

"I really love you," I tell him.

~

The campsite is cheesy. It's one of those family camping grounds with a pool and an arcade and pictures of cartoon bears and deer on all the signs. And it's muddy, because it's thankfully very warm for November. It's also deserted. The woman in the office smirks when she sees us. Because we're two teenagers, giggling, plastered to each other, and it's the middle of the afternoon.

"I honestly thought you'd be the backwoods kind of camper," I told him.

"Oh. I really thought you'd want a bathroom and warm water," he said.

"I was fully prepared to rough it," I tell him.

"Noted. We can go somewhere else, but, like, it's an hour to the state park where there's at least bathhouses. Otherwise you gotta dig to bury your poop."

"Yeah. I'm not into roughing it that much."

"Then this is home for the night."

Theo pitches the tent in about five minutes flat despite me being absolutely no help. It's a little mildewy, and it's very small.

"It's a two-man tent," Theo says defensively.

"Two very small men."

"Or two men very comfortable with each other," he says as he bends to kiss me.

He opens the car door and begins tossing things inside the tent. Pillows, blankets, an oversize sweatshirt that I'm pretty sure belongs to Evita, and our new plush toys. He doesn't set any of it up, but instead dives in with enthusiasm and then grabs my hands and pulls me in behind him. I laugh as I fall off balance and tumble into the tent. I'm impressed to see that Theo can actually sit up all the way in the small tent. It feels bigger on the inside than I thought it would. I was nervous about the idea of fooling around in here, like everyone would know and it wouldn't feel private, but at this moment, it feels like our own space and I suddenly don't care about anything outside of it. Especially when Theo zips the flap closed and pulls his sweatshirt off and then his T-shirt.

"You'll freeze!" I tell him.

"I won't." He grabs this scratchy Southwest-style blanket and burrows in right next to me. "I actually think you might get too warm." He tangles himself up with me, and I laugh, and we kiss. He's right. I warm up quickly, but the shock of air when he pulls my shirt over my head is still cold.

I let out a surprised breath, so Theo pulls the blanket tighter around me and presses his own warm chest against mine. His belt buckle grinds into my thigh.

"Ouch," I say. I reach to unbuckle it.

"Sorry." He grins. His grin gets wider still because I start to unbuckle his pants. Because I know. I want to do this.

"I think we should . . . ," I say.

"Should what?" he asks. He takes some of his weight off of me and lifts his head up enough to look into my eyes.

"I mean, you know, let it happen naturally and everything," I say, my face reddening to probably a record shade.

"I'm sorry, what are you talking about?" he teases.

"You know!" I say.

"I just want to make sure we are on the exact same page," he says. "I think that's important for both of our sakes, don't you?"

"I am consenting to sexual intercourse with you, so long as you take every measure to be gentle and safe," I say. My eyes start watering. It's weird. I didn't think this would feel so important. Or like such a big step. We're already so intimate. I've seen every part of him and felt every last inch of his skin. And I've been so vulnerable with him. Even if virginity is a construct, this is still new.

"You okay?" Theo asks quietly.

"It's just so big," I say.

He laughs, and I realize what I've just said.

"That's not what I mean!" I say, overcome with giggles myself.

"Just go with it!" he says.

"I cannot believe I just said that." I put my hands over my face.

"Don't worry about it." He moves my hands away from my face. And he looks at me, no longer laughing or smirking. "I love you."

"I love you, too. And I'm ready. Okay?"

"More than okay. But you're not ready."

"What?"

"I mean, I'm going to make you more ready." The smirk is back, and he unbuttons my jeans and kisses me down my body. "Did you still want to use a dental dam if we . . . ?"

"No. That's fine." I blush. "It's fine without . . . if you don't mind."

"Say no more," he says.

He continues to kiss my stomach and then the tops of my thighs. "Oh," I say when he puts his hands there, and then his mouth. "Oh," I say again, only this time it's completely involuntary.

It doesn't take me long. And I can't believe there's more we can do. But he's right. I am ready now. He pulls a condom out of his pocket, then hands it to me.

"You can check the expiration date," he says.

"I trust you," I tell him.

He grins, and then he's naked and rolling the condom on, and it strikes me then that it's a practiced move. I try to banish the thought.

But soon he's over me and his hand is there and he's guiding himself in, and all thought just goes away. Because I don't really care about anything else in the world right now.

~

"So. Was that okay?" Theo asks.

I roll my eyes, and when I *pfffff* Theo laughs. "You were there. I think you know it was okay."

"But just okay?"

"Are you trying to embarrass me?" I ask him.

"No, I'm just fishing for compliments," he says.

"You are a sex god. Okay?"

"That's more like it."

The question resurfaces. "So. I mean. You've done this before . . ."

"Yes . . ."

"I mean, and you were people's first."

"Yeah."

"Are you going to be all 'I don't kiss and tell'?"

"What do you want to know?" he asks. He sticks a foot out of the blanket, because it really did warm up in here.

"I don't want, like, tons of details or anything—"

"So, like, an overview. There were three other people."

Wait. This is news to me. "Three? Jesus, Theo, after hearing about you and Evita, I didn't think you kept that sort of thing from us."

"Yeah. Well, the first time for me was stupid. In a car after that party freshman year. You know, the one with all the older music kids?"

"Yeah. Pretty sure that was, like, the only party we went to that year."

"It was awkward. Like, we snuck out to the car and it was totally all her and I just went with it because, well, freshman guy."

"You never told me."

"I was sort of embarrassed. We didn't talk after that at all. Ever."

"Who was it?" I ask.

"Remember Michelle?"

"Cellist Michelle?" I ask, shocked. She was two years ahead of us. She was gorgeous and talented. She had this perfect long, straight, shiny black hair. And I'm sure her thighs didn't rub together when she walked and her chin didn't break out every month. The things I used to worry about resurface.

"It was so awkward. We were stand partners, too."

"Did Evita know?"

"Yeah. Why do you think she was so eager to try it herself? God forbid she be less experienced than someone. But Evita and I really only hooked up a couple times before she decided she didn't like having sex with me. So that was a huge confidence booster, as you can imagine."

"That sucks." I don't ask about Lily Ann. I really don't want to know. But I get the feeling maybe she gave him more confidence.

"Well. The confidence thing is a bit better. Because, well, you just called me a sex god."

I smile at him. "Well. If the shoe fits."

I sit up and start fishing through the pillows and blankets for my clothes.

"Where are you going?" Theo asks.

"I've gotta run to the bathroom. It's important to pee after sex to prevent bladder infections," I tell him.

"I'll start working on dinner," he says, reluctantly reaching for his own clothes.

I start unzipping the tent.

"Wait," he says. He kisses me on my nose. "I love you. I love that you are going to pee to prevent a bladder infection. And I love that you can relax around me. And that I can make you happy."

"I love you, too. But you're a doofus. What's for dinner?"

"Peanut butter sandwiches."

"Perfect."

We pool our pocket change and get M&M's for dessert. The cheesiness of the campsite melts away as it gets dark. All that's left is the quiet and the stars and Theo. Even though we're twenty minutes out of town, we are much higher in the mountains, and the air is now bitterly cold. But the mountain cold is somehow welcome while you look up at the stars.

"No mountains in Boston," Theo says.

"Nope. But they're not too far away." I lean into him. He doesn't have camping chairs, and we didn't get around to building a fire, so we're wrapped in blankets, leaning on a wheel of his car. "It's beautiful."

"I sort of forget our town's in the middle of this," he says.

"Hang on, you sap. Are you actually gonna miss this place when you're in Boston?" I elbow him.

"You keep saying that."

"Saying what?"

"Saying 'you' instead of 'we.' Like you aren't even entertaining the idea of Berklee anymore." He goes quiet. The arm around my shoulders squeezes a little tighter for a moment.

"It's just that you're definitely going, and I'm not necessarily. But I'll be close by either way. And I'm still not used to 'we.' Okay?"

"I realize it'd be stupid of you to hang all your plans on me. But I want you to be with me and Evita next year. Things could be so great."

"I realize it's not possible to totally forget about the future, but I kind of just want to focus on right now. And, well, how much fun we're having."

"This is the absolutely best kind of fun," he agrees.

"And we can have more fun," I say. I clap a hand over my mouth. I still can't believe it when flirtatious things fly out of my mouth. But he laughs and I go with it, leading him back to the tent for the night.

Thirty-two

My mom lets me stay home from school on Friday, but only because I made a case for our gig being an educational and professional experience. After Theo and I pack up the campsite we drive to Evita's apartment, where Alice and Evita are already running through some of our songs.

"Hi!" Evita says brightly the moment we walk in. She gives me a questioning look. But I roll my eyes at her. If I'm going to tell her about last night, it will not be in front of Theo. I feel my cheeks redden, though, which is enough of an answer for Evita.

We run through our whole set list, and we play without a hitch. "Isn't a bad last rehearsal good for a performance? Should we be worried that we sound awesome?" I ask.

"No way. I think things have clicked because we're all just having fun and not, you know, keeping any secrets," Evita says.

"Ugh. I totally played terribly last week. I'm so sorry," Theo says.

"Don't sweat it. We're on the same page now. But we do need to clean up that passage in 'Super Eighteen.' Like, crisp sixteenth notes. And the clapping needs to be sharper."

After we drill those sections, Alice asks if we can take a little break. "I just need some water," she says.

We decide to look at Boston apartment listings during the break. I don't remind them I might be living a couple hours away.

"We only need a two bedroom," Evita says. I glance at her, thinking she's going to tell me she thinks I should go to nursing school. "Like you two are going to need your own rooms."

"Good point," Theo says, putting his arm around me.

Evita looks at the time. "We need to pack up in an hour. I'm hoping we can run through some of the set when we get to the Map. Maybe we should just chill until then."

"That does not sound like my favorite dictator," Theo says.

"I think Alice is a little tired," Evita whispers.

Alice comes out of the bathroom. "Sorry, guys. I'm just not feeling that great."

"Let's tuck you in so you can get a nap in," Evita says, jumping up from the couch. "I'll find you a nightshirt or something." She's really turned into Alice's guard dog lately. She gets Alice set up in her room and then comes back out to where we are looking at maps of Boston and trying to make sense of the public transit system.

Twenty minutes later, Alice emerges but goes back into the bathroom.

"Is she okay?" Theo asks.

I get up and knock on the door. "Alice?" I can hear her get sick through the door. I wonder if she wants to be left alone.

"Just a second," she says.

I hear the water run, and I glance at Evita and Theo. They look a little freaked out. When Alice opens the door, she looks pretty awful.

"I hate to say this, guys, but I'm not feeling good. I think it might be a bug or something I ate," she says. "My stomach hasn't been right all day."

"That's okay," Evita says quickly.

"But our gig . . . ," Alice says.

"It's fine. Go lie down if you aren't feeling good." Evita has this pinched, worried face.

Alice puts a hand on her stomach. "I still feel sick," she says. She goes back in the bathroom.

Theo looks at me and whispers, "What do we do?"

"Alice?" I knock on the door again. "I know you probably want privacy, but maybe you could let me in?"

The door unlocks and I go inside. Alice is sitting on the toilet looking panicked. "I've got you, okay?" I tell her. Alice is always sunshiny and happy and relaxed, and seeing her this scared tells me that things are serious.

"I'm actually bleeding some," she says. Her face is splotchy, and her eyes are filling.

"Hey, Evita?" I call calmly. "Maybe just call an ambulance to be on the safe side?"

Alice starts to protest.

"Theo, maybe wait outside for the paramedics?"

I focus all my attention back on Alice. "Tell me what you're feeling?"

"My stomach's just not right. Crampy and upset. I think

maybe it's a stomach bug and it made me bleed? Does that even make sense? I threw up, and I still feel sick."

I nod. "I think you might actually be in labor."

"No!" she says. "It's too early!"

"It's a little early. But not unheard of. Do you feel any pressure?"

She nods tightly.

"I'm gonna wash my hands, okay?" I go to the sink and take a couple deep breaths while I scrub.

"Lacey!" Alice says sharply. "Maybe my water broke?"

"Okay. I think that means you're gonna meet Eli, okay?" I crouch next to her. "Do you want to stay on the toilet? We're calling the paramedics, and we'll get you to the hospital. Do you want a blanket or water or anything?"

"Did my water break?"

"I don't know," I admit. "Do you want me to look? I mean, I can't do an exam or anything, but . . ."

She grips my shoulder and sits on the bathmat, leaving her underwear on the floor. She's shaky and flushed and as soon as she sits, she spreads her legs and I know beyond a shadow of a doubt that she's in labor, because I'm pretty sure I see Eli's head.

"Evita!" I yell.

"Yeah?" She pokes her head in. She's holding the phone to her ear.

"You need to get me all of your towels. And then . . . a trash bag."

"The dispatcher is asking me if—"

"Evita, the baby is coming right now. Tell the dispatcher and say she has a doula with her. Just tell them what's happening."

"He's coming now?" Alice asks. "I don't want him to. Can you call my mom?"

"We will. Are you comfortable?"

"I think I should get back on the toilet," she says.

"I don't think you need to. I think you're feeling Eli's head. You can reach down and feel it if you want." I swallow. This is happening. Right now. Before the paramedics get here, before we can get to the hospital. Before Eli is full term. I push aside thoughts of what I've learned about infant distress and just concentrate on helping Alice get through these moments.

"Alice, you're doing really well," I tell her. "Just think about it—you've been going through labor and you've handled it all, thinking you just had an upset stomach! You're doing amazing."

"Paramedics will be here in just a few minutes," Evita says, dumping a bunch of towels on me.

"Tell them she's almost crowning," I say.

"I'm crowning? What does that mean?" Alice says.

"It means his head is very close to being born. Do you feel that pressure?"

She nods. Then she closes her eyes and groans. I feel her belly; it's rock hard and I know she's having a contraction. "Alice. Just take nice easy breaths and if you feel like you have to push, just do it gently, okay?"

She nods again. She's pushing. I know that it's an overwhelming urge that most moms don't have to think about. I remember when Dylan was born, and it only took a few loud pushes from my mom until his head was out. And I think of that first mom I helped, Shana, who pushed with all her might but didn't make progress for hours. I know that this experience is different for each woman, but I also know it's a time they'll never forget.

273

"Alice. I see him. I can see Eli's head. He has blond hair like you do," I say with a smile. "Even if the paramedics don't get here in the next minute, I'm here. I'm ready to help you meet Eli, okay?"

She nods, and she pushes again. Evita pokes her head around the corner. She lets out a gasp, and I put a finger to my lips. Evita just nods, the phone still to her ear.

I put extra towels underneath Alice's bottom. Because Eli is going to be here any second, and I'm going to be ready to wrap him up. I mentally go over what I need to do. I need to put him on Alice's chest, check his breathing, be careful with the cord, rub his back if he's not reactive. I need to keep an eye on her bleeding.

Eli's head emerges. I can see a wrinkled, smooshed face. Alice wails and pushes again, and the rest of his small pink body comes swimming out. Alice doesn't need instructions; she instinctively reaches for her baby, and I help place him on her chest.

"Oh my god. Oh my god," she says over and over.

"He's here!" Evita says. "You did it, Alice. Holy shit."

Then I hear Theo's voice as he guides in the paramedics. I drape blankets over Eli and rub his back. He's still quiet, but he's moving his little hands and feet. I rub and I rub, and he lets out a little shivery wail. We all breathe a sigh of relief. The paramedics crowd into the bathroom and immediately start taking vitals.

"Don't leave," Alice says to me, grabbing my hand. So I climb into the bathtub behind her and just marvel at little Eli with her.

"He's amazing. Look at how he's looking at you," I whisper in her ear.

"Holy shit. Did I just give birth?" Alice says with a laugh.

The female paramedic looks at her. "You sure did, hon. In a second we're gonna get you on the gurney and take you two for a little spin."

"Evita, what time is it?" I ask.

"It's three forty-five," she says from the doorway.

"So we'll say that Eli was born at three forty-four, okay?" I tell Alice. "Happy birthday, Eli."

The paramedics help her out of the bathroom. Evita and I move the towels and keep Eli covered. The paramedics cover Alice with a blanket. "Did I hear a name for the baby?" the second paramedic asks.

"Eli James," Alice says, beaming. She looks so much like her usual self now, radiant and happy and relieved. "Lacey can ride with us, right?"

"Sure," says the paramedic.

"We'll meet you at the hospital," Evita says.

"Should we call someone?" Theo asks Alice.

"Oh my god. Yeah. Eric. Holy shit. Someone call Eric and tell him he's a dad."

It's amazing how quickly new babies figure things out. As soon as we're in the warm ambulance, I see Eli's mouth searching for milk.

"Alice, I think he's looking for your breast. We didn't really talk that much about this. Were you going to breastfeed him?"

"Oh. Yeah. I think. What do I do? I thought maybe I would magically know."

"It's fine, you guys will figure it out. For now, just lower your shirt and put him near the nipple and he'll do his best."

I've done this before with other moms. I've seen my mom breast-feed. But I see the nerves on Alice's face. It probably feels strange for her to lower her shirt. But she does. "You can kind of hold your breast and brush his cheek with the nipple and he'll turn his head to find it. It's a reflex."

She does. Eli immediately does a hungry wide-mouthed yawn and smacks his lips. He latches on, and Alice's eyes fill with tears.

"Is that it? Are we doing it?"

"That's it. You're so awesome."

"Look at him!" she squeals.

The female paramedic looks at him again. She takes temperatures and counts pulses and breaths and before we know it, they're wheeling Alice into the hospital and up the elevators to the fourth floor where Kelly is waiting for her.

"Someone was in a hurry," Kelly says warmly. "He looks great. Good job, Alice. We're going to a delivery room just until you deliver the placenta, and we'll check you both over, but I think everything looks good."

I stay with Alice and Eli. I'm there when Theo walks in and almost faints at the sight of the placenta. Evita happily high-fives everyone she meets and also informs them of how awesome Alice is. When Eric and Alice's mom get there, we step out.

My knees feel wobbly. I'm shivering again. "I think I might be a little bit in shock," I say to Evita and Theo.

"About the baby or the sex you guys had less than twenty-four hours ago?" Evita asks nonchalantly.

Theo nudges Evita. "I leave you alone for ten minutes and you've already talked about that?" he asks us.

"No. We were too busy delivering a baby," I tell him.

"She didn't tell me. But I guess you just did. So, congrats, on both," Evita says.

"Yeah, but, Evita, virginity is just—"

"A patriarchal construct," Theo and Evita finish.

"Shut up." I laugh. My knees are still knocking together, so Evita and Theo wrap me in a giant hug.

"You are such a badass!" Evita says.

"Yeah. Pretty much," Theo agrees.

"You did do amazing," Kelly says, joining us. "I hope you don't mind, but I called your mom. I thought she'd want to hear that you delivered a baby by yourself. She'll be here soon."

"That's cool."

"Oh, shit. I should call my mom so she doesn't think I murdered someone in the bathroom," Evita says, panicked. She rushes off with her phone.

"I'm glad you got to do some birth work, even without your internship," Kelly says to me.

"I'm still so sorry about that," I say.

"I just hope you sort it out so you can start again," Kelly says. "You're obviously a natural at this."

"I hope so, too."

Theo and I check on Alice and Eli again while Alice's parents and Eric get coffee. Theo is a sap. He coos at the baby and remarks on his wispy hair and clear, alert eyes. Eli's tiny. Just under six pounds. But he's healthy.

When Eli falls asleep in Alice's arms, she announces that she's tired.

"He'll probably take a good long nap, so you should, too," I tell her.

"You don't have to tell me twice. Though I do just want to hold him for a bit."

"Absolutely." I give her a hug and give Eli a small pat on his head. His little plump lips are open and his little fists have unfurled slightly. He is out like a light. "He's perfect, Alice. Congratulations."

"I could not have done that without you," Alice says. "I'm sorry we missed the gig."

"Are you kidding? I don't care about that. This was probably an even better bonding experience for the Sparrows than a gig would ever be."

"I love you guys," Alice says. I give her a gentle hug, careful not to jostle Eli.

Back in the waiting room, Theo puts his arms around me, pulling me close. "You good?"

"Yeah. Wow. I really am."

"So, I hate to admit this, but I can see it. I can totally see this future version of Lacey, strolling through the halls of a hospital, making all these moms and families feel at ease. You're just so calm and positive and sweet, but, like, damn, you know what you're doing."

I smile at him.

"Though rocker-chick Lacey with the green top and sleek hair is pretty great, too," he says. Then he gets really close to my ear to whisper, "So is naked Lacey, by the way."

I elbow him when Evita rushes into the waiting room. "Okay, two things of note. My mom got home before I called her and she really did worry that there had been some horrific act of violence, so she might not forgive me for quite some time. And second: holy shit, you guys, I just got my acceptance email from Berklee!" She runs and dives into our laps.

Both Theo and I pull out our phones to check, but neither of us has heard. We submitted our applications the exact same second, but we applied to different programs, and since it's rolling admission we might hear at any time.

Theo looks at me with a sad little smile. I know he's still picturing nurse Lacey. Just like I am imagining a future as a midwife. But we can both just be happy for Evita, because she, without a doubt, is going to be in the right place for her.

She grins at me. "Lacey, I love you so fucking much and think you're a magnificent unicorn, by the way. It deserves to be said."

Thirty-three

"**W**e have to leave in half an hour!" Evita calls.

I'm a bundle of nerves. Public speaking is not my favorite thing in the world, but Evita and Theo and my mom all insist that I be the one to introduce our cause at the school board meeting. There are eleven students besides Theo, Evita, Alice, and me who are meeting us at the high school. I don't know why I thought our tiny town would have some sort of congressional meeting place. When I first pictured talking to the school board, I was picturing the US Capitol building that I saw last year on a field trip. It's a little reassuring that it won't be that formal.

Still, my hands are shaking. I keep going through my stack of papers. I have my written intro, the pages of signatures we collected, the printed-out anonymous comments from Tumblr, and my own speech. That's the part I'm the most nervous about. It's more than just citing facts and figures. I'm talking about shame and safety and what it's like to be a girl at our school.

Theo rubs my shoulders. "You'll be great," he says. "If you get nervous, just take a peek at me and I will be smiling and giving you a thumbs-up."

"Or at me, and I will be jumping up and down excitedly," Evita says.

"Yes, me, too," my mom adds.

"I might be bringing my stuffed herpes for luck," I say, pointing to the plush microbes that have been overseeing the operation. "Do I look okay?" I ask, looking down at my dress. I feel like maybe I dressed up too much.

Evita nods. "You look serious and pretty at the same time."

"Can we just get there early? I'm too nervous to sit around here," I say. "Plus, Alice is meeting us there, and I'm dying to give Eli a squeeze."

"Sure. Sure." Evita starts grabbing papers and notes and shoving them in her bag. She won't cop to being anxious like I will, but I think maybe she is.

"I wish I could come with you," Charlie calls from the couch in the living room.

"Dylan's so cute, he would distract from the cause," my mom says. "All right, kids, pile in the minivan."

"Shotgun!" Evita calls. "I have a playlist for this!"

"Of course you do." Theo laughs.

When we're in the van, I start to feel a little sick. It's more than just the public speaking. I desperately want my internship back. After helping Alice, it's all I can think about. I want the administration to realize that information isn't lewd. I will be so disappointed if our pleas are ignored. I'll be mad if I leave high school without making a lasting difference.

When we get to the school, I already see Paul and a couple kids from senior seminar and the GSA waiting by the main entrance. Cam is there along with another girl I helped, Amber. And some people I had to look up in the yearbook after they emailed me.

We gather around and go over the order we're going to be speaking. Then Alice pulls up in her car. I hand all the papers to Paul and jog over to her.

"Can I grab something for you?" I ask.

"Thanks." She hands me a diaper bag. "It's so good to see you."

"How are you feeling?" I ask her. She just left the hospital over the weekend.

"Super tired. Weirdly weepy and I'm basically leaking milk all the time. But I'm glad to be here."

"Okay, well, if you need help with anything or someone to hold Eli, my mom is basically dying for the chance."

"Thanks," she says. She opens the back door and carefully pulls the car seat out. Eli is all bundled up and sound asleep.

When we get to the sidewalk, everyone crowds around to get a peek at Eli.

"I helped deliver him," Evita says proudly to Paul. Paul looks suitably impressed. The way he smiles at Evita, I think he's got it bad for her.

"She did," Alice laughs, giving Paul a hug.

Once we're ten minutes from the start of the meeting, we file into the cafeteria. There are a few other parents or teachers from the school district here, but it's not as crowded as I thought it would be.

But then, with only five minutes until the meeting is set to begin, students start streaming in. The students have to unstack more cafeteria chairs. They line them up behind the rows that were already set up. My heart speeds up, but I'm exhilarated. Even Ms. George is here, looking coolly around at her students.

If I thought I got a lot of smiles and nods in the hallways, it's nothing compared to the smiles I'm getting now. Everyone here seems excited. We're taking a stand.

The board does some housekeeping, taking roll and going over the loose agenda for the meeting. And then they call on anyone who has "new business from the community," and before I can really process it, I'm giving my stuffed herpes a squeeze and standing up with my notes and walking toward the center of our chairs. There's no podium or anything like I pictured it.

"Hi. Thanks for allowing us to share some of our thoughts with you today. My name is Lacey Burke, and I am a senior. I would like to challenge the school board's definition of 'lewd literature' and expand the topics covered in high school sex and health education." I take a deep, shuddering breath. My nerves are making it feel like I can't breathe, but then I look at Theo in his cute shirt and tie, and he gives me the thumbs-up he promised. "Our high school currently teaches an abstinence-only approach to sexual health, and this is to the detriment of its students." I read lines of statistics and studies, and then I get to the fun part. I describe the blue fluid demonstration we had in senior seminar and talk about how I introduced a condom into the demonstration, and the students sitting behind me start to clap. I turn around and smile. I am suddenly armed with new bravery.

"My friends and I were suspended from school for distributing condoms, condom instructions, pregnancy tests, and other sexual health items. Because of this suspension, we've lost independent studies and internships that were vital to our education and our future. We were told that the items we handed out were lewd. But there are students here tonight who view that differently. Thank you for listening."

Next up is Theo. "I'm a male student who always rolled my eyes at our sex ed classes. They felt like condescending lectures that all of us would ignore. And I admit that I've struggled in the past with practicing safe sex. And the reason for that was stupid: I was embarrassed to buy condoms. I had been told by most of the adults I looked up to that having sex was wrong. Of course I was afraid to go into the only drugstore in town, with cashiers and pharmacists who go to church with my parents, and buy condoms. We wanted to help other students overcome that stigma so that if they were going to be sexually active, they didn't need to wonder how to be safe about it. They didn't need to be embarrassed or look up their questions about sex on the internet where there might be all kinds of misinformation. We all saw a pretty great change within the student body when everyone had easy access to condoms. Suddenly, there wasn't shame attached to having them. Everyone felt better about using them. Thanks."

He sits back down next to me, and Evita gets up.

"Hi. I was also suspended for my part in distributing this literature. And as such, I lost the time that I had dedicated to planning for the school's Gender and Sexuality Alliance. I'm the president of that, by the way. It's a really important group for a lot of the students at our school. I used my independent study to support the group and other LGBTQIA students. Like a lot of the other students in the GSA, the club has been really crucial to me feeling welcomed and included at school. Because, aside from the GSA, the school does very little to address the needs and questions of LGBTQIA students. In health classes in particular, I feel that by deeming sexual health information lewd, we are ignoring a real need in the community and stigmatizing sex so that students don't feel like they can find answers or help when issues around sex arise. I also want to point out that the current curriculum is really heteronormative and amatonormative, and that's especially damaging and stigmatizing to us LGBTQIA students. You can no longer, in good conscience, teach us while under the assumption that everyone is cisgender, heterosexual, and allosexual. I would urge the school board, while they examine their curriculum, to strive to make it as inclusive as possible."

This also garners applause from the audience, many of whom are GSA members.

Paul stands up and talks about how, because of our efforts, he spent more time thinking about consent and respect than he ever had before. Then Alice passes Eli to my mom, stands up, and begins to speak. It's possible she's even more nervous that I was. She looks back at us, and Theo, Evita, and I all give her goofy smiles and encouraging thumbs-up.

"It is probably apparent to everyone here that I am a teen mom. I just had my baby last week. I don't blame the school for my unintended pregnancy, but I do blame the culture of this school for adding to the shame and embarrassment I felt about my pregnancy."

"You rock, Alice!" Evita calls out when Alice pauses.

"I dropped out of school because I was embarrassed. When

Lacey told me about her senior seminar, I was really glad I had dropped out. But now I'm not. I've missed out on so much already this year. I missed out on having friends and a normal teenaged life. And, really, I should have been living as normal a life as I could before my baby was born. I know I'm not the first girl from this school who's had a baby. I'm probably not the first one to feel embarrassed, or even the first one to drop out. But I hope that the school board will find ways to help teenagers who are not ready for parenthood make informed choices about their health and their bodies. The statistics that Lacey shared show that teaching contraception in schools can be a powerful tool to combat unplanned pregnancies."

We all clap for her and wait for the next student to stand up and speak. My mom speaks. Then we pass around the petition and the information we've printed out.

"Does anyone have anything else to add to this discussion?" one of the school board members asks. We look around. Not every student has spoken, but they've all signed the petition.

"Thanks for your time and thoughts. We will take this under consideration, and address this issue and this regulation further."

Then they move on to other business. It wasn't exactly the grand finale I was hoping for. I was hoping someone on the school board would jump up and say, "These kids are right! Let's change the rules! Put it to a vote!"

Outside in the cool, we all hug one another. My mom gives me the tightest hug of all. "I honestly can't remember ever feeling as proud of anyone as I am of you guys," she says to our little group.

Theo gets a little misty-eyed. "You're the best, Ms. Burke."

"You're sappy," Evita teases.

"Yeah. I am," Theo says.

"The world needs men like you," my mom says.

"Oh my god, Mom," I say, rolling my eyes.

"The coffee's on me," my mom says to the kids who are still congregating.

Theo pulls me toward him and kisses the side of my head. "At the risk of sounding like your mom, I am so freaking proud of you."

"Me, too," I say. Then I cross my fingers and hope we made a difference. Or, more of a difference, since all the evidence in front of me is that we already have.

~

Later that week, Ms. George calls the three of us into her office.

"You'll be happy to know that I'm reinstating your independent studies," she says with a smile.

"Yes!" Evita says, jumping up from her seat and then sitting back down.

"The school board clarified their definition of 'lewd' to refer only to information that would be detrimental to the health and well-being of the students. Information on safe sexual practices does not fall under this new definition. So, your records have been cleared of the suspension."

"Seriously?" Theo asks.

"Okay, but what does this mean for sex ed?" I ask.

"While they didn't change any of the curriculum—so much of that is at the state level—they did make provisions for literature to be available at the school counselors' office. The counselors and I are looking into what pamphlets to include."

"Heternormative literature?" Evita asks.

"We're going to make it as inclusive as possible. And, in fact, I was going to ask, now that your independent study has been reinstated, if maybe you'd give us some resources you think might be helpful to LGBTQIA students," Ms. George says.

"Hell yes," Evita says.

The three of us look at one another, grinning.

"Thank you, Ms. George," I say.

"Thank you all!" she says, smiling. "I really admire how you presented your case to the school board."

"Can we get back to class?" Evita asks. "We're talking about applying for financial aid for college. It's riveting." She's totally deadpan, but, honestly, it is probably the most useful thing we've learned so far.

"Yes. Get back to class," Ms. George says.

When we get out to the hall, Evita lets out a whoop and hugs Theo and me. We get a dirty look from a history teacher who has her door open, but I laugh.

"We totally did that!" I say.

"We did," Theo says. "I'm super proud of my girlfriend."

"I'm proud of your girlfriend, too," Evita says, grabbing our hands.

Epilogue

It's May first, AKA college decision day. Naturally, Evita's turned this into an event. We have a gig later tonight. Theo and I are going to be debuting some of our new stuff. When Alice was getting used to life as a new mom, she didn't rehearse with us, so Theo and I suggested the idea of adding some acoustic, moodier stuff to our set list. It's a lot of me on piano, which I'm getting better at, and Theo on cello.

I keep writing cello solos for Theo. Each one of them is a grand romantic gesture, and I totally own that fact. All three of us sing now. None of us is as good as Alice, but together we are great at blending. It's not the Sparrows exactly; maybe it's a new musical project. Or maybe we'll marry the two sounds somehow, someday. But it's beyond exciting that we keep expanding and growing and finding our voices.

Alice is here today. Eli hasn't been put down once. One of us is always holding him, snuggling him, smelling the top of his head—which Theo thinks smells better than whatever shampoo he swears Evita and I use and keep a secret from him.

"So, I made a playlist for this moment," Evita says. She spins up a retro, upbeat playlist that blends new and old rock.

We've all gotten into Berklee. Theo and Evita are going no matter what. I got into UMass Amherst, too. Either way, the three of us are going to Massachusetts.

Janice buzzes around, setting out cookies, fruit, and sparkling cider. Evita, Theo, and I are planning on lining up our laptops and paying our deposits at the same time. And obviously we need to be well fortified for something as emotionally strenuous as this.

First, though, Alice taps a knife on her champagne flute. "I have an announcement." We turn to her. "Maybe it's crazy, but Eli and I want to come to Boston, too. Since I took my GED, I qualify to start studies at the community college up there. I might only take one or two classes at first, and establish myself as a resident. My mom thinks I'm nuts. She doesn't know why anyone would want to move somewhere so cold. But I think I need to prove to myself and to Eli that I can still make choices. So. I dunno. I hope you don't mind me tagging along on your dream."

"Are you fucking serious?" Evita says. "This is the best thing I've ever heard." She gives Alice and Eli a huge hug. "And you can totally live with us! We're going to look for apartments soon. We'll scope it out. We'll find one with a room big enough for a bed and a crib. We'll make it work."

"To the Sparrows," Theo says, raising his glass.

And I feel a pang. I don't think I'll be living in that apartment with them. Because I'm going to go to nursing school almost two hours from them.

My eyes start to water, and I'm not sure when I turned into such a crier.

"Lacey? Care to share with the class?" Theo says.

"I need to go to nursing school. For me. Which means I'll be living in the dorms and missing you guys like crazy during the week. I'm so sorry," I say.

"Don't be sorry," Evita says. "This is right. And you're going to spend every weekend with us, and we'll do family dinner once a week halfway between our schools. I already figured it out."

"I know. But it won't be the same."

"Hate to break it to you, pal, but nothing is the same. I mean, we've got a baby in our ranks. And you are a badass midwife and Tumblr star. Theo's hair is long. I started shaving my armpits for some insane reason. I mean, Evita of last year wouldn't recognize us now. But that's fine. I love us! I promise!" She gives me a giant hug.

Theo sniffs. Because of course he's crying. "I'm proud of you," he says with a froggy, sad voice. "But I did sort of want to sleep next to you every night."

"I know. I'm sorry."

"Are you guys going to make it official?" Janice asks. "Because I have a credit card that's just begging to have a deposit placed on it."

I nod. I'm doing this. Saying it out loud was scary. But now I know it's what's right for me. It's what I've known is right for a long time. I might not be all that confident in a lot of ways, but I'm confident in this: these friends of mine are in my future. If Evita is disappointed in my choice, she's not showing it. We're just laughing and paying deposits and eating way too many pastries.

Then we're all putting on massive amounts of eyeliner, dancing to pop music, and loading our cars with sound equipment. We're kissing Eli and hugging one another. We're facing whatever comes our way.

Acknowledgments

Writing the acknowledgments is something I've dreamed of, the way people practice their Academy Award speeches. (You don't do that? Just me?)

It's been amazing working with the Swoon Reads team. Thank you, Jean Feiwel, Lauren Scobell, and Emily Settle, for making Swoon Reads such a great place to be. Thank you, Alexei Esikoff, Melanie Sanders, Liz Dresner, and Raymond Ernesto Colón, for turning my story into a real book. Thanks, Kat Brzozowski. And giant thanks to Holly West. Every phone call and email with you has been such a joy.

Thanks, Uwe Stender and the entire Triada family.

Thanks, Susan Graham, for your insight and friendship. Thanks to Sarah Carter for the amazing sensitivity read.

Thanks to my Swoon Squad friends for welcoming me warmly into your group. A special thanks to Katy Upperman, who suggested I give Swoon Reads a try in the first place. And, holy cow, thanks to all the people who read this manuscript on Swoon Reads and gave me your feedback.

I'm extremely lucky to have the greatest village of young adult and middle grade authors that I'm proud to call friends. Kristen Lippert-Martin, Cat Scully, Katharyn Blair, Nikki Roberti, Andrew Munz, Allison Varnes, Natalie Blitt, Madi Ballenger, Sarah Glenn Marsh, Rachel Lynn Solomon, Katherine Locke, Lizzy Mason, Angele McQuade, Karen McManus, and Rachel Simon. Writing never feels like a solitary endeavor with you all!

Thanks to Daphne Key. Never underestimate the life-changing experience of having a great teacher. You were the first person to label me as a "writer."

To my friends who always have my back, even when I'm half-crazed from the whole writing-a-book thing. Lorac Lawton, Suzy Brown, Katherine Gilchrist, Rebecca Kammer, Lauren Kinne, Krista Carlson, Marynelle Losin, and Bridget Ballenger. I thank you. And my kids thank you! And thank you to my friends who support me from afar: Rachel Semigran, Maggie Johnson, Danielle Tinder, and Eamon McIvor. Thank you, Lauren Preti, for my awesome author photo and for reminding me to get back into yoga.

For the badass health warriors who taught me just how wonderful and supportive healthcare—particularly for a birthing person—can be. Thank you especially to Story Jones and Kelly Sicoli. Shout out also to Liz Reiner, Nancy Hazle, Brittany Averill, and Nancy Hall.

Thanks, Sara Raasch, for being one of the loveliest humans ever, and for being an inspiration in all the ways.

Thanks, Christina June, for being with me every step of the way and for always being up for a brainstorming session.

Thanks, Lisa Maxwell, for the near-constant texting and for your general awesomeness and for your honesty and your wit.

A brilliant, special thank-you to Danielle Stinson. I've known we were kindred spirits since the sinking of the *Titanic* (in movie theaters). I am so inspired by your writing. I love you so much. You are family to me.

Thanks to Kurt and Betsy Hinebaugh for all your support. And to Kent Hinebaugh, whose name is actually Byron. You all have listened to me talk about writing for a lot of years now, and I'm so proud to share this book with you. Thanks to my amazing parents, Tom and Susan Johnson. Not only are you wonderful parents and grandparents, but you also fight for what you believe in. Thanks, Mike Johnson and Owen Johnson. I don't understand hockey, but you guys still keep me around.

A huge thank-you to my partner, my love, and the jelly to my donut (and the cello to my viola), Jason Hinebaugh.

Last but not least, to the three humans who have taught me more about love than I ever thought one person could learn: Callum, Lucy, and Rowan, I love you guys a bushel and a peck.

DID YOU KNOW...

readers like you
helped to get this
book published?

Join our book-obsessed community and help us
discover awesome new writing talent.

1 **Write it.**
Share your original YA manuscript.

2 **Read it.**
Discover bright new bookish talent.

3 **Share it.**
Discuss, rate, and share your faves.

4 **Love it.**
Help us publish the books you love.

Share your own manuscript or dive between the pages
at **swoonreads.com** or by downloading the **Swoon Reads app.**

Check out more books chosen for publication by readers like you.